Claire Alla[...] [...] [...]orthern Ireland, where she still lives with her husband, two children, two cats and a hyperactive puppy.

I[...]er eighteen years as a journalist she covered a wide [...] of stories from attempt[...] [...] to court sessions, to the Saville In[...] into the events of Bloody Sunday, right down to the local parish notes.

She has previously published eight women's fiction novels. Her first thriller, *Her Name Was Rose*, was published in 2018 and became a *USA Today* bestseller, followed by *Apple of My Eye* and *Forget Me Not* in 2019. *The Liar's Daughter* was published in 2020.

When she's not writing, she'll more than likely be found on Twitter @claireallan.

Also by Claire Allan

Her Name Was Rose
Apple of My Eye
Forget Me Not
The Liar's Daughter

ASK NO QUESTIONS

CLAIRE ALLAN

avon.

Published by AVON
A division of HarperCollins*Publishers* Ltd
1 London Bridge Street
London SE1 9GF

www.harpercollins.co.uk

HarperCollins*Publishers*
1st Floor, Watermarque Building, Ringsend Road
Dublin 4, Ireland

A Paperback Original 2021
1

First published in Great Britain by HarperCollins*Publishers* 2021

A catalogue copy of this book is
available from the British Library.

ISBN: 978-0-00-838353-4 (TPB)
ISBN: 978-0-00-838352-7 (PB)

This novel is entirely a work of fiction.
The names, characters and incidents portrayed in it are
the work of the author's imagination. Any resemblance to
actual persons, living or dead, events or localities is
entirely coincidental.

Typeset in Bembo Std by Palimpsest Book Production Limited,
Falkirk, Stirlingshire

Printed and Bound in the UK using 100% Renewable Electricity at
CPI Group (UK) Ltd

MIX
Paper from
responsible sources
FSC
www.fsc.org   FSC® C007454

This book is produced from independently certified FSC™ paper to ensure
responsible forest management.

For more information visit: www.harpercollins.co.uk/green

For my agent, Ger Nichol,
who was the first to take a chance on me

Who's at the window, who?
Who's at the window, who?
It's the wee bogey man
With a sack on his back
Come to take you away.

Where will he take you to?
Where will he take you to?
To a wee dark shed
Over the hill
Far, far away.

Traditional song, sung to the children of
Northern Ireland, source unknown.

Prologue

Ingrid

I was ten years old when I found out that monsters are real and they walk among us. I can pinpoint the exact day that everything changed, when the world I'd found to be fun and innocent and good turned into something dark and frightening.

Looking back, I pity my mother having to find the words to tell my brothers and me what had happened. I pitied all the mothers and fathers who were forced to have that same conversation with their children at the dinner table that evening.

There'd be no playing out in the street any more. Not on these dark nights. There'd be no nipping in and out of neighbours' houses, or knocking on doors looking for a glass of water when we were parched from playing tig or Red Rover, or riding our bicycles all over the estate in and out of the dark alleyways.

We were never to go out on our own. Nor walk back from school on our own. Even though it would still be light then. We absolutely were not allowed to take the short cut through the overgrown fields at the back of the school, either.

And we were never, ever, ever to go into anyone's house on our own. No matter how well we knew them. No matter how many times we'd been there before.

Because Kelly Doherty had been found and she was dead. And someone, some bad man or bad woman, had hurt her and killed her and our mothers didn't know 'how they would ever be able to cope' if something like that happened to us.

I didn't sleep that night. I couldn't. For the first time, I hated that I had a room all to myself and my brothers got to share. They got to keep each other company. I curled into as tight a ball as I could manage, hugged Daisy, my tatty stuffed puppy, to me and squeezed my eyes tight shut. But every noise, every creak, every sound from the street had my imagination running wild.

I was scared to move. Scared to breathe. I prayed over and over again, channelling my earnest childhood belief in prayer and a greater good, for Jesus himself to protect me.

'Oh, Sacred Heart of Jesus, I place all my trust in you,' I muttered over and over and over again until I was stumbling over the words and trying to shake the image of Kelly, dead – like actually dead – from my head.

What did dead people look like? I wondered.

Had she been scared?

Had she been alone?

Who was the bad man?

Or the bad woman?

At some stage during the long, dark night I heard voices on the street. Whispers. I couldn't make out the words, but I guessed they could only be talking about one thing. One person. It was all everyone was talking about. It was all everyone was thinking about.

I wondered if I crept to the window, if I ducked my head through the curtains, would I be able to hear more? I slipped out from under my duvet, still grasping Daisy tightly, and tiptoed to the window. My breath was loud, heavy, misting against the cold glass. My heart thumping so fast I wondered was it possible for a ten-year-old to have an actual heart attack and die.

I almost, almost, didn't look out of the window, but I steeled myself, took a deep breath and opened my eyes.

There was a man, dressed in black, a woollen hat pulled down over his forehead, a scarf, or jumper or something high on his neck. But I saw him, and he saw me.

He looked straight up at me, raised a gloved hand to gesture to me, to bid me to come to him, and I fell to my knees, then curled into a ball, squeezing my eyes as tightly as I could. Because monsters were real.

The bogeyman we had always been told was just make-believe stalked our streets.

Chapter One

Declan

Thursday, 3 November 1994

Declan and Niall Heaney had gone against their mother's express wishes and had not come home straight after school. They had been on their best behaviour all day in their stuffy classroom and now all the energy they had managed to control for six long hours needed to be expended.

And they had a den to visit, one they went to every day. Little more than a hole in the large bushes and trees that ran along the side of the reservoir at the Creggan Country Park (or 'the rezzie' as they called it), it was the Heaney twins' favourite place on earth.

One day it could be headquarters for the Power Rangers. The next a soldier's dugout. Or a ninja training camp. Most of all, though, it was theirs. It had just the right amount of foliage cover to provide a shelter of sorts in the rain and shade in the summer. And the old lunch box they had buried, telling the long-suffering Mrs Heaney it had been lost, held a trove of treasures fit for any ten-year-old boy. Chewing gum. Match Attax trading cards. A box of matches. Two cigarettes they'd secreted from their daddy's stash but hadn't dared smoke yet, half a packet of bourbon creams, fifty-six pence exactly in loose change, a pair of dice, a knife that had been blunted a long time ago and a folded page from one of their school jotters in which they gave the girls in their class marks out of ten.

They didn't need much more. They had their imaginations, after all, and they used whatever they could get their hands on as props for whatever world they created that day.

They knew that Kelly Doherty was missing. Of course they did. Everyone in the estate did. They imagined that probably everyone in Derry, maybe even all of Northern Ireland knew about Kelly. She'd gone out collecting for Halloween with her friends and had become separated from them at some stage. It was now a whole three days later and she still hadn't come home, so the search had shifted to the land surrounding the reservoir.

Kevin McCay had told them that he heard his mammy and daddy say that poor Kelly was probably dead now and it was probably better for her that she was. Neither Kevin nor the Heaney twins understood what that meant, but they were happy to parrot it anyway.

'We have to go and maybe help look for her,' Niall had said. 'This is like something off the TV or a movie.'

Declan had resisted at first, but his brother had a point. It was a big deal and besides, if they went home, their mammy would just make them do their homework straight away like she always did. It would be more interesting to see the search in full swing, but he didn't actually want to look for her, especially if Kevin McCay's mammy and daddy were right.

They'd watched as a group of maybe a hundred grown-ups had set off walking around the country park at the top of the reservoir. They were wearing bright yellow jackets, carrying torches and sticks, which they used to poke around in the grass. From where Niall and Declan sat in their den, close to the water's edge, they could hear the repeated shouts of Kelly's name.

'They've a van up there with tea and soup and biscuits and stuff,' Niall said. 'For all them people searching. Do you think they would give us some?'

Declan had considered this for a moment and had shaken his head. 'Nah. I bet it's only the grown-ups that get that.' He sniffed, drawing the sleeve of his duffel coat under his nose. It was cold and the sky looked like it could open and dump buckets of rain on them at any time.

'Da says he's going to go out and look with them later,' Niall said, digging out the old lunch box from its bed of leaves and dirt and taking out two bourbon creams.

He bit into one and handed the other to his brother. They didn't need those free biscuits or the soup anyway. They had their own supplies.

'Do you think he'll want us to go, too?' Declan had asked. He'd shuddered at the thought of searching in the dark.

Niall shook his head. 'Not a chance. Even if Da wanted us to go, Ma wouldn't. Besides, we've homework to do tonight.'

'Bloody sums. I hate the seven times tables,' Declan had said dejectedly, finishing his biscuit. Declan lifted the stick he had been using as a sword earlier and started to poke at the leaves and mud, sending a fat black beetle scurrying for cover. 'There's no craic here today at all,' Declan added. 'And I'm freezing. Shall we just go home?'

Reluctantly Niall, the younger of the two by seventeen minutes, agreed and stood up, hefting his school bag onto his back.

'C'mon, then,' he said to his older brother and the pair started their walk along the banks of the reservoir, Declan still dragging his stick, leaving a line in the dirt as they went.

It was Declan who saw her first. Not that he knew what it was he saw when he first looked. He thought it was a piece of rubbish. Discarded carrier bags, floating on the water, lapping towards the shore. Dirty white plastic. He didn't think anything of it at first glance. Then, as he bowed his head against the squally shower that had started, he spotted what looked like a black school shoe, patent leather, mired in the mud at the water's edge, and he glanced up again.

The dirty white plastic had morphed into a white dress — lace and satin. A mottled hand, bloated and grey, had floated to the surface. He knew that Kelly Doherty was dressed as Glinda the Good Witch of the North from *The Wizard of Oz* when she disappeared. Recycling her first communion dress from the year before. And still, he couldn't make sense of what he was seeing. It couldn't be . . . His vivid imagination was playing tricks on him. This was just rubbish. The hand, it looked so unreal, so fake, it was probably a discarded Halloween prop. It couldn't belong to a person.

It, this shape that refused to make sense, floated closer to him. The edges started to become more defined.

He put his hand out to block Niall, to stop him from coming closer. He had to protect his more sensitive brother. But he'd not been quick enough.

'Is that . . .' Niall's voice faded out.

Declan was stuck somewhere between horror and morbid fascination. Imagine if he, just ten years old, could be the person to find Kelly Doherty. If it was Kelly. The body in the water, now just a few feet from the boys, was face down. Dark strands of hair floated like weeds to the surface. Kelly had blonde hair. He knew that. He used to see her running around the playground with all of her friends. Screaming in that annoying high-pitched way wee girls do. This hair was dark, though, splayed in fronds on the top of the water. Maybe it was the water that was dark, he thought.

He wanted to step closer. To look more closely. But his legs didn't want to move. The noise around him faded out, replaced with a buzzing in his ears.

He felt Niall take the stick from him. Watched as his brother stepped closer to the bank, his shoes sinking into the mud. Mammy would be raging, Declan thought, but Niall was undeterred. He waded into the water, gasping at the cold as the water covered his feet, his ankles, up to his knees. He reached out with the stick, caught it on the dress and pulled. The shape – the body – moved a little towards them and Niall turned back towards Declan. 'C'mere and help me!' he shouted, but Declan was frozen to the spot. He couldn't even shake his head.

Niall swore and took another step towards the shape, getting a better hold of the dress. Then he heaved it towards him until it was close enough that he could grab the material with his hands and pull it to shore.

As her legs, her arms, her hands all became visible, Declan knew it had to be Kelly – it had to be – but she was face down, her features hidden.

He watched as Niall gently prodded at her prone body. He tried to tell Niall to step back, but his voice wouldn't work, either. He knew they should get a grown-up. Niall turned and gestured to Declan to follow, but he didn't, shaking his head. He still couldn't move, afraid if he even tried, he might wet himself with fear. He knew Niall would say he was being a baby, and maybe he was, but right at that moment, he didn't care.

His stomach clenched as he watched his brother poke some more. He didn't expect there to be any give. He watched in horror as the stick pushed through an already shattered skull into the soft matter of Kelly Doherty's brain.

He doesn't remember much from after that, except that was the point he did wet himself, and he threw up, undigested brown Bourbon biscuit splattering on the muddy ground.

Chapter Two

Ingrid

Wednesday, 16 October 2019

The archive room in *The Chronicle* isn't anywhere near as grand as it sounds. It's not a fancy library, lined with mahogany shelves housing every copy of *The Chronicle*'s 200-year-old history. I don't select the bound copies I need and carry them to a leather-topped desk to pore over them under the gentle glow of a reading lamp.

Instead, I shiver as I try to make sense of a long-ignored filing system to find the papers from 1994. Twenty-five years before. When I was ten and Kelly Doherty was eight.

I got to grow up, though. Kelly didn't.

I'd been nervous about digging out these files. Uncharacteristically so. Normally, the grittier the story or more gruesome the crime, the more eager I am to be assigned to cover it. But this was different. This was the anniversary of a murder that had shocked to the core the community in which I grew up. We'd been used to violence, of course, in Northern Ireland.

Bombs and guns and masked men were something we were almost, but not quite, immune to. But murder, like that? Of a child? That didn't happen. That changed everything. Changed everyone. I never really understood fear or grief until then. I've never forgotten them since.

I wish I'd lifted my grey cardigan from the back of my chair before I came down here. It's ugly and not at all my usual style, but it comes in very useful during long hours in the archive room. I suppose I could walk back to my desk and get it, but I'm happy to hide out away from everyone.

I had a couple of glasses of wine last night and my head is the worse for it. I should know by now never to drink on a school night, and certainly never to drink cheap wine. The combination of the two is lethal, especially when faced with working my way through pages and pages of minute typeface, blurring against yellowing newsprint.

Sighing, I rub my eyes and wish the lighting in the archive room was better. I stop flipping over pages when I see her face. Angelic. Gap-toothed. The picture is black and white, but I can see her hair was blonde, ringleted. Just as I remember it. There's a clip holding it back from one side of her face. She's in school uniform – the same school colours I wore myself – and it looks like it was taken by one of those official school photographers who charge an arm and a leg.

The headline is stark: 'Bring her Home.' The subhead speaks of the hell the family of missing schoolgirl Kelly Doherty are going through. The byline is Ryan Murray's. He's since climbed the ranks to editor, but must have been only a junior reporter then. This would've been a huge story for him to cover.

The Chronicle was published just twice a week in 1994, instead of daily like today. It was an era when local journalism bloomed. Circulation was high. Advertising was healthy. Competition was almost non-existent. *The Chronicle* was a flagship paper. Not like now, I think. The Internet has almost wiped us out. Why pay for news when you can get it for free?

Looking at the date on the front page, I see that by the time this paper hit the counters in the newsagents, it would only have been a matter of hours before Kelly's body was found. I shudder, an icy coldness running through me. I blink and it's like I'm there again, on Halloween night.

We were all dressed in our fairly basic costumes, throwing together whatever our parents could find to make us into a bunch of amateur monsters, vampires, witches and fairies. We were armed with plastic shopping bags, which we carried from door to door. This was before Halloween was Americanised. We didn't say trick or treat – we would parrot in sing-song voices 'Anything for Halloween?' to our neighbours, and we would be rewarded with nuts and apples and grapes; if we were exceptionally lucky, we might get a lollipop.

Then, bundled in our duffel coats, we'd move on to the next house and the process would begin again. We didn't need parents to chaperone us then. It was a different time. We watched out for each other. Our neighbours looked out for us. The only thing to fear was the thought that our bags of loot could be 'raided' by the bigger boys from the next street – taking our collections and leaving us to go home empty-handed.

That night, it was cold and wet. I remember my breath curling in soft white in front of me and the nip of the cold at the tips of my fingers, the strength of the wind catching the hood of my coat and pushing me backwards. I wished I'd worn my gloves and a hat – not that I would've admitted that to my mother. The smell of smoke from the coal fires in each home hung thick in the air.

I remember, or at least I think I remember, seeing Kelly. Those curls. Her white dress. A star on a stick covered with tin foil to give it the appearance of a magic wand. She was running down the street, following her friends, laughing. Jumping in puddles as she went. I remember her waving at me. And I waved back. Or I think I did. Memory is a funny thing.

I didn't see her again after that until the day of her funeral, when I saw a little white coffin being carried into the chapel.

I spend an hour making notes, snapping photos of the relevant pages on my phone and searching through boxes of negatives for the relevant original images from the time. By then the chill in the archive room has become too much and I need a coffee.

I'm walking back to my desk, when the door to the editor's office opens and I hear my name being called.

'Ingrid,' Ryan says from behind his desk as I walk in. 'Sit down.'

I take a seat for a minute or two while Ryan taps at his computer, sending emails or proofing pages or possibly just scanning Twitter. Anything to keep me waiting, to remind me that he is my boss. Eventually, he looks up.

'You've been researching the Kelly Doherty anniversary story?' he says.

I nod. 'I have. And I've put the feelers out to see if Jamesy Harte will talk to us. He's not come back to Derry, by all accounts, but I've been able to track down one of his cousins, who made positive noises. I'm sure as his campaign to clear his name grows, Harte'll want to talk. Something about him . . . well, it never added up to me. It would be interesting to hear his side of things.'

Ryan sits back and steeples his fingers together in an exaggerated 'I'm thinking' pose. 'The thing is, Ingrid, I don't think we want to be seen to be backing Jamesy Harte in any way. He was convicted and he served his time. The law says he was guilty and I think digging too deep into that . . . well, it won't make us popular.'

'It's not like you to shy away from a big story,' I tell him, and it's true. It's one of the reasons I have stayed at *The Chronicle* for so long – Ryan's willingness to push for answers, no matter how uncomfortable the questions.

'I'm not shying away from anything, Ingrid,' he says, his tone harsh. 'Cover the story by all means. A measured anniversary piece. But I don't think we should be coming down on the side of a convicted child killer.'

'Even if he claims he's innocent? There's a growing body of evidence . . .' I begin. 'I've only started to look into it, but there seems to be something in what Jamesy is saying. This could be huge. What if there has been a huge miscarriage of justice here, Ryan? Don't we want to be on the right side of championing that?'

The thought that a man might have spent the better part of two decades in prison for a crime he didn't commit – and one of the most heinous crimes a person could commit at that – makes my blood run cold. But it also fires up the journalist in me. This is a once-in-a-lifetime chance to be at the very heart of a major story.

'Don't be fooled by him and all the do-gooders jumping on the "innocent man" bandwagon. I covered that story at the time, Ingrid. That murder was stomach-churning. You're too young to remember. Too wet behind the ears. Believe me, Harte doesn't deserve redemption. He doesn't deserve to become a figure for the miscarriage-of-justice bleeding hearts to get their knickers in a knot over. We don't give child killers voices.'

I stay quiet. I don't tell him that although I was young at the time, I probably have a more vivid memory of it all than he does. He wouldn't listen anyway. When Ryan gets a bee in his bonnet about something, nothing on this earth will make him change his mind. If he doesn't want an interview with Jamesy Harte, that's one thing. But I'm not personally prepared to stop working on the story. It would kill me. Yes, I'll give Ryan the hearts and flowers piece he wants, but that doesn't mean I can't do a bit of investigating in my own time.

'Stick to a colour piece, Ingrid,' Ryan says, cutting through my thoughts. 'Use some of the old pictures. Talk about the sense of shock. Go easy on this one. Your "bull in a china shop" approach won't get you very far here.'

Funnily enough, he has never objected to my 'bull in a china shop' approach before – not when it was getting him exclusives and sending his sales, as well as his website click rate, soaring.

'Okay, boss,' I say, trying to hide my annoyance but not managing to do so.

'I mean it, Ingrid. Or I can assign someone else to it if you think you can't follow instructions.'

I tell Ryan what he needs to hear. I don't want to get on the wrong side of him, even if I don't agree with his stance. He's been in this game a lot longer than I have. Then again, maybe that's his problem – he's been doing this job so long he has lost his fire for it. That burning desire to tell the story and fuck the consequences has been extinguished by bonuses, promises of early retirement and a nice leaving package from the company if he doesn't rock the boat.

Me? I'm not opposed to a bit of boat-rocking every now and again.

Chapter Three

Ingrid

I'm the last to leave the office. That's not unusual. Ryan went home an hour ago. The rest of my colleagues left a good hour or more before that.

'Do you not have a home to go to?' he asked me, his earlier terseness forgotten, as he slipped into his coat and pulled his scarf around his neck.

He asks me that question every night. And every night I tell him I work better here. When I'm alone. When there are no distractions.

Sometimes he tries to distract me before he leaves. He leaves his office with a wolfish smile on his face and I know immediately what's on his mind. He's an attractive man. Older than me, of course. In his mid-fifties, but he looks after himself. Dresses well. He's well groomed; tanned and toned, but not too much. He's not vain. He has the bluest eyes I've ever seen. Piercing – that's how I'd describe them. When he turns on the charm, I find him impossible to resist, even if most of the time he enrages me with his arrogance. Some would say we have a love–hate kind of an arrangement. But it's more complicated than that. I wouldn't say that I loved him, and yet I find myself drawn to him anyway. I'm pretty sure he feels the same.

He wasn't in a predatory mood tonight, though. 'I'll have to talk to HR about this,' he said, which is a threat he makes at least once a week. He always follows it with waffle about 'lone working protocol' as if, as reporters, we aren't dispatched to talk to dodgy people in dodgy places on our own all the time.

I didn't argue with him. I just rolled my eyes. Nodded. Told him I'd see him in the morning.

As soon as he left, I looked at the negatives I'd retrieved from the archive room earlier. They were from pictures of the funeral. Pictures of Kelly Doherty's grieving family. Pictures of me and my school friends standing, shivering in the cold, as a guard of honour outside of the chapel. Thankfully, I seem to be hidden behind one of my classmates, the top of my head just about in view, but that doesn't stop me from remembering the day. The wind was icy-cold, whipping around our legs. School uniforms – skirts and knee-high white socks – were not enough to protect bare legs from the cold. I shivered so hard that my teeth chattered together, giving me a headache.

I remember the sense that this was something very, very important. Our teacher had told us we weren't to show her up. We were to be on our very best behaviour and if we were, we would get no homework for a full week and we could go home with our mammies and daddies after the Mass. I remember the sense of solemnity about the whole thing.

But I also remember the fear. This was our friend. And she was dead and in a box – and we didn't, none of us, quite understand it.

And then I saw Kelly's mammy and daddy crying. Her mum roaring with grief, like nothing I'd ever heard before. The grief of a mother who had lost her child. It haunts me still, even though I'm the least maternal person in the world. Maybe that's *why* I'm the least maternal person in the world. Much too scared ever to risk experiencing pain like that. I remember there were people holding her up, helping her to walk into the chapel while she was bent double with the pain of her loss. I couldn't look away, even though I couldn't bear what I was seeing.

I remember I saw my mother crying. And my teachers. And the neighbours. And my friends. I remember my own lip trembling but being determined not to cry. Not even one little bit. Even though I was sad and scared and it all felt very grown up.

I remember thinking if only Kelly had been with us that night. With our gang. None of this would have happened. I was ten years old and riddled with guilt. We were the older kids on the street. We should have watched out for her more, but she had her own friends. I couldn't even start to imagine what they were feeling.

I slip another strip of negatives into the old scanner, watch the full images appear on screen and study them. It's all, more or less, as I remember. I look at the crowd. A sea of heads bowed in procession outside St Mary's Chapel. I see a face I think I recognise. Head up, looking directly at the cortege. I zoom in closer, only to have the image pixelate and blur. But I'm sure, or as sure as I can be, that it is Jamesy Harte. He looks just as I remember him – younger maybe. I know I'm older now than he was when he went to prison. He doesn't look like a killer, but then again, what does a killer look like?

I save the file on to my computer. Then I email it to myself, just to make sure I have a second copy.

I work until my eyes threaten to jump out of my head and go home on their own. Only then do I switch off, lock up just as Ryan reminded me and leave for home, stopping at Sainsbury's to pick up some sort of ready meal on the way. And a bottle of wine – for the fridge, of course. I promise myself I'll do more work after I've showered and eaten, but I find my eyes drooping as I sit on my bed and towel my hair. I lie back on my pillow, vow I'll just rest my eyes for five minutes, but I can already feel myself drifting off. The world is swimming somewhere between reality and my imagination.

It takes a minute then for me to realise that the sound I hear is not the siren of an approaching police car in my dream, but the ringing of my phone. Head fuzzy, eyes heavy, I reach out and answer, muttering a garbled hello.

'Is that Ingrid Devlin?' a male voice asks.

It's deep, husky, as if its owner smokes thirty a day, but there's also a nervous edge to it.

'Yes. It is,' I reply.

'Good. Good,' he says before he clears his throat. 'This is Jamesy Harte. I heard you were looking to talk to me.'

I'm immediately awake, reaching to my bedside table for a pen and the notebook I keep there just in case. First rule of journalism: never be beyond reaching distance of a notebook and pen. I'm surprised to find my hand is shaking. I take a deep breath. This is Jamesy Harte. Fucking Jamesy Harte! The man who changed everything. Who made monsters real.

'I am, Mr Harte. Thanks for getting in touch. I wasn't expecting to hear from you so quickly.'

Second rule of journalism: always be polite when first talking to a new source. Build a relationship of trust with them from the very beginning, even if they are suspected of being a very bad person.

'No need to call me mister,' he replies. 'Jamesy will do. And if I'm right, you're wee Ingrid Devlin from Creggan?'

'Well, not so wee any more,' I tell him. I'm about to remind him of my age, that I'm just a little older than Kelly Doherty would have been, but I think better of it. 'But yes, you've a good memory. I am indeed from Creggan. Although my mum has moved away from Leenan Gardens now.'

'There weren't many wains called Ingrid around,' he says, pausing to take a breath. 'You remember a name like that.'

There's something in the timbre of his voice that makes me uncomfortable. The thought that he remembers me, maybe. That maybe it's more than just my name. I shiver, the hairs on the back of my neck standing up. I can't escape what he was convicted of.

A memory of him comes to my mind. In the small front garden of the house he shared with his mother. He would be there every day, just in time for all of us walking home from school. He'd chat to us. Sometimes he gave us sweets. Sometimes we gave him some of ours.

I heard grown-ups say there was 'no harm in him', but my mother warned me not to talk to him for too long. 'You let Jamesy get on with his gardening and get yourself home to do your homework,' she'd say.

After he was arrested, of course everyone in the neighbourhood had something to say. They no longer thought there was no harm in him. 'There was always something about him,' they'd whisper to each other over hedges and fences, or gossip over shop counters. They didn't think, or care, that we could hear them, too.

I'd always thought he was a nice man. At Halloween his mammy would make a batch of toffee apples and if you were really quick, you'd get one for your goody bag. It was Jamesy who would hand them out, grinning, at his front door, delighted to see our excited faces.

I realise I've paused for a moment or two too long. I will myself to get it together. 'Well, okay, Jamesy,' I say. 'I do want to talk to you. You know I work for *The Chronicle* now . . .' I begin.

'*The Chronicle* hasn't been a friend to me,' he says slowly.

His voice is thick with sadness. I clear my throat. 'I'm aware of that, Jamesy,' I say. 'But I also do a bit of freelance work, you know. Write for other papers. I've even written a couple of books. True crime stuff.'

'Aye,' he says. 'I saw that one you wrote about that Grahame woman's death. It was a good read. Awful business altogether.'

'Thank you,' I say, trying not to think about how that entire episode had complicated my life way too much. 'The thing is, I'd love to help you tell your side of the story. I know you're claiming you were set up.'

'I *was* set up,' he says. 'I didn't do it. I wouldn't do anything like that,' he continues, his slow, deep voice losing its soft tone. 'I didn't deserve to go to prison. I never touched that wee girl, never mind did all those things they said. I'm not like that. I'm not a bad man. I wouldn't ever do something like that. I wouldn't do those things. Those dirty things. I never killed anyone. Not even a spider. Mammy would call me and I'd put them out the window. Those people, back then, the police and all, they just told lies, and made everyone believe they were telling the truth.'

'I'll help you tell your story if you let me,' I say. 'I'm looking into everything surrounding Kelly's death. I'd like to meet you and talk to you about it.'

'But it's not for *The Chronicle*?' he asks. 'I don't want anything to do with that paper.'

I suck in a breath. 'No, Jamesy. It's not for *The Chronicle*. It's for the other papers I told you about. Maybe even a book.'

I hear him suck air in through his teeth. 'A book? About me?'

'Maybe,' I say. 'I mean, I have to run it past my editor and all, but we could start to chat.'

'You won't tell people I'm a monster,' he says. 'I'm not a monster. You have to believe me. I can't talk to you if you don't believe me.' There is a childish pleading quality to his voice now.

'I just want to hear your side of the story, Jamesy. So I can tell it to people. Don't you think it's time you had a voice in all this?' I purposely don't tell him whether or not I believe him – because the truth is, I'm not sure where I stand.

But I won't break the third rule of journalism – flatter and cajole your subjects. Make them feel they are in control of the narrative.

'I do, I really do,' he answers.

'Then can we arrange to meet? Talk about this face to face?'

He pauses for a second. 'Well, I'm not in Derry,' he says. 'I've never gone back there. Not when I got out eight years ago, and not since. And sure, there's nothing for me to go back to anyway. Mammy's long gone. The house passed on to someone else. Derry forgot about me,' he says.

I hear him sniff, wonder if he's crying.

'Where are you staying?'

He pauses, clears his throat. 'Ingrid,' he says, 'can I really trust you? Because if the people here knew what they said I did, I think they might try to hurt me. Or if people from Derry knew where I was . . . I'm scared, you know. I know there's a price on my head.'

'You can trust me,' I tell him. For the most part I mean it, certainly when it comes to his location anyway.

He shares his address with me; a small seaside town on the Antrim coast. The kind of place flooded with children in the summer looking to play on the beach or at the amusements. It strikes me as an odd choice for him, but then again, if he is as innocent as he says he is, why would it matter if there are children running around all over the place? He's no threat to them.

I arrange to meet him at the weekend. Outside normal

working hours. I want to keep this from Ryan as much as possible.

When I hang up, the details scrawled into my notepad, I punch the air. I've got him and I've got the story. I push away the niggle of fear – my nerves at the thought of coming face to face with the man we'd come to think of as the bogeyman who'd stolen our childhood innocence from us.

Chapter Four

Ingrid

Thursday, 17 October 2019

It's a brisk morning. The sun is high in the sky and if this had been three months earlier, there's every chance it would have been a scorcher of a day. But it's not. It's heading towards the end of October and in the last couple of weeks the temperatures have taken a marked dip. This morning is the first time this autumn that I have noticed my breath rise like steam in clouds in front of me. The first time I've noticed the dew on the grass now has a sparkle of frost to it.

I've parked the car on Broadway, in the Creggan Estate. It's much less glamorous than its New York namesake, but it's the council estate where I grew up and even though my father has passed away, and my mother has long since moved, it always feels a little like coming home to be here. I sit in my car and look around. It hasn't changed all that much. Most of the houses now have white uPVC double glazing. There are more cars on the street, satellite TV dishes decorating the skyline. But apart from that, it looks much as it did twenty-five years ago. Rows of uniform terraced houses, tidy gardens to the front.

I've come here just to look around. To walk the same streets again. To try to ground myself in this place that I rarely return to. I want to make sure I'm remembering the geography correctly. I wonder if many of our old neighbours are still here, or have a whole new generation of families moved in and started their lives?

Although, no doubt, there will be less children running around the streets than when I was little. Children don't play out any more. Not in the way we used to.

I put on my gloves and get out of the car, pulling up the collar of my coat to keep my neck warm. I retrace the steps that were once so familiar to me until I find myself standing outside what used to be Jamesy Harte's house. The garden he had once been so proud of has been paved over. A few wilting pots of flowers, long past their summer bloom, sit beneath the window. A blue wheelie bin, emptied of its contents, waits to be taken back through the house to the back garden.

From the garden wall I can see all around me. I picture how he would have been able to watch us as we walked home from school in a pack, small groups of us drifting off at each street that broke off from Broadway. He would've had a clear view all the way up to St Mary's Chapel from his preferred spot.

Do I think he was being predatory when he stood watching us? Chatting to those of us who passed him? I know I didn't at the time. I think of the sad, scared man I spoke to last night. Something about it feels off to me, but God knows I've been taken in by protestations of innocence before.

Digging my hands deeper into my pockets, I start to walk

up towards the chapel. A slow movie of my childhood memories is playing in my head as I do so.

I can see the garden we used to hide in during our more adventurous games of hide-and-seek. Can see the low wall I sat on making daisy chains while waiting for my friends to finish their dinner. Those were such innocent times.

I'm so lost in my own thoughts that I almost don't hear someone call my name. A male voice, low, gravelly – as if fighting off a cold or a cough – breaks through my reverie and grabs my attention. I look up, see a tall figure maybe fifteen feet away from me. A black beanie hat pulled down on a weather-worn face, a dark beard that needs trimming. A bulky khaki coat, dark blue jeans. Hands, like mine, buried in his pockets, shoulders hunched. A pair of once white trainers, now scuffed and grey, on his feet. He could be any age from twenty-five to forty-five. I can't quite tell, but he is looking at me, and he definitely knows who I am.

'Are you too good to say hello to me now?' I hear him say.

There's a cheekiness to his voice and I look closer until something about him becomes familiar to me.

'Niall?' I ask.

He laughs, which ends in a coughing fit that causes him to fold over onto himself, his hand covering his mouth until he catches his breath. 'You're almost right. To be fair, it's a fifty-fifty chance.'

'Declan,' I say, and I know that I'm right. I'm talking to one of the Heaney twins. They sat three rows back from me in primary school and liked to pull at my plaited hair and steal my fruit for break. But they were actually funny and sound and let me join in their games back in the street.

'You've got me!' he confirms. 'I have to say it, Ingrid. You're looking well. I like the blonde hair! The years have definitely been kinder to you than they have been to me.'

I don't think it's arrogant that I agree. Up close Declan looks much older than our thirty-five years. I don't say that though. I simply shake my head. 'Not at all,' I lie.

'Ah now, I'm here like death warmed up,' he says, the thick lines of crow's feet etched into the side of his face, his cheeks and nose ruddy, showing the signs of someone who enjoys a drink too often. 'And you're all glam in your fancy coat and your swish haircut. I always thought ye'd do well in life,' he says, sniffing loudly, accompanied by a wet rattling sound, which makes my stomach turn ever so slightly. 'You still writing for the paper? Writing those books of yours?'

I nod. 'And yourself?' I ask him.

'Ah, well, I'm what you would call in between jobs at the moment. On a career break, so to speak.'

He laughs, but there's a hollowness to it.

'And Niall, how's he?'

'Ah! the prodigal son. He's doing the very best,' Declan says, and I think I hear a hint of bitterness in his voice. 'Teaching in some fancy primary school up near Belfast. Deputy Head, don't you know.' He adopts a faux posh voice. 'Doesn't come back here as often as he should, according to our ma, anyway.'

'That's great that he's doing well,' I offer.

'Aye, I suppose it is,' Declan says, but there's a coldness in his eyes that I can't ignore. 'Anyway, what brings you up this way? Out on a big story? Is there scandal brewing?'

'Actually, I'm just doing a wee bit of research. The paper wants me to do an anniversary piece on Kelly's murder.'

He looks down at his feet. Shifts uncomfortably. 'Christ,' he mutters under his breath. 'Hard to believe it's twenty-five years.' He takes one of his bearlike hands from his pockets, rubs at his bearded chin. 'Christ,' he mutters again. 'Awful time. All of it.'

And it comes back to me. He, and Niall, were the ones who found her.

'Shit, I'm sorry,' I tell him.

He looks up. 'Why? You didn't kill her,' he says with a shrug, his eyes darting to Jamesy Harte's old house.

'But I forgot there, for a moment. I forgot that it was you who found her.'

I watch him for a reaction. Watch to see if he looks open to talking about it more. I can usually get people to talk about things, but this is different. These are people I know, or knew. This was my childhood.

'Aye, well. You're lucky to forget,' he says. 'I wish I could.'

I remind myself to tread softly.

'Do you want to talk about it?' I ask him and his eyes widen. 'I don't necessarily mean for the paper or anything. But sometimes talking helps, and I remember what it was like back then. How awful it was. All the grown-ups losing the run of themselves. We weren't allowed out past the door for months.'

He shook his head. 'I didn't want to leave the house for months,' he says and he looks again towards Jamesy's old house. 'It messed me up, Ingrid, ye know.'

I remember that he changed overnight. He wasn't the boisterous messer he had been. He became withdrawn. Sullen. A meanness in him emerged that had never been there before. In hindsight, I could hardly blame him.

'I can't imagine,' I tell him, but I can. I'm blessed or cursed with a very vivid imagination and working this job has opened my eyes to a lot of the darker elements in the world. I've seen and heard things that I will never be able to forget, no matter how hard I try. 'Look, why don't we get a cup of tea?' I say to him. 'It's freezing out today and I'm not exactly dying to get back to the office. We can have a chat. I'll even buy the tea.'

He looks at me and smiles a weak, watery smile. I wonder

what his life has become. This man with the sad eyes who is 'in between jobs' while his twin brother excels.

'A cup of tea would be nice, Ingrid,' he says. 'Throw in a sausage roll or two and it's a done deal.'

I smile, wrap my arm through his and lead him to my car so we can drive the short distance to the café at the Rath Mor Centre. It's only as I spend more time with him that I realise his clothes have definitely seen better days. He's really just skin and bone, and there's a shake in his hands that doesn't go away.

Chapter Five

Declan

3 November 1994

His ma had hit Declan square around the head before pulling him into the tightest of hugs. The slap, he knew, was because he'd not come straight home after school. The hug, because she knew what he had just seen and she could see he was traumatised.

Not that he was crying. He had stopped crying by then. He had stopped almost everything except breathing. He couldn't speak. No words would come out. He wasn't even thinking in words now, just images. Just sensations. How his stomach had fallen through his boots when he saw the stick sliding into the soft grey matter of Kelly Doherty's brain.

Niall was talking, though. Telling her. Telling everyone what he saw. What he did. 'But she was dead already, Mammy. I didn't kill her!'

Declan had run to find the search party once his stomach was completely empty of all its contents. He'd run, crying, his tears mixing with snot and spit as he shouted as loud as he could for help. Mortified in his piss-stained trousers, his own vomit down the front of his duffel coat. He tried to be brave, but he couldn't. He could only scream until he was heard and then he led the men back to the water's edge. He'd prayed all the way back that he was wrong and it wasn't Kelly. It was just a pile of rubbish and the figure he had seen had been a product of his vivid imagination. But it wasn't. It was all too real.

And it was worse than he could've imagined. Kelly's da arrived and could not be held back. He was roaring like a wounded animal and lashing out at anyone who tried to stop him. He was up to his knees in the water and he hauled Kelly towards him, turning her over, pushing the tendrils of her hair away from her face so that he could see her. Her face. Blue. Grey. Black in places. Her lips were black. Declan remembered that. Her eyes glassy, open. Like those of the fish he saw on the counter at Stewarts Supermarket. She looked funny. Funny peculiar, not funny ha-ha, he had thought to himself – the phrase his own da would use popping into his head.

But funny wasn't the right word. Or peculiar. Maybe just wrong. She looked wrong.

Her features were bloated. Almost a caricature of what she once was. Her father took her hand, the same black and blue and grey and green. He remembered that. He'd always remember that. Just as he would remember how the tips of her fingers were bloodied, nails black. Her hands twisted and bruised. Her dress ripped. He saw her knickers. He was mortified at that. How he saw her knickers, how, even in the circumstances, he registered that it was something he wouldn't normally see. Just like with everything else, though, he couldn't look away.

That would haunt him in the days, and weeks and months ahead. That he didn't look away. Did that make him a pervert? Did that make him wrong?

He couldn't bring himself to talk about any of it. Not to

Niall. Not to his ma or his da. Not to the policeman who sat on the good armchair and asked him questions while drinking tea and eating chocolate biscuits.

He'd just shrug his shoulders and shake his head. 'I dunno,' he'd mutter if pushed. But mostly he just wanted people to stop asking questions. What chance would he have to forget any of it if people kept going over the same old questions, time and time again?

It started to make him angry.

Chapter Six

Ingrid

Thursday, 17 October 2019

'Ingrid!' Ryan calls from the depths of his office, the door wide open to the newsroom.

The tone of his voice is enough to let me know that he is in a shit mood. Dropping my bag at my desk, I grab my notebook, take a deep breath and plaster a fake confident smile on my face.

'You called, boss?' I say, sitting down opposite him, my tone light.

'Were you up in Creggan this morning?' he asks.

I see no reason to lie. 'Yes. I went for a walk around. Just to get a sense of the place again. See if any of the old neighbours are still around.'

'And you got talking with Declan Heaney?' His face is serious.

'Jesus! Word doesn't take long to spread around here, does it. Are you having me followed?' I say, and I'm joking. Mostly.

Ryan doesn't reply, just keeps his expression neutral. Clearly, he is not in one of his more playful moods today.

'But yes, I did get talking with Declan. I bumped into him when I was walking up Broadway. We went for a cup of tea and a chat. You know it was him and his brother who found Kelly's body . . .'

I think to the look on Declan's face as I asked him how well he still remembered it. His eyes had glazed over a little. His face darkened as if he were watching some awful movie clip that only he could see.

'You don't ever forget something like that,' he'd told me.

'Declan Heaney doesn't keep well,' Ryan says, sitting back in his chair and looking at me. 'You know that, Ingrid. He's fond of the drink and smokes. Likes to get himself in trouble. Scan our archives – you'll see he was a frequent flyer in the courts a few years back.'

'Well, I imagine I might be the same if I'd gone through the trauma he did at ten years old,' I tell him. 'But you've said yourself, it was a few years ago now, and it was petty stuff, wasn't it?

'Look, he's an old school friend. We were in the same class and we used to pal around with each other when we were small. We chatted over tea and I bought him a couple of sausage rolls because he didn't look like he'd had a decent meal in a couple of days. If you're not happy about me taking the time out of my working day to help someone who clearly needed it, I'll make up my hours this evening. Just like I always work over my hours anyway.' I look directly at him, at how his blue eyes narrow.

He rubs his chin.

'You know I told you to go easy on this one. You've no need to go wandering the streets of Creggan looking for witnesses,' he says. 'You never know what you're getting mixed up in with Declan.'

'I wasn't looking for witnesses,' I tell him. 'I was just getting a sense of the place. How it's changed over the years. You know, that famous "colour" you talk about. I was just doing my job.'

'Your job is to follow the instructions given to you by your editor and bring me the copy I ask you to write. You don't get to set the news agenda, Ingrid. That's my job and you'd do well to remember that.'

'As if I could forget,' I tell him, my voice barely hiding my frustration. It's not often Ryan pulls rank with me. He has always trusted my judgement and my methods. I don't like feeling as if I've annoyed him. 'And hopefully Kelly's family will talk,' I say. 'I know it's more than colour, but it's an exclusive. They've never spoken to anyone about what happened.'

'Well look, here's my advice. Don't push the Dohertys too hard. We have to do all we can to maintain our reputation as different to the gutter press. We don't want to be seen to be hounding a grieving family.'

'I'm not hounding them,' I say, my tone sharp. 'I'm going through appropriate channels. I've made an approach through Lorcan Duffy, their local councillor,' I continue. 'I do my job, Ryan, and I do it well, but if you don't want the story this time, I won't pursue it. For you.

'But that doesn't stop me taking a personal interest and if another newspaper feels braver, well, I'm not going to rule out helping them. In my own time, of course. We all know this paper is in trouble and I'm not prepared to sink with it. I want to make a name for myself.'

He blinks; his mouth opens and shuts. Just as I'm not used to him pulling rank, he's not used to me pushing back.

I stand up, ready to make a dramatic exit from the room.

'Ingrid,' he says as I turn to leave.

I face him, arms folded across my chest, expression stern.

'I know you think you're the big "I am" these days, but pride comes before a fall,' he says. 'You might think you know it all, but there are times when experience matters more in this industry. There are things more important than bylines and flashy headlines.'

He is speaking in what I call his 'arrogant arsehole' voice. If we were alone, properly alone, I'd call him out on it. Tell him he gets an A plus for being patronising.

He doesn't give me a chance to respond. He bows his head and directs his attention at one of the two computer screens in front of him. As far as he is concerned, the conversation is over, but he's wrong. It's just on pause. It will resume the next time he slips his arms around my waist and pulls me to him, moaning in my ear that he needs me.

I stalk back to my desk and sit down. Trina, one of my fellow reporters and the closest thing I have in the office to a real friend, gives me an 'Is everything okay?' look.

I shake my head, roll my eyes. 'I'll tell you later,' I mouth, and she nods.

The newsroom is, unusually, deathly quiet. Everyone is hard at work, or hard at pretending to work. Even Tommy, our junior reporter who is usually up for a bit of banter, has his head bent low and his fingers are battering his keyboard with unnecessary force. I catch Jim, our very old school and nosy subeditor, glancing up at me, but he looks downwards as soon as he spots I'm looking at him. I know they were all listening. Now I'm seething.

How did Ryan know I was in Creggan, or that I was talking to Declan Heaney? I take my phone out of my bag, where Declan's number is now stored along with a recording of our chat in the café. I knew I'd only scratched the surface with him and if I got to speak to him again, I could get more out of him. I just had to be patient. And defy Ryan.

I'm not denying that Declan is a damaged individual. He'd not been shy about telling me how he has struggled to cope, and hasn't always made the right decisions, or even good decisions. He has an acute reminder in the shape of his overachieving twin brother that his life could have been very different. I've arranged to meet him again next week to chat some more. His story is powerful. It makes for good emotive copy. It illustrates how Kelly and her family were far from the only victims that day.

I don't understand why Ryan isn't crawling all over this.

I log in and check my email to find a note from Lisa on reception.

Councillor Duffy called. Can you call him about an interview with the Doherty family.

He said you'd know what it was about.

I allow myself a self-satisfied smile.

Chapter Seven

Ingrid

'You won't over-sensationalise it, will you?' Councillor Lorcan Duffy asks me.

He's been appointed as media go-between for the Doherty family and is taking his role exceptionally seriously, even if his understanding of how the media works is limited.

'Of course I won't,' I say, and it's true.

Some stories don't need to be sensationalised. They are huge of their own accord. I could outline nothing but the facts of this case and it would be hard-hitting enough. I mean, of course, I will have to write it to have the most impact it can, but I don't intend to make life more difficult for anyone by over-playing things. I need Lorcan to understand that.

'Look,' I tell him. 'Today, it's me approaching you – but I'm willing to bet I'll not be the only one. Everyone will want to do an anniversary piece, especially with Jamesy Harte making renewed claims about his innocence. The difference is that I know the Doherty family. I knew Kelly. We went to the same school. I can make this as painless for them as possible. If they tell me the story, give it to me as an exclusive maybe, it might just stop everyone else rattling at their door.'

There's an audible intake of breath on the other end of the line. 'Oh, they wouldn't like that. Everyone coming to talk to them. Mr Doherty isn't all that keen in the first place. He doesn't want to talk at all. He says he doesn't want to draw attention to them and have everyone poking into their lives.'

'This is how he can take control of the situation,' I tell him, pulling all of my persuasive tactics out of the box. 'As you know, the media can be unscrupulous at times. And persistent. If he tells their story to one reporter – a local reporter who they know – that could put an end to it all.'

'That really will be an end to it?' Councillor Duffy asks.

'Any further queries can be directed to me and I'll fend them off,' I say.

'Well, if that's the case, I think I can persuade them to talk to you. I'll have a word with them. I assume you want to get this in the bag sooner rather than later. When suits and I'll run it past them?'

'Wednesday is best,' I say, knowing my diary is usually quiet on that day. I can take my time. Do it properly. Ask questions I can use outside *The Chronicle* and Ryan's retrospective and unambitious colour piece. 'But look, I'll work around them if Wednesday doesn't suit. The only request I have is that they don't talk to anyone else.'

'I'll make sure of it,' he says.

This is perfect. An exclusive, and after I've spoken to Jamesy, too. 'Great,' I say. 'I owe you a pint, Lorcan.'

'I'll have to take you up on that offer sometime,' he says, and I know he means it. This is not my first encounter with Lorcan Duffy and he has made his intentions quite clear in the past.

'As soon as things are a bit quieter for me,' I say, knowing full well I've no plans at all to slow down on my workload any time soon, never mind meet him for a drink.

I hang up – and fire a quick email to Ryan letting him know the interview is as good as in the bag. It's all coming together very nicely indeed.

I've barely noticed the transition from day to evening and from evening into night. I've been vaguely aware of my colleagues leaving, of the newsroom getting quieter and eventually falling silent. Another paper has been put to bed and we get to start all over again in the morning.

Ryan walks up to my desk before he leaves.

'Are we okay?' he asks.

I look up at him, blinking.

'Well, I'm okay,' I tell him, looking back at my screen where I was just putting the finishing touches to an unrelated feature piece set to run in the weekend edition. 'I wouldn't dare try to speak for you.'

'Look. Sweetheart,' he says, and I cringe, biting back the urge to tell him that I am not his sweetheart. We're not playing that game now. 'I don't mean to come across as heavy-handed, but I'm not telling you to go easy for the good of my health. I'm watching out for you.'

'I appreciate the concern, but I can look out for myself,' I say, still not looking up. 'And before you get your knickers in a knot, don't worry, I'll make it very clear any extra stuff I look into isn't for *The Chronicle*. Our precious reputation will be protected.' Only then do I look back at him. See him shaking his head.

'You can be such a brat at times. You're going to get yourself in a whole lot of trouble one of these days, Ingrid. Maybe then you'll realise I was only trying to help you.' He perches on the edge of my desk, and I feel him hook a finger under my chin and lift my face towards his. 'You know I care about you.'

I'm too angry to listen to him. Too angry to show him any respect, begrudging or otherwise. I shake my head, pull away from his touch.

'Then stop patronising me,' I say. 'You're not my father, so stop treating me like some stupid junior reporter without the sense I was born with. I know what I'm doing.'

'I'm not saying you're stupid. But I am saying you're in too deep, Ingrid. You're too close to this and it's never a good idea to get too close to any story.'

'Ryan, if you don't mind. I have a lot to do here.' I nod towards my screen. 'Can I just get on with it?'

He shrugs. 'Just think about what I'm saying,' he says before he reminds me to lock up when I'm done.

I mutter 'Arrogant arsehole,' under my breath as he leaves, resisting the urge to give a two-fingered gesture to his retreating figure.

My feature article complete, and filed in the system for editing, I turn my attention back to researching the Doherty case. I want to find out as much as I can about Jamesy Harte's campaign to have his conviction overturned before I speak to him. But our archives don't give much to go on. It's not a case that people have wanted to throw their support behind, not until recently, anyway.

I figure the best way to start is to look at any contemporaneous court reports from the trial, of which there are many. Putting my cardigan on, I make my way back to the archive room, which is now cold enough that it could double as a fridge if it wanted to. I lift the heavy bound tomes of the relevant year's papers and carry them back to the newsroom, where I make use of an abandoned desk to flick through them.

Time passes. I'm not sure how long. The reports are a mixture of long legal arguments and details that make me feel sick to my stomach. I'm sitting, pen in hand, making notes, when a loud rattle of thumping at the doors of the office startles me. Ryan will have locked the door on his way out, brought the shutters to half mast, but it's not usual for anyone to come near the building in the evening. And certainly not at this time, I think, looking at the clock on the wall to see that it has passed nine.

Despite the thudding of my heart, I try to convince myself it's just someone making a nuisance of themselves. If I ignore them, they'll go away. Still, my attention has been pulled from my work and I'm too jittery to focus on it. Another loud bang, followed by a rattling of the shutters, has me grabbing my phone. I can call the police. I probably should. But then Ryan really would get on his high horse about lone working regulations and I'd not be permitted to stay on past hours any more.

If I just stay where I am, whoever it is will eventually get bored and leave. I'm sure of it. It's not like they'll be able to break in, is it? I sit in silence. Afraid to move. I hear several loud, indiscriminate noises, crashes, something smashing, but it sounds too muffled to be one of the windows. Eventually, it goes quiet and I slowly exhale, only to be startled again by a loud thump to the newsroom window. The blinds are closed. Whoever it is can't see in, but I can't see out, either. I look at my phone. Maybe I really should phone the police.

But there is no more noise. Not a peep. I try to get back to work, but I'm too rattled and even though I'm sure whoever it was is long gone, I don't want to be here any more. After fifteen or so minutes, I decide to go home.

My nerves are on high alert as I lock up and I keep my keys bunched in my hand ready to hit out at any attacker who might jump out at me. I scurry to the far end of the car park, cursing myself for parking so far away from the building. Only when I get closer to my car do I see that the driver's window has been smashed and something has been spray painted across the bonnet.

I look around, again worried someone is watching and waiting. My heart thuds and I'm not sure what to do. Do I run back to the office and try to get back inside? I'm gripping my keys so tightly I can feel them threaten to break the skin. A car passes, its lights illuminating all around me. There is no one else here but me, but still I can't stop shaking.

In the darkness I struggle to make out what the spray-painted word says, but as my eyes adjust, I clearly see the word 'scum'. I decide the best thing to do is just to get the hell out of here, as quickly as I can, so I pull on my leather gloves and open the driver's door, prepared to brush any broken glass out of the way so I can drive off. But there is a rock there, obviously the one used to smash in the window, and around it is a lined page of a notebook, bound with an elastic band. I pull the paper free and unfold it.

Words are scrawled in thick black marker, in block capitals: LET THE MURDERING PAEDO ROT OR IT WON'T BE A WARNING NEXT TIME.

Chapter Eight

Ingrid

Scared. Scared and embarrassed. Shamed. Angry. Scared again. Emotions swirl through me, clashing and changing and smashing together as I drive home. My heart is still racing. My foot is shaky on the clutch. I have already stalled at two junctions. What will people think when they see my battered car drive along the streets? When they read 'scum', what conclusion will they draw about me?

I'm not scum. I'm a reporter doing my job. People want to read the news. They gobble up whatever we provide them. But people are never considered 'scum' for reading, are they?

I hear the loud honk of a car horn, glance up and realise I've cut someone off without even realising. I shake my head. I have to stay focused.

I'll have to get the car to the garage first thing, I think. Get them to fix it as soon as possible. Get them to keep it quiet. I don't want to report this to the police. If I do, there isn't a hope in hell that Ryan won't find out about it and he'll be all over me with his 'I told you so' smugness. He might pull me from the story.

My head is throbbing now, my face blazing as I drive – too

embarrassed to stop at the off-licence for a bottle of wine, or at the Chinese for a takeaway. I don't want people seeing. I pray that the dimly lit parking space at the far corner of the communal car park is empty. I want to park where as few people as possible can see my car.

For a moment I wonder if I'm being followed. I look into the rear-view mirror and notice the same silver car has been behind me for at least the last five minutes. I'm starting to get really spooked, when it indicates and turns off to the left. Still, I don't relax. I don't relax even when I park in the mercifully free parking spot, or when I cover the broken window with a makeshift repair of a bin bag and duct tape.

I stand in the rain, shivering with a mixture of adrenaline and cold. I just want to be in my flat. Behind a locked door. With the safety chain on, the curtains pulled, the entire world locked outside.

I'm still jittery as I pour the dregs of a bottle of wine into my glass and gulp it down. I drop two slices of bread into the toaster for a quick dinner and flick the kettle on. I'm not used to feeling unsettled, even though I am used to people hurling abuse at me, or threatening me. I've even had one or two death threats in my time. It comes with the territory of journalism, I suppose. But this? This feels different.

Normally, it's just people letting off steam. They shout and roar and send angry emails in a pique of their own grief and fear. People who are programmed to think all journalists are bottom feeders. Their anger fizzes out as quickly as it erupted. The death threats are more likely to come from bored keyboard warriors who only know how to talk the language of extremist Internet messaging boards. All bluff and bluster. But this . . . this is not like that.

Nothing about this story feels right.

Not Ryan's reaction to my suggestions.

Not the way Declan Heaney had refused to say more after telling me he was sure that Jamesy Harte couldn't have been Kelly's killer.

'We don't need to talk about that any more, do we?' Declan had said, pouring a second cup of tea out of the pot, hot tea leaking from the tin spout and trickling onto the table.

He didn't make eye contact, but I knew he was done talking about Kelly and Jamesy and the aftermath of that horrific afternoon, and it would be unfair of me to pursue it further.

I'd reached across the table to rest my hand on his. He'd startled at my touch as if he wasn't used to feeling the warmth of human contact. His hands were cold, thin, and his knuckles protruded like pebbles.

'Of course we don't. Well, not all the time, anyway,' I'd said. It wouldn't have done to go too far off topic for too long.

'Dead on,' he'd replied with a weak smile. 'You know, sometimes it messes with my head too much.'

'I'm not surprised,' I'd told him, and that much was true.

'And I'm fed up of listening to my own voice anyway,' he'd said. 'How're you, Ingrid? Life seems to be treating you well.'

I'd smiled at him. Life was treating me well. It had its ups and downs, of course. But in the grand scheme of things – especially compared to Declan – I couldn't, or shouldn't, complain.

That's what I'd thought earlier, anyway, before my car was attacked.

Maybe I'd have to watch my step a little with this one. Someone clearly wasn't happy at having me snoop around.

Chapter Nine

Ingrid

Friday, 18 October 2019

I've had the nightmare again. The one I had throughout my teenage years. It's been a long time since it bothered me, but here I am, shivering in my bed, my nightclothes damp with cooling sweat as scattered images jump about in my mind.

I woke myself up with my shouting. I've put the bedside light on. It's past 5 a.m. and already I'm thinking I won't go back to sleep. I don't want to risk slipping back into that dream.

The details always change slightly, but he is always the same. The man dressed in black. Looking up at me as I stare out of my childhood bedroom window, raising his hand to gesture at me to come to him.

Over the years I've convinced myself that he isn't real. He was never real. That I had never seen him outside my dreams, that he had never beckoned me to him, holding one hand up. But sometimes, I wonder. I try to pick out a detail in his build, or his clothes, or the glint of his eyes that will allow me to place him.

For all the good it will do. I can hardly go to the police and decry someone as a murderer because of dreams that haunted me and a memory I no longer trust.

Pulling my hands through my hair, damp with sweat, I glance at my clock again and decide it would be best just to get up. Change my bed sheets. Grab a shower. Wait until it's reasonable to phone my mechanic and arrange for my car to be collected. If I keep busy, I can push the dream out of my head. I can tell myself that the bogeyman in the black suit isn't real. And he certainly isn't coming for me.

'You're late today,' Trina, one of my colleagues at *The Chronicle*, says, raising her eyes from her computer screen and glancing at the clock.

It's not as if I'm not painfully aware that I should have been here at least forty-five minutes ago, but it took a while to get through to my mechanic. It took longer to try to feel calm enough to leave the flat and come into work in the first place. This has got under my skin and I don't like it. I'm not used to feeling rattled.

'Is everything okay?' she asks.

I like Trina. She's one of life's good people. Our lives are very different outside work – she is married with two young girls – but we each harbour an unspoken respect for each others' life choices. Still, I can't bring myself to tell her the whole truth.

'Car trouble,' I tell her, pulling my coat off and hanging it on the back of my chair. 'I had to get a taxi.'

There's no tremor in my voice and I tell myself that's a good thing. If I can fake being calm and in control, maybe I'll actually start to feel that way.

'Oh, I hope it's not too expensive to fix,' Trina says, lifting her coffee cup and nodding towards mine. 'Do you want a coffee? I'm making one.'

I smile and nod. 'Yes, actually. I'd really love one. Thank you.'

I don't tell her about my bad night's sleep. I don't want to get drawn into any conversation that might lead to awkward questions being asked.

'Black, no sugar?' she asks, and I nod again.

She turns on her heel to go to the kitchen. Tommy yells after her that he'll have a cuppa if she's making one and she asks him what his last slave died of. But her tone is light and I know she'll come back with a tray of hot drinks for everyone.

I switch my computer on, listen to it whirring slowly to life. I look around my desk and something nips at me. I'm not a tidy freak by any means, but my desk looks more dishevelled than normal and the top drawer on my locker is slightly ajar. I start to wonder if someone has been going through my things, then chide myself for being paranoid.

Nonetheless, opening it, I try to assess if anything is missing or has been moved, but I can't see any obvious signs. I look at my desk again, at the sheaves of paper I've left sitting around. At my pen pot. At a couple of old editions of *The Chronicle*, folded and waiting to be put in the recycling. I lift the papers, expecting to find my contacts book underneath it, but it isn't there.

I lift all the other sheets of paper looking for it. I check my bag. And then double-check my top drawer. I start to feel a little on edge. My contacts book contains the phone numbers and email addresses of all the people I've had cause to interview or speak to over the course of my journalism career. It's more reliable than any online equivalent. It won't outdate or be vulnerable to hacking attempts. It's my bible and I'd be lost without it.

'Did anyone borrow my contacts book?' I call out, resisting

the urge to use the word 'steal'. 'Because it doesn't appear to be on my desk.'

I'm met with silence. When I look up, I see a few people are shaking their heads, shrugging their shoulders. Trina walks back into the room, carrying a tray of mugs. I ask her, but she hasn't seen it, either.

'Did you look in your out tray?'

I nod, because I've looked everywhere. Someone is lying to me, but I'm not sure who. I want to stand up and ask again, louder this time maybe, but I doubt anyone would own up. So instead I just say to the room, as calmly as I can, 'Perhaps if any of you find it, you could return it to my desk and we'll say no more.'

No one answers and I swallow down my frustration. Instead, I sip from the coffee mug, ever grateful to feel the caffeine start to flood my system. Even if there's a chance it will also start to make me feel more jittery than I already am.

My mechanic has told me he's very busy and he'll get round to fixing my car when he can, but it might not be until next week. He raised a very bushy eyebrow when he saw the graffiti on the bonnet, but thankfully didn't ask any questions. Maybe he's one of a select group of people who wonder why this hasn't happened to me sooner. People who believe I'm the gutter press.

My phone rings and I answer only to hear Ryan's voice. He wants me in his office. Now. Once again, it doesn't sound as if it's likely to be a fun conversation. I take a long drink of my coffee, which burns as it slides down my throat, before going to see him.

I barely have the door closed before he asks me if I know anything about the broken glass in the car park.

'It was where your car is usually parked. Must have happened overnight. Is your car okay?'

I blush. I can't hide the fact I don't have it with me today, but nor am I willing to tell him the truth.

'Short of a problem with the clutch, my car is fine. But it will be in the garage for a bit.'

'So, the broken glass has nothing to do with you?' His left eyebrow is raised so high, it's not that far from his hairline.

'Why would it?' I ask, deciding a brazen approach is the best way forwards.

'I'm not sure, Ingrid, but I can't help but feel you're not being totally honest.'

'I'm sorry you feel that way,' I tell him. 'Is that all you were looking to talk to me about?'

His voice softens. 'Ingrid, this is me you're talking to. Let me take off my boss hat for a moment or two. As your . . . erm . . . friend . . . are you sure there isn't anything you want to tell me? I can help you, you know. Keep you safe.'

This is Ryan Murray on a full charm offensive. It's almost as if he can switch on the extra twinkle in his eyes. It dawns on me that even though I have looked up to Ryan for years, and even though our relationship isn't always strictly professional, I don't trust him entirely. Something I can't quite put my finger on is nagging at me.

'I'm fine. I've told you what you need to know. If you want to call the garage and ask them to confirm that it's my clutch that's banjaxed then feel free.'

'No. No. I'll take you at your word,' he says, just like I knew he would.

'Grand,' I say, fake smile plastered on. 'Is there anything else you need?'

His twinkle has dimmed just a little. 'No. Just go and get started on your work.'

Before I leave, I turn to him. 'Ryan, you didn't lift my contacts book from my desk, did you? It seems to be missing.'

He nods. 'Actually, I think you must have left it here earlier this week. I found it on my desk this morning.'

He lifts some of his paperwork and I see my black hardback notebook. I am simultaneously relieved and suspicious that it is on his desk, because I'm as sure as I can be that I did not bring it into his office at any stage. I would have no reason to.

I take it from him, my mind going into overdrive. I don't know why, but I have a strong suspicion that he knows more than he's willing to admit about what exactly happened to my car.

Chapter Ten

Declan

Why did he have to bump into Ingrid Devlin there in the middle of the street when he was looking rough as a badger's arse? He lit a cigarette directly off the back of another one, tried not to think about the fact he only had four left in the packet and was short of money to buy more. Maybe he'd ask Paddy in the shop to sub him a fiver for one of those cheap packets he sold under the counter.

'You shouldn't be smoking them!' his ma was always telling him. 'You shouldn't be smoking at all, but especially not those. You never know what's actually in them. Rat poison or arsenic or something.'

Most of the time he is able to let her rants wash over him, thankfully. But sometimes he wants to tell her that cheap fags are all he can afford, that and the occasional bag of grass when he wants to forget his worries. He tries not to drink so much these days. It doesn't agree with him. But the grass makes him forget, for a wee while at least. Maybe he'll ask his dealer to sub him some of that, too. He's good for it. He pays his debts as soon as his dole lands in his account.

He sits back in his armchair and takes a long drag of his

cigarette. He knows they're crap. There's an acrid quality to the smoke that he does his best to ignore.

Fuck, he thinks again. His jeans had been dirty, his face in need of a shave, and he was sure he didn't smell the best when he had seen her. Ingrid fucking Devlin, looking beautiful. Her hair soft, her skin . . . he didn't want to think about how soft her skin would feel. How good it would feel to touch her. Caress her. Fuck her.

He feels himself start to get hard. He'll think about her later. When he's in bed. When he can block out the feelings of shame at her seeing just what a disaster he's made of his life. Practically begging her to buy him a cup of tea and a sausage roll. Has he no pride left?

He laughs, a short, harsh laugh. He hasn't had pride in a long time. He has little to be proud of. Living alone, surviving fortnight to fortnight. Always intending to get a job. Never quite managing it. He's not lazy, he tells himself. Declan Heaney is not afraid of hard work. He's just broken. Troubled.

His life changed forever that day, twenty-five years ago. Shouldn't he be over it now? He sucks on his cigarette again. But people keep reminding him of it. Even Ingrid fucking Devlin. He'd have given anything to have her notice him back at school. Here she is and that murder is all she is interested in. What he saw that day. Not who he is. Not his hopes or his struggles. Everything in his life has been framed by those moments on the banks of the rezzie.

Then again, his brother, Niall, was able to get over it. Wasn't he? Saint Niall in his smart suits and with his posh voice. He lost all trace of his Creggan roots as soon as he could – now, his accent has more hints of snobby Belfast than the lyrical Derry twang.

It's been a while since he has spoken to Niall. Maybe he should phone him and give him the heads-up that Ingrid might want to talk to him. No, he doesn't want to speak to Niall. He doesn't want to talk to him about Ingrid. He can picture it now already, Niall on the charm offensive, and he bets he would be just the kind of man Ingrid Devlin would go for. Polished and proper. Not wondering whether he should buy fags or grass on tick again.

Trying to ignore the beeping that warns him his electricity is running low and he'll need to top up the meter, Declan Heaney takes another drag on his cigarette. Maybe all those carcinogens in the cheap fags will do him a favour and finish him off sooner rather than later.

Chapter Eleven

Ingrid

Saturday, 19 October 2019

The train is cold as it trundles along the north coast, through Castlerock, past Benone. There aren't many people on the beaches today. Just a few tourists, by the look of it. Hunting out the *Game of Thrones* locations, no doubt.

I wrap my scarf a little tighter around my neck and wish that I'd put on my thermal tights instead of ordinary opaques. I also wish my car wasn't in the garage so that I could have driven up to meet Jamesy Harte instead of having to rely on the fairly archaic rail system that exists outside Belfast.

I've been told I'm a control freak. I like to do things my way. I don't see that there's anything wrong with that. My way hasn't let me down too often in the past, but the upshot of it is that I feel out of sorts when things can't happen the way I would like. When I have to rely on other people instead of doing everything under my own steam.

I sigh, look down at my laptop again, read over the old

newspaper stories that I'd scanned and saved. I glance at the old picture of Jamesy as he was then. I didn't realise he had been so young when it had happened. Just twenty-two. My hazy childhood memory had him as a grown-up, therefore an 'old person' in my head. He isn't even old now. He'll be in his late forties, with still a lot of life left to live. But he's lost so much.

I study his picture from 1994. I wonder how he'll look now. Older, obviously. More serious. The picture from the paper shows him as I remember him. There was a softness to him. A gullible air. In those non-PC days, he was referred to as 'a bit slow' by those who knew him. 'Not the sharpest knife in the drawer' by others.

Maybe that made it all the easier to pin the blame on him for what happened to Kelly. Or maybe he actually did kill her.

I've met murderers before. I've been charmed by them. Mostly I know how to keep my distance, not to believe all they say. But in my experience, the most dangerous people of all are those who can lie so convincingly, with such emotion, that they can pull the wool over your eyes.

I'm not sure that Jamesy Harte has the wherewithal to be so manipulative. But no other murderer has had the impact on my life that he has. He was the near miss. The scary figure. The proof that it's not just strangers who are dangerous. He became a man to be feared. And I did fear him. For years.

As the train pulls into the station at Coleraine and I prepare to take the final leg of my journey by taxi to Portstewart. The fear that has been ingrained in me for the last twenty-five years rises up in me. I have to focus on my breathing. I am here to do a job and this man, who will sit opposite me, is no threat to me at this time. I will be okay.

★　★　★

We've agreed to meet in a café, and not a very salubrious one at that. Neon cardboard stars with handwritten prices battle condensation on the inner windows to advertise the fare on offer. 'Tea's and Coffee's' are cheap and cheerful, and possess unnecessary apostrophes. I don't imagine I'll be able to get a green tea or a chai latte here – and I'm right.

I take a seat on a slightly wobbly walnut chair and order a pot of tea and a scone. Though the café itself is dank, dark and in need of some TLC, the waitress is warm and welcoming and calls me 'pet' at the end of every sentence.

'Awful day out there, isn't it, pet?' she asks as she busies herself behind the counter, dropping three teabags into a small metal teapot, and setting a mug and a side plate on a tray.

'It is. Cold, too. I don't imagine you've many people about on days like this,' I say, finding comfort in the distraction of small talk.

'You'd be surprised. There's some who love a walk along the promenade in all weathers. They come in here in their wet coats with their runny noses and heat themselves up again while they dry off. The smell of wet coat and wet dog can be fierce in here, pet,' she laughs.

I smile a little.

'What brings you here yourself?' she asks.

'Work,' I tell her. 'I'm meeting someone.'

She raises a not-so-perfectly drawn-on eyebrow. 'Jesus, times must be tough if this is where work gets done these days, pet. Not that I'm trying to get rid of business, but there are better places to make a good first impression.' She laughs, loud and brash.

'I'll be grand where I am,' I say and open my laptop in front of me.

I don't want to continue the conversation. I don't need her to be too interested in why I'm here and what I'm doing. This has to be on the quiet.

She settles herself, sniffs and plonks an anaemic-looking scone on a side plate along with two pats of butter then brings the lot over to me. The tea is as dark as tar as I pour, overflowing and running down the spout, spilling onto the table. I hate strong tea, but I don't ask her to remake it. I just add as much milk as I can without turning it cold and sip gingerly from it, the ashy tang of the scalded leaves burning my tongue.

I hear the door open letting in the noise from the street and an influx of cold air. I turn my head and look to see a man. Tall, thin and wrapped up against the cold. He stares at me and I feel uncomfortable in his gaze. This isn't Jamesy Harte. Or at least it's not the Jamesy Harte I remember from my childhood, or from the pictures I'd looked at on the train.

'Ingrid?' he asks, his voice soft.

There's a familiarity to his tone that I can't deny.

'Jim?' I ask, just as he had instructed.

No one calls him Jamesy any more, apparently. Not to his face. 'People hear my name and they've already made up their mind about me,' he'd said.

He nods, a flash of nervousness crossing his face, before sitting down opposite me. I realise he's as scared as I am.

'Can I get you a cup of tea?' I ask him and he nods.

But I don't want the waitress, no matter how nice she is, to come to our table, so I get up and go to the counter and order it there, waiting for it to be ready and carrying it back myself. With a shaking hand, I place the tea on the table, then I sit down. My mouth is dry and I can feel my body tense up. A moment or two passes. I'm at a loss for words. What do you say when you come face to face with your nightmare?

I sag with relief when the door opens again and a sodden family, loud and complaining about being out in the cold, bundle in and start to discuss what to order at the top of their voices. I feel marginally less nervous when there are more people around and I pull myself together enough to speak.

'Thanks for agreeing to see me,' I say as I try to find something recognisable from my childhood in his features. 'You've changed.'

'Well, so have you, young Devlin. All grown up now.'

He speaks in the same slow way he did on the phone. As if the words are struggling to come from his mouth. I can see his knuckles are white as he lifts his teacup, tension evident in his grasp.

'Well, it's been a long time,' I tell him.

'It most certainly has,' he says wistfully. 'Too long. Sure, it was another life. It's like I was a different person then you know. Before . . .' He speaks with sincerity, his eyes misty with emotion.

'You been here long?'

'Coupla years,' he says with a shrug. 'When I got out, they found me a place in Ballymena, but it wasn't for me. I didn't like it, so my social worker, you know, she helped me find a place here. It's not much, but at least it's near the water. I always liked the water.'

An image of Kelly's broken body lying on the banks of the reservoir comes into my head. I push it away.

'There was never any question of me going back to Derry,' he says. 'There's nothing for me there. It's not home, you know. It stopped being home a long time ago. Then when Mammy died . . .'

A tear, followed by another, rolls down his cheek. He brushes it away as if he is ashamed of it. It strikes me that shame seems to hang over him like a cloud. It lines his face. It spills out of his mouth with his words. Shame, for something he said he didn't do. Shame that so many people have piled on top of him. Me included.

'It broke her heart, you know. Me going to jail. The things

they said about me. The things they said I'd done. How does a mother get over that?'

I set my phone to record as subtly as I can. He glances at it, looks up at me as if he is realising for the first time that this is an interview and not just two people chatting.

He takes a deep breath.

'She wouldn't visit me in prison. Did you know that? Said she wouldn't be able for seeing her son behind bars. She'd rather not see me at all. I think she was worried if she did come, well, some people wouldn't like that. She'd be run out of town. My poor mammy. She didn't ask for any of this.' His eyes, bloodshot, tired, blink at me. 'The last time I saw her was at the sentencing. The last time I got a hug from my mother . . .'

He sips from his tea, looks out of the window, past the thick drops of moisture running down the inner panes. He doesn't finish his sentence. He's lost to the memory playing out in his head.

'But you spoke to her? Or wrote?'

'I'm not one for writing. Not much. Not like you, Ingrid. You've a gift for it. I get muddled up too easily. They told me in prison, you know, they told me I've dyslexia.' He breaks the word down into syllables. 'Die-slex-ee-ah.' As if it required herculean effort to remember it and say it correctly. 'We spoke on the phone. Sometimes. But it upset her, ye know. And then that would upset me – and there's no lonelier place in the world to be than back in your cell worrying about someone outside being in bits over you.'

'Did she stand by you? Believe you?'

'That I didn't do it? Honestly? I don't know. She said she believed me, but she would ask, you know. The odd time. Ask if I had anything to get off my conscience. If I wanted to go to confession. I never liked confession,' he said, his eyes focusing on mine. A dull grey matching his pallor. 'Too claustrophobic.

Too small and too dark – those confessionals. Felt like climbing into a coffin.' He shudders. 'I don't like small spaces. I never did. I like to be outside.'

He pauses and I don't speak, waiting for him to collect his thoughts and continue.

'Anyway, there was a part of her that must have thought I did it. Or else she wouldn't have kept asking.' The sadness radiates from him.

'Sometimes I wondered if I lied and told her it was me, after all, if I went to confession and lied to the priest, too, it would've been easier. She'd have found it in her heart to forgive me if she thought God had forgiven me. And sure, I could always confess then tell the priest I'd also sinned by lying. I'd get round it that way.'

He shrugs, wraps his hands around his mug of tea and looks out of the window. His logic makes me sad to my very core.

'Why now?' I ask him and he looks back at me, confused. 'You're declaring your innocence now. Why?'

'I always said I didn't do it,' he said. 'But I'm tired of people believing I did. I thought, maybe, it would be easier when I got out. Well, I'm out eight years and it's no easier. I'm tired of hiding and being scared. I'm tired of taking the blame for it. This anniversary – it made me think and then I was contacted by that human rights group. They had heard about my case. Looked into it. Said there were problems with the conviction.'

'What problems?' I raise one eyebrow.

'You'd need to talk to them. I get confused in the details,' he says, 'but it made me think, things have changed since then. If the police looked at it again, they might find something now that they didn't then. All that fancy DNA stuff or some-thing. They might ask questions. Why would I have done it? I wouldn't hurt anyone. I wouldn't do that to a wee girl. What he did. That monster. I'm not a monster.'

His voice is shaking with emotion. He has put his mug down and is wringing his hands. I can feel his legs jiggling nervously under the table.

He takes a deep breath. 'I know I don't have brains, you know. I'm not smart. And I'm a wee bit different. I never fitted in. It was just so easy for them to blame me for it all, wasn't it? As soon as they knew I had been out on Halloween night – that I'd no alibi – they just decided it was me and that was that.'

'Where did you go on Halloween night?' I ask, knowing that this was one of the key factors in the prosecution's case.

Jamesy Harte liked to be outside, but he rarely left the safety of his front garden. Mass on Sundays, maybe. A walk with his mother into town. But he was a loner. He didn't go out with friends.

He fidgets in his seat. 'I told everyone where I was,' he sighs. 'But no one believes me. I liked the costumes. I just wanted to see more of them, so I went for a walk up and down the streets. Up Greenwalk and down Broadway. I wasn't even gone very long. Maybe fifteen minutes. But Mammy was asleep when I got back and she couldn't back me up.'

'And what about her wand?' I ask him and he pauses. 'They found it in your house, didn't they? Her wand from that night. And a bobble from her hair. One of her dolls.'

'I didn't take them,' he says, sitting up straight, his voice tight and angry now. 'I knew nothing about them. I've no idea how all that ended up in my house. Someone must've put them there,' he sniffs. 'Someone set me up.'

That was the substantial evidence, you see. That he couldn't get away from. The wand – the simple little accessory covered in tinfoil that Kelly had carried around with her, a bobble from her blonde hair, a Barbie doll – they had been found in his house. His fingerprints had been found on both the doll and

66

the wand – which he said were there from when he had found and picked them up, from behind the sofa.

With that, his lack of alibi and testimony that he used to stand outside his house and wait to talk to school children every day, that some thought he had an unhealthy interest in some of us, the jury had found him guilty.

'Who would have done that?' I ask. 'How?'

I shake away my growing feelings of pity for this poor creature in front of me. Her stuff was found in his house. His house that he rarely left. It seemed impossible that they could've been planted there.

'I don't know!' His voice is loud and thick with emotion.

The family across the café stop chatting and look at us. Jamesy drops his head in his hands.

'I don't know,' he says again, quieter. 'I've spent twenty-five years trying to work that out. Seventeen of those years in a prison cell. You can do a lot of thinking in a prison cell.

'I should have fought harder at the time. But I trusted them, the police and the lawyers. The policeman, he said to me, he said, "If you did nothing wrong, you've nothing to worry about." And I thought, sure I didn't do it. I can't get into trouble if I didn't do it. I kept telling myself that. But that policeman told lies, didn't he? Because I did get into trouble.'

Jamesy rubs at his temples, pressing the pads of his thumbs into the soft flesh. I can feel the stress radiating off him in waves. I glance around and the waitress is eyeing us suspiciously. The family are whispering among themselves and shooting furtive glances our way.

I reach my hand across the table and place it gently on Jamesy's arm. He looks at me and his sadness washes over me. This man is broken. I see his truth in his eyes and I want to believe he is telling me the truth.

'How about we go for a wee walk?' I say to him. 'Free up this table for other people.'

He nods, not questioning my desire to free up a table in a café that has only six customers in it, and at least eight other empty tables already.

I pack up my stuff and watch as he shuffles back into his grey anorak. Everything about him is grey, bleak and diminished.

Before we leave, he thanks the waitress.

'Mammy said there's no excuse for forgetting your manners,' he tells me.

I thank her, too, as she moves to wipe down our table, her eyes never leaving us.

The rain is still falling as we walk up the promenade. It's now a fine drizzle and actually, it feels good to be out in the open air. Jamesy stops and watches as the waves crash to the shore.

'I love the beach,' he says. 'Any time of year. It's beautiful, isn't it?'

I think of all the years he missed this sight. Missed the rain and the tang of salt in the air.

'Jamesy,' I say. 'Tell me about the people who are helping you now. The campaigners. Are they happy enough that you're talking to me?'

He smiles. 'Well, no. They won't be. They take on old cases, test the law or something. I can't remember how they said it. You know what? Sometimes I feel like they talk at me and not to me. Does that make sense? A lot of people like to do that. Well, they – I can send you their details – they told me they'll do the talking for me and I should stay quiet, but you're different, aren't you? I know you. We were sort of friends.'

He smiles, a silly kind of a smile. There's a childish glint to it and I'm reminded of how he was all those years ago. I think of how trusting he is now, telling me his story. I realise I have a responsibility to him to tell it fairly.

I smile back at him. 'We were,' I tell him.

'So, will you support me? Do you think you can get someone to publish my story?' he asks, his expression painfully hopeful. 'Will they tell people that I was set up?'

I blink. I have to be truthful to him. By the sounds of it, enough people have already lied to him.

'I can't make any promises, but hopefully. I have a few ideas of who might use it, but you never know with these things. It's controversial, you know. So, you have to be honest with me. You have to tell me the exact truth. We have to trust each other.'

'I won't fib,' he says, lifting his hand in the Boy Scout salute. 'Scout's honour.'

'And your campaigners,' I add, wary that they probably have an agenda all of their own. 'You've to tell them to trust me and that I know what I'm doing.'

He nods enthusiastically. 'I will. I promise I will, Ingrid.'

'That's good,' I say. 'So, let's get walking, find a quiet spot somewhere and we can start at the beginning.'

He nods. 'There's another coffee shop just up the road a wee bit. We can get in out of the rain before we catch our death of cold.'

'That sounds like a good idea,' I say and again he smiles, as if he's delighted to have said the right thing.

'Can I ask you something first?' he says as we walk.

'Of course.'

'You believe me, don't you?'

'I think I do,' I say softly.

He smiles, a genuine smile that stretches across his face, and claps his hands together. 'That's good, then,' he says. 'That's really good.'

Chapter Twelve

Ingrid

It's dark as I get out of a taxi outside my apartment block and fumble in my bag for my keys. The wind is picking up and whistling through the trees, showering leaves and other detritus all over the street. It has started to rain and it's that thick, heavy, icy-cold kind of a rain that stings when it lands on your skin. I'm almost tempted just to pour everything out of my bag onto the wet ground to find my keys quicker, but luckily my hand brushes against them and I pull them out.

It's only when I go to put them in the front door that I notice it's already ajar.

'For fuck's sake,' I swear under my breath.

I'll have to leave another passive-aggressive note on the communal noticeboard in the hall about this. Surely it's not that difficult to double-check that a door has actually closed tight behind you as you leave. They might as well issue an open invitation to burglars and street drinkers to come on in and make themselves at home. I'm cold and tired, and in no form for people who can't perform the simplest of tasks. My mood worsens.

I just want to be in my flat, under a hot shower, before

slipping into warm pyjamas and pouring myself a glass of wine. I try to focus on that and not my annoyance at the open door as I climb the stairs to my flat, which just so happens to be on the top floor of the four-storey building. I only ever use the lift when I'm weighed down with shopping. The rest of the time I allow myself a smugness at choosing the healthy option. There's a satisfying ache in my calf muscles as I reach the top of the stairs and turn down the corridor towards my own front door.

Except the motion-activated lighting, which should automatically switch on when I enter the corridor, doesn't click on. I swear again. That's another thing I'll have to speak to the management committee about. Although I shouldn't need to. I pay hefty enough fees for the upkeep of the communal spaces. I use the torch on my phone to illuminate the short distance to my front door which, I realise quickly, is ajar, too.

Suddenly, the open front door and the banjaxed light don't seem like mere inconveniences any more. A shiver runs down my spine and I feel my breath catch in my throat. I know I pulled the door shut on my way out. I'm fastidious about it. I always give it a little push afterwards, just to be sure. I freeze, not sure what to do. Do I push the door open, fumble for the light switch inside? Do I call the police? And tell them what? 'My door is open, officer. Please come check my flat for me?' I can only imagine their response – and that's before considering how I haven't always seen eye to eye with the police in this city. They're not fans of me 'sticking my nose in' and I'm not a fan of their sweeping incompetence.

Still, some incompetence might be better than no support at all around now. I try to quiet my breathing, to listen for any unfamiliar creaks. I don't hear anything, but I keep my phone in my hand – unlocked – just in case. And my keys, too, in case I need to defend myself.

Slowly I push open the door, reach my left hand towards the wall and find the light switch. To my utter relief, it comes on and floods the hall with brightness. At first glance nothing looks amiss. My bedroom door is closed, as I left it. The bathroom door is ajar, as is the door to the open-plan kitchen and living room. I cough, loudly. A cough that sounds just as fake as it is. I'm not sure why I do it. It's unlikely an intruder will suddenly introduce him or herself on hearing it.

I look down at my phone, wonder if it's too late to call a friend – or ask someone to come over for a bit. I'm feeling edgy. First my car and now this? I can't ring Trina. It's gone nine and she'll be settled down for the evening, probably a few glasses of wine down. Married life and parenthood have combined to make her predictable. Besides, I don't want to embroil her in this.

I edge my way into the living room, keeping my back tight to the wall so no one can jump up from behind me. Switching on the light, I see the room is untouched and I wonder as I look around if I've been making a mountain out of a molehill. Maybe I wasn't so thorough pulling the door closed as I thought – and it does stick a bit.

I feel brave enough to slip off my coat and hang it over the back of one of the two kitchen chairs. I don't drop my keys or my phone, though. Not yet. And my heartbeat hasn't slowed.

I turn, walk out of the room, push open the bathroom door and pull the light cord. Everything is as it was here, too. Not a thing out of place. I've just my bedroom left to check and for some reason, before I even open the door, I have a feeling I'll find something. A chill is creeping up my spine and my mouth is dry as I put my hand to the door handle and open it.

I see the bed first. My crisp white bed linen now soaked

in red. My stomach tightens, then threatens to turn. Then the wall catches my eye. The same red, streaked on my walls.

There's blood on your hands.

I hear a door slam. My door? I don't know. I can hardly think. I can't breathe. I step back, push my back against the wall and look around me, my hands shaking. I'm trying to unlock my phone, to call for help while I'm not sure if I'm alone. Fear has rendered my fingers all but useless. I'm trembling too much to bring up my contacts list.

Is someone here? Has someone left? And the red? Is it blood? It's as dark as blood, I can see that. It's running down the wall, over the fresh white paint. It's spattered on my headboard. My heart is beating so fast I'm sure it might just jump out of my throat. I catch a hint of something on the air, a smell. Paint, I think. Could it be paint?

Gingerly I reach out, try to touch the red liquid on my bed. It's cold, thick. I bring my shaking hand to my face and sniff. I was right – it is paint – and I almost, almost sag with relief. But even though it might not be blood on the walls, and on my bed, there's no doubt what the intention behind it is. And I can't escape the fact that someone has been here. Someone knows where I live. Someone knows how to get into my house, into my bedroom. Someone wants to scare me.

They've succeeded.

I want to leave. I want to rewind ten minutes, come back and find that this is all a figment of my imagination. I don't want to stay here, like a sitting duck, on my own waiting for the police to come. The tightness in my chest ramps up – it feels like someone is squeezing my heart and lungs and I'm struggling to gasp at the air around me.

I wish my mother hadn't moved away. That my father wasn't dead. That I could run to the family home that had provided me with such comfort when I was small. I wish I could run to Trina's, but we're not that close – not close enough for Saturday night break-ins and breakdowns. I mentally scan through a list of friends and acquaintances and realise, with a thud, that there aren't many – if any – I can call on right now.

The sensible part of me screams at me to call the police. The part of me that feels fear and wants comfort screams at me to run to somewhere I feel safe and cared for.

My hands sweaty, my fingers still clumsy and shaking, I scroll through my phone and hit the call button.

I'm almost weak with relief when I hear his voice.

'Can I come round to your place? Jen and the boys are away, aren't they?'

'They are and of course you can.'

'Good, I'll be there as soon as I can get a taxi over.'

'Are you okay? You sound shaken?'

That question. Suddenly, I'm not sure I want to tell him the truth. I don't want him to know just how shaken I am. I don't want to see pity in his face, hear the undertones of 'I told you so' in his voice.

'I'm fine,' I lie. 'I just fancied some company.'

It's a huge understatement. What I want is a distraction. Something to lift me out of this scary, dark place. It doesn't matter if that distraction is good for me or not.

'Good. Okay. See you soon.'

He sounds cynical. He probably doesn't believe me, but he'll forget that when I get there. He is easily distracted.

'Yes, see you soon, Ryan,' I say, hanging up and already feeling ashamed of what I'm about to do. I'm not the kind of mistress who feels devoid of shame at sleeping with another woman's husband.

Chapter Thirteen

Ingrid

'This is a nice surprise,' Ryan says, helping me out of my still-damp coat. 'Were you out walking in the rain?'

I'm shivering and my teeth are chattering, but I don't think it's with the cold. I can't deny it. I'm glad to see him. To hear his voice – it's comforting.

'Sure, I got the taxi to drop me at the bottom of the street. Can't be seen pulling up outside. What would the neighbours think?' I reply, turning to face him.

'Stuff the neighbours,' he says, putting one hand to my face and brushing my hair back. 'I don't care what they think.'

His breath is warm and smells of beer as he presses his lips against mine. I pull him close. I want to feel the weight of his body tight against mine. I want to block out the noise and the fear. I want to block out my guilt at needing him – a married man – so badly.

Because I do need him. Right now, I need him – and I know if he can hold me so close that I can feel what I do to him, then I can forget it all for a time. I can become lost in the most basic of instincts and the most animal of feelings.

I won't even think about who he is – how we have promised

each other time and time again that we aren't going to do this any more. That it's not good for either of us. Not professional. Not fair to Jen and the boys. Not fair to each other. Because this is not love. This is not even 'like'. This is sex. This is scratching an itch for both of us and nothing more.

It's angry, physical sex that distracts and makes my nerve endings tingle, to the point that all I can focus on are the sensations coursing through my body. The wrongness of it is part of what makes it so irresistible, even though each time I find myself alone with Ryan, his hands groping at me, making me melt time and time again, I swear it will be the last time. I swear I won't ever show him how weak I am again. Because this, this need for something animalistic on a wet Saturday night when his wife and children are out of town, and I'm trying to block out how scared I am, this is very much a sign of my weakness.

I lose myself in it as he groans, moves inside me until he calls my name and gasps, his body juddering then stilling, his breathing heavy. 'Jesus Christ,' he mutters. We've not even made it out of the hall this time.

I pull away from him, go to the bathroom to freshen up. Looking in the mirror, I stare at my flushed face. A sheen of sweat covers my forehead. What remained of my lipstick is gone, my hair is frizzing from the rain, my eyes are tired. I try to catch my breath because it still hasn't settled. I try to fight back the urge to cry or scream. I don't want to be scared. I don't want to tell Ryan I'm scared. That will just show him even more of my weakness. In this moment, I wish this could be something more. He could be someone else. That he is someone who loves me and that I love him. But he isn't someone else and we don't love each other.

I stand and breathe in and out in this lovely family bathroom. There are traces of Jen everywhere. Soft grey towels against the polished white tiles. A reed diffuser from Next, a bottle of Jo Malone Lime Basil & Mandarin handwash, with accompanying hand cream. One of those faux cool signs on the wall, black frame, words in black print: Wash your hands, you filthy animal.

Jen is a nice woman. Friendly. Stylish but not overdone. Quiet. A good mother, by all accounts. I have eaten dinner, prepared by her, at her table. I have drunk her wine and laughed with her sons. I have discussed my favourite TV programmes with her, sitting on her sofa, drinking a cup of tea she has made.

But I have also fucked her husband. And not because I love him, because I don't. I admire him, for the journalist he is. For the life he has led. He can make me laugh and he can infuriate me. He can challenge me and inspire me. But I don't love him. There is little point. He has made it clear, always, that he will never leave Jen. Not now. Not when the children have grown up and moved out. Not ever.

Not that I want him to. Maybe there was a time when I entertained that little fantasy, but that's long gone.

I wash my hands, using Jen's expensive soap, and I dry them on her perfectly fluffed towel.

My breathing is no calmer. I'm horrified to find that the fear I'd felt at home hasn't eased. It's not become any clearer to me what I should or shouldn't do. Whether or not I should call the police. Actually, I know I *should* call the police. I just don't want to.

I walk back to the living room, which is as tastefully decorated as the rest of the house. A picture of Ryan, Jen and their two teenage boys smiles down at me from the wall. It's one of those arty 'look at us in our jeans and white T-shirts' shots that screams 'happy family'.

Ryan is sitting, smiling like the cat that got the cream, on his sofa. Two glasses of a rich red Malbec are poured and sitting on the coffee table in front of the fire.

I sit down on the other end of the sofa. My itch has been scratched and I have no desire at all to be close to him physically any more. Lifting the glass, I fight the urge to down the wine in one go. I don't want to do anything that will belie my emotional state.

'Jesus, Ingrid. You're like a woman possessed. Not that I'm complaining,' he says with a satisfied grin.

I cringe internally at my own neediness but do my best to keep my expression neutral.

'Things were so tense between us all week at work, I never thought you'd be up for meeting this weekend,' he adds. 'I thought I'd give you some space to calm down.'

I look at him, drink deeply from my wine glass, shrug my shoulders. I can play this part. I'm well-practised at it.

'I didn't intend to come here. But, you know, Saturday night and I was bored . . .' I lie. It surprises me how easily it trips off my tongue.

'Well, I'm happy to provide a distraction, and I'm definitely happy to see you. Will you stay over? You can, you know. Jen and the boys won't be back until tomorrow dinner time at the earliest, so you know, we could make the most of it. It's not often we get the opportunity.'

'I didn't think this was a stay-the-night kind of arrangement,' I say, staring down into my glass.

'It can be,' he says, and there's a longing in his eyes.

Whether it's for another shag or something more meaningful, I don't know. I don't want to consider the latter scenario. There is no good that can come out of developing anything more than a colleagues-with-benefits relationship with him. Even if I wanted to continue to hide here, it would only be a temporary fix. I would be fooling myself.

I shake my head. 'We've been over this before. Why it's a bad idea. Jen doesn't deserve this.'

'I hate to burst your bubble, but if by "this" you mean us sleeping together, then that has already happened,' he says. 'Many times. Not least twenty minutes ago when you threw yourself at me.'

Shaking my head, I say, 'I mean this as in us sharing a bed, your marital bed, in your home. You've made it clear you're not going to leave her — and I don't want you to, either. So, let's not make it more than what it is.'

'Don't you ever get lonely?' Ryan asks, putting his wine glass down on the floor, sitting forwards so that he can look in my eyes.

Those big blue eyes, searching my face, trying to read me. I break the stare. Look down at my glass.

'We all get lonely, Ryan. Even those of us in big houses with partners and children.'

This is all starting to feel a little claustrophobic now. He wants to have a big chat. One of those deep and meaningfuls, and God, it's the very last thing on my mind. I came here to escape my worries, not add to them.

The thought of the red paint sliding down my wall in long, skinny drips comes back into my head.

'Actually, I think I should probably go. I'm going to call a taxi.'

I put my glass down, fish in my bag for my phone.

'Are you serious?' he asks, incredulous. 'You've not even been here an hour and you're off again?'

'You got what you wanted, didn't you?' I ask him.

'You're a total bitch at times, Ingrid,' he says.

'Maybe. But I'm also right. Look, I'll wait for the taxi at the bottom of the street.'

'But it's lashing it down.'

'I'm not made of sugar and I won't melt,' I tell him as I put my coat back on and lift my bag. 'Thanks for the wine.'

I hear him swear as I pull closed the front door, but I walk on anyway. When the taxi pulls up, not only am I soaking, but I'm also shaking again – a mixture of anger, fear and exhaustion coursing through my veins. I don't want to go home. Not tonight. Not in the dark. But nor do I want to land on the doorstep of family or friends. I don't want to answer questions.

I ask the driver to drop me off at the Maldron Hotel in the city centre, praying they aren't fully booked. I'll deal with everything else in the morning.

I toss and turn. My head is too full to allow me to sleep, even in the comfort of a super king-size bed. I'm not sure what I should do next. Clear up the mess in my flat? Add some more security measures? Look for somewhere new to live? None of the options are ideal. Some are not even possible. I can't add to the communal security of the block, and I sure as hell can't afford to move right now.

Massaging my temples and giving up on sleep, I accept that I really shouldn't waste any more time before I call the police. I should've called them straight away. No doubt they'll ask all sorts of questions about why I didn't, about where I went instead. I'll have to lie. Fuck. I can't have them landing at Ryan's door asking questions. What if Jen is back?

What will Ryan say if he finds out the real reason for my unexpected visit?

I sit up, make a cup of tea in the hotel room, trying not to think about all those stories that fly around the Internet about people boiling their underwear in hotel kettles.

I run the power shower, stand under the pulsing stream, grateful beyond words to feel the thrum of the water pummel my skin and reinvigorate me.

I remind myself that I'm only doing my job and sometimes my job gets a bit scary. Not everyone wants the truth to come out, but that doesn't mean we stop trying to find it. I don't bow to intimidation – no matter how intimidating – although it does strike me as odd that it seems to be the case that someone knows I'm in contact with Jamesy Harte.

After talking to him yesterday, I've no reason to think I shouldn't be speaking to him. He made quite a compelling case and I'm even more of the mind that he wouldn't have had the wherewithal to commit such a crime, never mind try to hide it.

He has as much of a right to have his voice heard as the Doherty family – more even, if he is telling the truth.

I turn the shower off, wrap a towel around me and play back the interview with Jamesy on my phone while I dry off and get dressed. His voice. His naivety. His pain.

He's either telling the truth, or he's as good a liar as they come.

Chapter Fourteen

Ingrid

Sunday, 20 October 2019

Detective Sergeant Eve King arrives at my flat just over an hour after I call the police. In the cold light of day, as the early winter sun streams in through the window, I feel less spooked. Not much less spooked, but enough that I don't want to throw up every time I look at the paint on the wall.

I've just made up a pot of fresh coffee, when the door buzzer sounds, and I let DS King in. She's accompanied by her tall, gangly colleague, DC Mark Black. All of our paths have crossed before and I know DS King sees me as a thorn in her side. I wonder if she is experiencing a sense of *schadenfreude* right now.

'Ms Devlin,' Eve King says as I open the door.

I spot a uniformed officer further down the corridor. No doubt this will be talk of the whole building.

'I think we know each other well enough that you can call me Ingrid now,' I reply.

DS King neither smiles nor tells me I'm okay to use her first name in return; instead she glances around, takes a pair of latex gloves out of her pocket and puts them on.

'You said you had a break-in?'

'That's right. I did. When I came home last night, just after nine, the door was open. My door, and the door to the complex. I went into my bedroom and saw this . . .'

I turn to lead her to my room, but she doesn't follow. When I reach for the handle to open the door, I hear an intake of breath.

'Try to touch as little as possible,' she says. 'In case there is trace evidence.'

'Sorry,' I mumble. It unnerves me how having the police in my own home makes me feel much more vulnerable.

'So,' she says, 'you found the doors open when you got home last night?'

She has one eyebrow raised when I look at her.

'Yes. About nine. I'd been working all day and came home . . .'

She raises a hand to stop me, mid flow. I'm pretty sure she's enjoying this.

'If you discovered a break-in last night, why are you only calling it in now?'

DC Black stifles a smile. I glare in his direction and he straightens up. I don't have to remind him that I know exactly how to land him in deep trouble if I was so inclined.

Turning my attention back to DS King, I speak, doing my best to be honest, but not too honest.

'I . . . I freaked out, I suppose. I was tired and scared and I certainly wasn't thinking straight. I just wanted to get away from here. I know Saturday night is a busy night for the police. I couldn't stand the thought of waiting around. I just needed to go somewhere else. So I went and checked in at the Maldron for the night.'

I don't mention my stop-off at Ryan's house on the way.

'We could've helped. Someone would have been with you as soon as was possible,' DS King says.

'I'm hoping you can help now,' I say, turning back towards my bedroom door and opening it.

DC Black moves around me, walks to the far side of my bed and examines the wall closely.

'This seems to be the only room he, or she, touched,' I say. 'Everything else was in its place.'

'Nothing stolen?'

'Not that I have noticed.'

'And that's paint, isn't it?' DS King asks, nodding her head towards the wall.

'Thankfully, yes. It appears to be nothing more sinister.'

'There's blood on your hands,' DC Black reads aloud. 'And do you know what that might be referring to?' he asks me.

He speaks to me as if we are total strangers, as if we don't have our arrangement on the side. As if I've not seen him slightly the worse for wear from alcohol.

I blink. Direct my answer primarily to Eve King.

'I'm not sure, but it could be to do with a story I'm chasing at the moment. It's the anniversary of a child's murder. Kelly Doherty. I'm not sure if you'll remember that . . . Not everyone is happy about it. Especially now Jamesy Harte is making noises about an appeal.'

DS King nods. 'I know the case,' she says, and of course she does – DS King is the kind of woman who knows everything.

She takes her phone from her pocket and snaps a picture or two of the wall.

'You do seem to like getting yourself into all sorts of trouble, don't you?'

Her tone is friendly, but I believe it to be little more than an act.

'Well, if you mean I'm not afraid to do my job and ask tough questions, then I suppose so,' I say, my heckles rising.

'Well, that's not what I meant, but . . .' She looks around the room again, turns to DC Black and tells him to call in SOCO and check for any CCTV images at the main entrance.

'Those cameras have been out of action for weeks now,' I tell her. 'I've complained about it, but nothing's been done.'

'There might be some footage from the walkway. The council offices' cameras might have caught something,' DC Black says. 'I'll get that checked.'

'Great,' DC King replies. 'And, Ms Devlin . . . I mean, Ingrid . . . maybe we can have a sit down and go over some details.'

I nod and lead her to the living room. I even offer to pour them both a cup of coffee, which they both decline, and then I go over the events of the previous night, down to the broken lights in the corridor outside my flat.

'I didn't get overly alarmed when the lights weren't working in the hallway last night. Things here break. A lot. If it's the weekend, you can forget about them getting fixed, even though we pay through the nose for management fees. But now, I think someone might have tampered with them.'

'I'll look into that, too,' DC Black says.

DS King speaks. 'And you went to the Maldron. How did you get there? Did you drive? Phone a taxi?'

I shift awkwardly, wondering if I can get away with not telling the entire truth.

'I got a taxi. It was late and it was raining. My car's in the garage . . .'

She nods and I take a deep breath; I might as well tell her the truth about that at least.

'It was vandalised on Thursday night. So it's in for repair.'

'Vandalised how?' she asks.

'A window put in. Someone spray-painted the word "scum" on the bonnet. They left me a note.'

I watch as she looks back to DC Black. She sighs.

'And you didn't report this?'

'No. I just took the car to the garage. Thought it was just some yob, annoyed I'd reported his court case or something. It happens.'

'And you say there was a note. What did it say?'

I blush. Damn it. I'm about to be caught out in my own lie.

'Something about letting the paedo rot,' I say, my face blazing.

'Doesn't sound like the words of just some yob, does it?' Eve King asks.

'No. No, I suppose not. I just didn't think it was anything serious.'

She raises an eyebrow. She's not even trying to hide the smirk on her face now.

'Didn't think it was anything serious,' she says slowly as she writes the words into her notebook, shaking her head at the end.

'Look, officers, here's the thing. I'm a journalist. If I contacted you every time I got a nasty letter in the post, you'd never have time to do any other work.'

'Surely you don't get the window of your car put in on a regular basis, though?' DS King asks.

'Well . . . no . . . But you can't help but make enemies in this job. Journalists fall foul of everyone at some time. Even the police,' I say, looking directly at her.

She doesn't blush, but then again, it's not her toes I've trodden on. Her boss, the inimitable DI Bradley, might not stay so quiet if he were here.

'I'd say someone breaking into your home and leaving this message escalates things, though,' she says.

I can't argue, so I nod. 'And that's why I called you.'

'You say you were working all day. At the newspaper office?'

'No. I was in Portstewart. Doing an interview. Research for a book.'

'Another true crime book on the go?' she asks.

I nod. 'Well, hopefully. I don't have it signed off by my editor yet, but that's the plan.'

'Related to the Kelly Doherty murder?'

I wonder if she knows that Portstewart is where Jamesy has been housed. I imagine she does.

'As it happens, I was interviewing Jamesy Harte yesterday.'

She raises an eyebrow again while she writes his name in her notebook – as if she is ever likely to forget it.

'The aforementioned "paedo" alluded to on the note in your car, perhaps?' she asks.

'He claims he was framed. That he was an easy target.'

'The police investigation and trial jury clearly thought differently,' she says. 'And I'd hazard a guess he's not come to Derry because he knows he might not be welcome here.'

'Yes. That's correct.'

'And are there many people who knew you were talking to Jamesy? Who know you're working on this book.'

I think for a moment. There's Ryan and Declan. Lorcan Duffy, the councillor, knows I'm doing interviews. I'm sure some of my colleagues have an idea. But none of those people knew I was in Portstewart yesterday.

I give DS King a list of all those names and tell her, honestly, I can't imagine any of those people being in any way responsible for the break-in, or the attack on my car.

She tells me she'll have to talk to them and I cringe at what Ryan will say. So much for keeping this quiet. I jump at a buzz at the door signalling the arrival of the SOCO team.

Chapter Fifteen

Declan

It's cold in the flat. So cold that Declan really doesn't want to get out of bed, even though his bladder is fit to burst. Through bleary, bloodshot eyes he looks at his phone to see what time it is. The darkness in the room, coupled with the time of year, means it could be any time at all in the day. He hopes it's close to afternoon – that he has slept away a large portion of the day.

His head hurts. Self-inflicted. Too much to drink last night, followed by a few joints. He'd felt good last night, for a while. But now the self-hate has come crashing in, and as he finally gives in to the desperate need to pee and climbs out of his warm bed into the icy coolness of his bedroom, he shudders.

He'll ask his ma to sub him some money for the electric. Again. At least he can put a heater on, for an hour. Take the chill off.

His bladder emptied, he walks to his kitchen – around which lies the detritus of the night before – and opens the cupboard, looking for something to eat. There isn't much to whet his appetite and he wonders if he should go up and see his ma early. Try to cadge a Sunday dinner off her. There's not a Sunday goes by that she doesn't have a roast dinner of some description on the go and she always cooks extra. Besides, he really does need to try to get some money to top up the electricity before the power goes off altogether and he can't even charge his phone.

If he gets to his ma's early enough, while his da is still at Mass, he might be able to score a bacon sandwich for breakfast too. If he's lucky he'll get to eat it without his da chiming in about how spoiled he is and how he needs to get his life together.

It takes too much of his mental energy to challenge his da, to tell him he's one to talk. And he's not in the mood for a row.

Declan throws some clothes into a bag, along with his razor and deodorant. Timing it properly, he'll be able to make use of her hot water while he's there to have a long soak in the bath. It will be much more enjoyable than standing under the pathetic trickle of never-quite-hot-enough water that passes for a shower in his flat.

He feels better for it. For getting up and getting out of the house. It would be pushing his luck, he surmises, if he showed up with a bag of washing, too. Although his ma would do it for him. She never says no. She might complain, roll her eyes, but secretly, he thinks she's delighted to help out. She's guarded with her public displays of affection, aware that she will be accused of being 'too soft' on him, but she has other ways to show her love.

She takes care of him, still. She'll lend him the money for the electricity, which she never wants back. She'll also drop a few items into a bag for him to take home and fill his cupboards. He used to feel a bit ashamed when she did that – that he wasn't able to provide fully for his own needs – but now he sees it for what it is.

It's love.

Or that's what he tells himself.

His mood dips, however, when he turns into his street and sees Niall's car — a shiny 4x4 with all the latest auto gadgetry — parked outside. Niall, the only person in the world who can make him feel worse about his life than his da can. He's tempted to turn and go back home, but he's come this far now and his stomach is grumbling, anxious to be fed. The lure of a warm bath is also too strong to ignore, especially walking in the icy-cold rain with the wind blowing a gale. He'll offer up his time with Niall for the holy souls, he thinks — not sure if he believes that souls exist, holy or otherwise, or if they go anywhere after a person dies.

An image of Kelly Doherty, on the banks of the reservoir, comes back into his mind. Her eyes wide and glassy when they turned her over. Her mouth open just a little. Mud and blood. Filthy water trickling out between her once pale pink lips. They weren't pink any more. She was translucent. Except for the places where decomposition had already begun.

He pushes the image from his head. Wishes there was a way he could push it from his mind permanently. This bloody anniversary is stirring up too much. He pauses at the end of his mother's garden path and wonders does Niall think about it much. Does it keep him awake at nights? Does he have to self-medicate to try to forget? Probably not. He's too happy. Too successful for that. He self-medicates maybe with his designer clothes and his fancy car.

The sight of smoke curling from the chimney and the promise of a warm fire are what finally persuade him not to turn round, after all. He doesn't have to talk to Niall. Not much, anyway.

Washed and shaved. In clean clothes that his mother pressed for him before slipping a twenty-pound note in the back pocket of his jeans. Declan is sitting in the same seat at the kitchen table that he sat at as a child. Niall is directly opposite him, as it always was. His parents fill the remaining two chairs, and Snoopy, his mother's beloved mutt, is asleep at his feet.

The table is laden with a good Sunday dinner with all the trimmings. Roast chicken, mashed potato, roasties, carrots and broccoli. Gravy so thick you could stand a spoon up in it is sitting in a measuring jug. There's no need for a gravy boat here. The jug does the job. A tall glass of cold milk sits in front of Declan and it's all he can do not to shovel the food into him like a savage. He has long passed 'hungry' and moved on to ravenous, despite the bacon sandwich he devoured not two hours before.

He feels the gentle pat of his mother's hand on his, a signal that he can start eating.

'No potatoes for me,' Niall says. 'I'm shredding at the moment, so chicken and veg will be fine. I'll avoid the gravy, too.'

'Christ, Niall. That's no dinner at all. You need more than that!' Declan hears his ma proclaim.

He himself has two reactions. The first that it means there is more food for him and that's no bad thing, and the second that his brother really has become a self-important prick recently. 'Shredding.' For fuck's sake. Why? To compete in the primary school teachers' Olympics? He bites back a smile at his own joke, spears an especially crunchy-looking roast potato on his fork and takes it for a swim around the gravy on his plate before eating it in one bite.

'I'm not getting any younger, Ma,' Niall says. 'I'm just trying to look after myself. No one ever died from going easy on the spuds now, did they?'

'Apart from all those people in the Potato Famine,' Declan quips.

His brother glares at him. Niall Heaney doesn't like being

bested by anyone. Declan allows himself to enjoy the warm feeling of smugness at making his brother look stupid.

He ignores his da, who straightens in his chair. Declan knows this body language well. 'No messing about at the table allowed.' It was drummed into them from an early age. He decides not to make any more jokes.

'How's the hunt for work going?' Niall asks him, knowing full well that Declan hasn't been able to secure any work, despite his efforts.

Admittedly his efforts could be better, but there are days he can barely lift his head, never mind fill in some stupid application form that won't even secure him an interview in the first place. His criminal record – petty crimes: drunk and disorderly, breaking and entering business premises – hasn't endeared him to prospective employers.

'Well, you know. Irons in the fire and all that,' he says.

'I'd think those irons would be well heated by now,' Niall says, eyeballing him.

When, Declan wonders, did they drift apart? They were as thick as thieves as children – impossible to tell apart – and now he barely recognises his brother when he looks at him. He's certainly nothing like the reflection Declan sees in his own mirror. And it's not just because of his brother's shiny suit and the moisturised skin. It's the look in his eyes.

Contentment? No, he doesn't think it's that. Coldness, maybe? There is a bitter streak in his brother, buried below the surface but there all the same. Maybe it's just smugness, he thinks. Niall Heaney certainly thinks he is better than the family he left behind in Derry. That much is obvious.

'Here, Declan. I was talking to Paddy up at the shops and he told me he saw you talking to that Ingrid Devlin girl the other day,' his ma says.

He notices how Niall's eyes widen just a little.

'What's the great Ms Devlin doing slumming it back in Creggan?' Niall asks. 'Surely she didn't come here just to see you?'

'Niall, don't be such a brat to your brother,' his ma chimes in, and Declan feels all of fourteen years old again.

'She was working, as it happens,' he says. 'What with Kelly Doherty's anniversary coming up and Jamesy making noises about appealing his conviction.'

A silence descends on the room. Knives and forks stop clattering against plates. His da puts his cutlery down altogether, sips from his glass of milk before putting it down, a little too heavily, on the table. The room is silent now, apart from the ticking of the kitchen clock.

'I don't see the need to be dredging any of that horrible business back up again,' his ma says, lifting the tea towel she had draped over her knee as a makeshift napkin and folding it before setting it on the table and getting up, her dinner barely touched.

'You know, he's saying he's innocent,' Declan said. 'That he was set up. He has campaigners and all.'

'Jesus, Mary and Saint Joseph,' his da says. 'He must have a death wish. Was it not proven in court? Is that not enough for him? He'd be best to keep his mouth shut.'

The volume of Declan's da's voice has increased just a fraction with every word. Declan notices the muscles tense in his da's jawline.

'Shame on him – putting that poor girl's family through all this again. Have they not suffered enough?' his ma says, her voice soft.

But she's agitated. He can see that.

She gets up and walks to the sink to run herself a glass of water from the tap. She holds the glass to her forehead as if trying to cool herself down.

'But if he didn't do it?' Declan says.

Just as his ma gives him a warning glance, Declan hears the thump of a fist on the table, feels the vibration of the impact, sees the plates and cutlery shift as if they are startled, too.

'For Christ's sake, Declan, the dogs on the street know he did it. He didn't get put away for nothing,' his da says.

Niall says nothing. Just lifts his glass of milk and takes a long drink from it.

'I hope you're not going to talk to her again,' his ma says. 'Don't be stirring things up. There are a lot of painful memories there, son.'

'Really?' he asks, unable to keep the sarcastic tone from his voice. 'Of everyone, I think I might be aware of that.'

'Don't you dare speak to your mother like that!' his da barks. 'Sauntering in here like the layabout you are, taking whatever your mother will give you – and don't think I don't notice. Because I do. I'm not stupid. And then talking back to her. You've a cheek, Declan.'

'Frankie,' his ma urges. 'Don't be getting upset. Your blood pressure.'

'Then tell this buck eejit here he hasn't the first notion. Talking to Ingrid bloody Devlin! She'd sell her granny for a good story. And who is it she works for again? *The Chronicle*, is it? That Ryan Murray is editor there . . . I thought he'd more sense. Stupid bastard.'

Declan watches as his ma rests her hand on his da's shoulder. His heart is in his mouth because he knows this could go one of two ways. The soft touch of her hand will calm his father into submission, or it will enrage him further. He doesn't want to feel responsible for what might happen.

'Message heard,' he says. 'It wasn't on purpose, you know. We just bumped into each other. It's not like I can tell her anything, anyway. Not anything new.'

His father settles down, appeased by his response. Even if he hasn't exactly told the truth. Yes, their meeting was accidental, but he does know things about that night, things he hasn't dared to speak to anyone about. Not even Niall.

But he won't antagonise things further. He'll just finish his dinner and go home. He already has twenty pounds from his mother stashed in his pocket, thankfully. He doesn't need to ask her now.

His father declares he has lost his appetite. Stands up and leaves his plate on the table for someone else to tidy away.

'I'm going for a walk,' he says, grabbing his coat.

They all want to ask him if he means he's going to the pub. Declan hopes not. It's been years since his da was drunk, but memories of those days have never left him.

'I wonder if she wants to speak to me,' Niall says eventually as the three remaining members of the Heaney family pick at their plates.

Their dinner is cold now. Nowhere near as appetising as it was.

Declan says nothing. He doesn't want his brother anywhere near Ingrid. He has already decided that he isn't going to tell Niall that he has her number saved in his phone, or that she did actually mention wanting to talk to him. He doesn't lie, just gives a non-committal half nod and says no more.

'I always liked her,' Niall says, a wolfish look on his face.

Declan tries to remember when he started hating his brother.

Chapter Sixteen

Ingrid

Monday, 21 October 2019

I had double-locked my front door and put a chair in front of it. I'd also locked my own bedroom door, but none of that had helped me sleep particularly well. I'd never realised before how noisy my flat can be. I wonder how I'd ever been able to tune out all the rattles and creaks before, not to mention the noise of the traffic outside.

I have a coffee before I leave for work, and then stop and grab another coffee – extra large – on the way in. If I could source an intravenous caffeine drip and attach it directly to my veins, I absolutely would. At least, I console myself, it's a Monday and, as the song says, Mondays are manic. Hopefully, a busy day will keep me distracted from the waves of exhaustion that are just waiting to wash over me.

My head hurts, so I rifle through my drawer to find the strip of paracetamol that has been there for the last six or seven months. I'm not one to reach for pills, but these are desperate times.

Once I've logged in to my computer, I check my emails. There's the usual Monday morning stuff. Court lists, press releases on upcoming events, a round robin from the police press office detailing any incidents of note over the weekend. My stomach tightens when I see a paragraph headlined 'Break-in at city centre apartment complex.'

Police are looking for information about a break-in at a flat in the Riverside Complex, which took place sometime between the hours of 11 a.m. and 9 p.m. on Saturday evening.

The female resident of the apartment returned home to find her front door open and threatening graffiti sprayed on the walls of her bedroom. Nothing appears to have been taken in the break-in.

Police are appealing for anyone who may have seen anyone behaving in a suspicious manner, or who may have information about the incident, to contact them at Strand Road Police Station.

'Fuck,' I swear, not quite under my breath, as my phone rings that single tone of an internal call. I already know it will be Ryan.

'Was it you?' he says as I answer. 'Is that why you called over on Saturday night in such a strange mood? Was it your place? I've a message here saying that a DS Eve King wants to speak to me. What the fuck, Ingrid?'

His voice is quiet, but there's no denying the angry intonation in his speech. It's grossly unfair of him to do this over the phone while he very clearly knows I'm sitting in a busy newsroom and not at liberty at all to comment on any late-night visits to his home while his wife was away.

'Yes,' I say, keeping my tone professional. 'It was my place, but I'd prefer not to talk about it. I've a lot of work to do here, so do you mind if I just get on with it?'

'A threatening message, Ingrid. What did it say?'

'It was just some nonsense. Didn't even make sense. The police are exaggerating,' I lie. 'But look, I'm due in court in half an hour, so I really need to get going.'

I'm actually not due in court. It's not my day for sitting on the press bench reporting on the city's penitent petty criminals, but I'll do it anyway. Tell Trina she can stay at her desk and that I don't mind going. Anything to get me out from under Ryan's watch. And tonight, for once, I'll make sure to leave before him so as to avoid another one of his lectures.

As I pack up my bag, swig back the rest of my coffee and throw a new reporter's notebook into my bag, I glance through the window that separates Ryan's office from the rest of the newsroom. He has a face like thunder as he talks to some other poor unfortunate on the phone, possibly even poor DS King. In fact, by the look he fires in my direction, the expression of shock closely morphing into anger, I'm almost sure he is talking to DS King. I grab my phone and rush out of the office. I'll get a taxi to pick me up from the side of the street and I'll definitely ring the garage to find out just when they expect my car to be ready.

It's dark when I get home and I can't lie – I feel nervous heading back to my flat, even though the police have promised extra patrols in the area. The lights in the corridor are, thankfully, working again and when I reach my door, it is closed and locked. I let myself in to where I'd left a lamp on in the hall so that I wouldn't be returning to darkness. Everything is calm and as I left it.

I flick the switch on at the kettle and drop two slices of bread into the toaster. It's a lazy dinner, but it's all I have the energy for. I make a cup of tea and sitting down at the table, I rifle through my post, checking for anything of importance. I'm examining my latest credit card statement (very depressing, as it happens), when my phone vibrates with a notification.

It's a friend request on Facebook. I click to open it and am greeted by a semi-familiar face. He's older now, of course. The years have been kind to him – he is very handsome, as it happens. There's a cheeky glint in his eye, one I remember from twenty years ago. One that is most certainly no longer there in his brother's eyes – Niall Heaney, Declan's twin.

I'm intrigued enough to accept the request immediately and start to stalk my way through his Facebook page, looking at all the pictures of him smiling, shirt and tie, clean-shaven face. His shirtsleeves rolled up, exposing toned and tanned forearms. Him on what looks like a sunny holiday. Him standing in front of a group of gap-toothed children, all of them giving the thumbs up to the camera. The caption reads: 'Great work in our accelerated reading programme this year from Primary 5. This is my favourite part of teaching.'

The flurry of likes and comments from his, mostly female, followers leaves me in no doubt that Niall Heaney is popular with the fairer sex. I'm reading the responses, some of the blatant flirting, when my phone pings with a Facebook Messenger notification.

Hey stranger, thanks for accepting my request! Hope all is good with you. You certainly look good;)

I cringe a little at the compliment. I know he most likely says this to all the women in his life – or at least all the women of a certain age who he thinks he might stand a chance with. I'm familiar with his type.

I was in Derry at the weekend, catching up with the family. Declan was saying you're researching Kelly's murder, for the anniversary. He said you might want to chat with me.

I smile. I do indeed want to talk to him.

I don't suppose you have any more plans to be back down in Derry? I type. *These kinds of interviews tend to go better face to face.*

He replies with a smiley-faced emoji, which isn't entirely appropriate given the seriousness of the issue we are due to discuss, but I hope it means he's amenable to it. There's no doubt you can draw more out of a story from someone sitting across the room from you than you can over an online chat, or even a phone call. I watch the three little dots appear on the screen that indicate he is typing and I wait for his response.

I didn't have plans, but I can make them. Working all week, but how does your Friday night look?

Friday night is not usually a time I choose to work, but there's no doubt it will add to the narrative to have Niall's side of things in his own words. I'm sure I can manage to keep things on a professional level. I reply that Friday night would suit and we arrange to meet in Starbucks in the Foyleside Shopping Centre.

After what has been a stressful day, I feel the tension start to slip from my shoulders. I decide a bath will relax me completely, so I go to my bedroom to gather my dressing gown and my book to read while I soak. I look at my bed, stripped bare. I've thrown out all the paint-stained bedding. I'll buy a new duvet and pillows tomorrow. The graffiti on the wall is still there — vivid and stark. I've arranged for a painter to come and cover it, and he's coming tomorrow, too.

I stare at the words, examine every detail. A chill runs through me, followed by a burst of anger. I don't have anyone's blood on my hands.

I never did.

I decide to sleep on the sofa in the living room again, a throw pulled over me for warmth.

It's a fitful night, one where I question everything. Where I question if I do make the world a worse place because of the job I do. Ask myself how much I have given up to get to where I am in my career. I'm not proud of myself. I have lied. I have manipulated people. I have done what I've needed to do to get the story before my competitors. I have worked harder and longer to establish myself. To prove I'm as capable as any of my male colleagues. That I'm better than Ryan Murray. That I've taken what he has taught me but exceeded his ambition.

Is it wrong to be so ambitious? I ask myself that often – more so at four in the morning. Especially when I feel alone. When I realise I've put my work over almost everything. When even my romantic life is entangled in career progression. Or at least it was to start with.

I think of Ryan, of the push and pull of our relationship. There was affection there once. Maybe it's still there, buried somewhere. But now, I don't want to see him. I don't want to be summoned to his office again. To be berated like an errant child.

At five in the morning I send him a text. Tell him I'm taking a personal day. I *need* a personal day. Time and space to get my flat, and my head, together. He replies with a cursory 'Okay.'

Chapter Seventeen

Ingrid

Wednesday, 23 October 2019

Liam and Bernie Doherty still live in the same house that they lived in twenty-five years ago. Their surviving children have grown up and moved out, starting their own families and building their own futures. But apart from the absence of bikes abandoned in the garden, or football boots left on the front step, there is very little about the exterior of the Doherty family home that differs from how I remember it looking all those years ago.

The same wooden fence lines the front garden, the same metal gate sways in the wind. I close it behind it me. I remember that being one of the things Ryan did teach me when I was a cub reporter. Show everyone respect – always close the garden gate after you. It's a small gesture but it tends to work. People see you are more considerate.

Looking up towards the front door, I try to remember when I was last in this house. Was it that night? I try to remember did we carry our plastic bags to the front door of the Dohertys' house looking for loot that evening. My memory is hazy.

Before I have time to reach the top of the path, the front door is pulled open and a tired-looking woman, her bobbed hair greying, looks out at me. There's a soft smile on her lips as she welcomes me in – but I know that it's not genuine. It's an act. I imagine Bernie Doherty has become quite the expert at false smiles over the years. It's not exactly a secret that she is out of her head on prescription medication most of the time. Diazepam and whatever other mood stabilisers she can get her hands on.

I remember hearing my mother saying that it was as if Bernie Doherty went into the ground with Kelly. The woman who was left behind was little more than a shell of the person she used to be.

'Ingrid,' she says, 'c'mon in and go through to the living room. I'm just making a pot of tea.'

The fifth rule of journalism, after always close the gate, is never to refuse a cup of tea. It's an easy conversation opener – it relaxes people.

There is a fire blazing in the hearth and the TV has been muted. I can see Phillip Schofield is very animated about something. I slip off my coat and sit down, taking in the dated décor around me. The pictures on the walls – of all the Doherty family. Liam and Bernie on their wedding day. The three Doherty boys, JP, Christopher and Liam Jr, and, of course, Kelly. She was the baby of the family. The only girl.

There are more pictures of her on the walls than anyone else. The pictures look dated now, too – have that fuzzy quality of snapshots taken in the late Eighties and Nineties, slightly blurry and faded over time. One professional photo of Kelly hangs above the fireplace – her hands together in prayer, her blue eyes looking directly at the camera. Her expression is solemn as she stares out of the mahogany frame, the picture of innocence in her first communion dress. The same dress she was wearing when she was murdered. Despite the heat, which is verging on overpowering, I shiver.

Bernie walks back into the room, with a tray laden with two mugs, a small bottle of milk and a plate of chocolate digestive biscuits.

'Do you take sugar?' she asks. 'Or are you sweet enough?'

'Sweet enough,' I reply, reaching out to take a mug from the tray and refusing the offer of a biscuit. 'Is Liam joining us?' I ask.

She sits down, her tray now resting on the coffee table in the centre of the room.

'I don't know. He doesn't handle this well, you know. He's not mad about the idea of this story. It's hard for him, you know. Still. He's up at the cemetery. Do you know, he never misses a day. Sometimes he even goes more than once, if he's having a bad day. And with her anniversary coming . . . and that man wanting to appeal . . .' Her voice breaks and she drops her gaze for a moment, staring into her mug, before taking a deep breath and looking back up at me. 'Well, it's extra hard at the moment.'

'It must be,' I say. 'I can only imagine.'

I try to age Bernie Doherty, putting her early sixties at the very most. But she looks older. Like she's had enough now. Her face is lined with wrinkles, her knuckles swollen and arthritic. Her eyes look as though they have been permanently bloodshot from the moment she heard about her daughter until now.

She shrugs. 'People always say that, you know. They can imagine what it's like. Truth is, they can't. Unless you've gone through it, unless you live knowing that your child most likely died in absolute terror and you didn't keep her safe . . .' She pauses for a moment. 'Well, unless you've been through it, there's no way of imagining just how awful it is. Not accurately, you know. And you wouldn't want to, either. Nobody should have to have the thoughts we've had to live with.'

I feel a blush creep up my neck. She's right, of course. 'I can only imagine' is such a nonsense phrase faced with something like this.

'I'm sorry,' I say. 'You're right, of course.'

Bernie goes quiet, stares off into the middle distance. She worries at the wedding ring on her finger, blinks and looks at me. 'Nothing to be sorry for,' she mutters. 'You didn't kill her. You were just a twain too, weren't you? It could've just as easily have been you, but Kelly was the unlucky one. That's one of the hardest things to get our heads around. That it was just bad luck. It could've been anyone.'

A chill runs through my bones, again because she's right. It could've been anyone, which means it could've been me.

Liam Doherty looks haunted when he arrives back at the house. He's painfully thin. Old. His hair is grey, his beard unkempt. He stops at the door of the living room, taking off his coat, and looks at me before looking at his wife. She, by now, is clutching a tissue, which is disintegrating with her tears. Her cup of tea is untouched.

'Liam,' she says. 'You're back. There's tea in the pot. I took the bag out so it wouldn't stew.'

He looks at me, then back at Bernie, before he turns to leave without speaking.

'You will come in and talk to Ingrid here, won't you? You remember Ingrid? Went to school with Kelly and the boys. She's going to make sure no one forgets our girl. Especially now,' Bernie calls and he stops walking.

For a moment he just stands very still.

Then he looks at me, his eyes cold. 'Yes, I remember her,' he says, still looking directly at me before turning his head sharply towards his wife. 'I'm not in the form for talking. I told you I didn't want us to do this. I don't think any good can come of it.'

'But it's her anniversary coming up,' Bernie says. 'It's time we finally spoke. People should know about her. How amazing she was.'

'The people who matter already know,' he says, his voice tight. 'All this will do is have people talking about how she died, like it's some form of true crime TV show. Well, I won't have it. Those who knew and loved Kelly will always know and love her. I don't need some gutter journalist telling the world how my girl was murdered.'

He glares at his wife, but she drops her gaze. He swears under his breath and storms out of the living room towards the kitchen.

'I'm sorry,' Bernie says, her face beetroot with embarrassment. 'I'm sure he doesn't mean it. I thought he'd come round.'

'It's okay,' I soothe, even though I'm bitterly disappointed. 'I know this is unbearably hard for you both.'

'He thinks he let her down,' she says, staring at the open door. 'He should've protected her. He's never been able to forgive himself for that. He blames himself more than he blames Harte. Always has. It's a daddy's job to protect their children, he says.' She glances down at the floor. 'I'll never forget it, you know. The noise that came out of him when they brought her home. I was off my head on sedatives from the doctor, you know, but I still remember it. That would've cut through any haze.

'He was like a wounded animal, roaring over her coffin.' Her voice is breaking and tears are flowing freely. 'He kept telling her he was sorry. Telling her she could have anything she wanted if she just opened her eyes and came back to him. Promised he'd take her to Disney World. If she'd just get up. Kissing her face, stroking her hair. His wee baby.

'I couldn't even stand up to pull him away, and the boys squealing, crying beside me. Him trying to rub some warmth back into her hands. "C'mon, pet," he said to her. "Time to rise and shine. Don't you be leaving me now." It was more than we could take, you know. And then . . . well, then she was buried and Christ, do you know what it's like to be expected to leave your child in the cold ground? To walk away from them? How were we supposed to do that? How is any mammy or daddy supposed to do that?'

Bernie sniffs. She is lost in her memories and I'm taking notes, recording her words, and my heart is cracking for her. But I can't lie. I'm also thinking this is incredible stuff. Will make for a brilliant story in the paper, or chapter in the book. This is gold. Sometimes I wonder if I am nothing more than the gutter press, just like they say.

She keeps talking.

'At the start, he'd go there every day. For hours. He'd bring a book and read to her, you know. Buy her some of the toys she wanted, the dolls and teddies, and put them on her grave. When the snow fell that year, I had to wrestle a blanket from him. "She'll be cold," he told me. "It's too cold up there."

'He had a breakdown, you know. Ended up in Gransha for a spell. The "madhouse" as he called it. I remember being jealous of him, that he got to escape it all for a while. They had him so doped up he didn't know his own name, while I was left trying to pick up the pieces. With three boys who didn't have a clue what was going on and that trial coming up. There's days I wonder how I'm still standing at all.'

I look at the fragile, broken figure sitting opposite me. I know she's just existing. She stopped living the same time Kelly did.

Chapter Eighteen

Ingrid

Thursday, 24 October 2019

On Thursday morning I pick up my car before work and I'm glad to do so. The mechanic has done a good job and even though I'd rather be spending my money on something nice instead of paying for a respray and new window, I feel comforted to get back behind the wheel.

I drive the short distance to the City Cemetery and sit for a while, trying to take in all that I have heard over the last few days. The interview with Bernie Doherty has got under my skin and my sleep last night was fitful at best.

There is an air of sadness hanging over me. I am not made of stone. I cannot escape the feeling that I'm now somehow touched by their pain, too – that it has been added to the mountain of tragic stories I've heard over the years that now keep me awake at night. Not that I wasn't touched by what happened to Kelly all those years ago anyway. We all were.

The streets we used to play on remained deserted for months. At school, there was a silence that was never there before. I remember seeing a teacher, Miss McDowell, crying in the corridor. There was a special assembly, where we were told it was okay to be sad. It was okay to miss Kelly. And then a policeman told us all about stranger danger and what to do if anyone tried to kidnap us.

I was terrified. We all were, I think. Terrified of every car or van that passed us. Terrified of the dark. Terrified each time we passed the framed picture of Kelly that had been erected outside the principal's office and were reminded of what had happened.

I shake my head to try to focus on what I'm doing. I have a vague idea where she is buried. Towards the far wall, close to the edge of the maze of pathways that wind down the hill from Creggan to the Brandywell. The graves in this part of the cemetery are well settled now. Mostly just a long line of frost-covered lawn, occasional floral arrangements or ornaments showing them to be well-tended, their inhabitants still loved and missed.

It doesn't take me long to spot Kelly's grave – the tall angelic figure, chiselled out of white marble, glistening as if she has been freshly hewn. The gold lettering that spells out her name has been retouched, Bernie told me. Fixed up for her anniversary. They retouch it every few years. Liam takes cleaning cloths and spray to the cemetery with him at least once a week to make sure the stone is kept sparkling. Looking at it now, I wonder how on earth they had been able to afford such a stone. 'Debt and danger' probably, as my mum used to say.

Bernie had told me, 'You know, we had all these hopes and dreams for her and in the end, all we can do for her is make sure her resting place is well-tended. So we do that.'

Kelly Doherty
1986 – 1994
Taken from us
Beloved daughter, sister & granddaughter

Be Not Afraid

Instantly the words and the tune of the hymn 'Be Not Afraid' come back to me. I remember it was sung at Kelly's funeral. I had wondered if she had been afraid. I'm sure she had been. Even then there was something about the reassurance that God was with you in your most trying times that didn't ring true.

I felt it even more now, after listening to Bernie Doherty tell me how she'd had to listen to her daughter's injuries outlined in a cold, methodical manner. As if it hadn't been her baby girl who had died but instead just a collection of bones and muscles and organs.

'He took her humanity away,' Bernie had told me. 'When he killed her. You know. He took away so much, but what I can't forgive him for is taking away the very sense of who she was. She wasn't my wee girl, who would roar laughing watching Mr Bean, or who would constantly be on at me to save the empty toilet roll tubes and milk cartons and to buy her poster paint so she could make some monstrosity she'd seen on *Art Attack*.

'Nobody cared that she loved being read to still each night. That writer, you know. The famous one . . .' She'd paused for a moment or so as if trying to pull a name from the depths of her memories. 'Dahl!' she'd said triumphantly. 'That Roald Dahl. She loved him.

'And nobody cared that she still sucked her thumb sometimes when she was really tired, or that her favourite dessert was Viennetta. All people knew, and cared about, after she died was what that Jamesy Harte had done to her. If he'd touched her. Done things, you know.'

I'd nodded because I did know. I knew that some signs, abrasions and bruising, had been found on Kelly Doherty's legs, but there was no evidence she'd been sexually assaulted. No evidence of penetration.

'The thought that they'd had to check, examine her private parts, even in an autopsy, made me feel she'd been violated anyway. I know that's irrational, but I can't help it,' Bernie had told me.

'Then, how they spoke about her. She became a collection of bruises and fractures. She was so much more than that.'

At the time, I'd been shielded from the worst of the information about how Kelly died. All I'd known was that a bad man had killed her. He'd hurt her. Then I'd been told it was Jamesy Harte and I remember how that seemed so strange to me, because the Jamesy I knew wasn't a bad man.

Kelly's face stares out from a picture on her stone. It's the same picture that hangs in the Dohertys' living room. I don't know why, but I'm suddenly overcome with the urge to reach out and touch it – so I do, and then I trace my finger along the golden letters spelling out her name and I close my eyes.

A memory comes to me. It had been raining that day, although it had stopped by the time we went out to collect our nuts and apples. My mother had asked me did I want to wear my welly boots to keep my feet dry – but no. I hadn't wanted to. Princesses don't wear welly boots, I'd reasoned, so I'd slipped my feet into my black patent school shoes and left before my mother could force me to change.

I'd been running down the street, away from someone or something, when my foot landed square in the middle of a wide puddle, which was deeper than it had appeared. Ice-cold water and silt had splashed up around me, soaking my foot through my shoes and dirtying my socks. I was flung forwards, dangerously close to losing my grip on my plastic shopping bag which, by then, was half full.

I remember that I'd put my hand out to block my fall – the same hand I was now using to stroke the letters of Kelly's name. It had landed, palm down, onto the wet, gritty road. I can still feel the burn and sting as a layer of skin was scraped from my body, tiny stones embedding themselves into my flesh.

I remember scrambling to my feet. The shouts of 'Stop!' and 'Raid!' and 'Hurry Up!' and 'No!' ringing in my ears, bouncing off the houses around me. I didn't have time to think about the pain or the cold. I didn't have time to think about how my wet sock was now slipping into my shoe.

Righting myself, I had run on and I hadn't looked back to see who was shouting. I've never thought about it. Not until now. My memory is too faded to try to distinguish the voices. Male, female, adult or child. Was it Kelly who shouted 'No!'?

I take out my phone, step back and take some pictures of the stone, of the fresh flowers, the small teddy bear ornament that adorns the grave. The snaps on my phone won't do the story justice, so I make a mental note to arrange for a professional photographer to take pictures of Kelly's grave for the book I'll write. As well as a picture of Declan. Niall. Of the Doherty house. Our old school. Jamesy? Will Jamesy want his photo taken now, trying as he is to conceal his identity?

I decide that when I get home, I'll start making proper plans for the book. Start planning the structure, now that I can see it starting to come together. Once I have an outline, I can approach my publisher to see if they are interested, but I already know they will be. This has everything. Grief, fear, pain, destroyed lives, a possible miscarriage of justice.

I feel the little flutter of excitement that comes at the beginning of a project. It takes over, for the moment at least, from the feeling that I might just be a little too close to this story.

Chapter Nineteen

Ingrid

'The wanderer returns,' Ryan announces as I walk back into the newsroom.

He is holding court in the middle of the room, notepad and pen in hand, no doubt brainstorming with my colleagues about tomorrow's edition.

'I was starting to wonder if you still worked here. You left yesterday lunchtime and we're only seeing you now?'

It has just gone ten in the morning. Ryan's tone is light, but the expression on his face is anything but. If looks could kill, I'd be a corpse on the floor right now. I've no doubt that any number of my colleagues have picked up on it, too. Tommy gives me a sympathetic nod.

'I was out with the Doherty family yesterday,' I tell him. 'For the anniversary piece. I thought it best to take my time and do a good job. I didn't leave 'til almost five, so I thought I'd just go on home. This morning I was at the cemetery, getting pictures of her grave for the story.'

'Oh, I bet that was tough,' Trina says, always one to try to calm any incoming storm.

'Yes, well it was. Their grief is still very raw. More at the moment, of course. Given the anniversary. But Bernie was very open and honest. It's powerful stuff.'

'Sounds like front-page stuff,' Trina says.

'I'm the editor here and I make the decisions,' Ryan says brusquely. 'Write me a lead piece and a feature for four and five. Keep it focused on Kelly, not on who is responsible. We want heart, not blame. Let's not give Jamesy Harte any more attention.'

'Not even if Bernie Doherty has said she'll never find it in her heart to forgive him?' I ask.

'I don't want him mentioned outside of outlining the facts as they stand. He was convicted of her murder and served seventeen years in prison. No more and no less.'

'Really? Nothing at all?' I raise an eyebrow. It's a strange approach, to put it mildly.

'Don't question me, Ingrid. Just write your piece.'

'I'm on it,' I tell him, trying not to sound too annoyed.

'Well done, Ingrid. On getting the scoop,' Trina chimes in, and I offer her a smile of gratitude.

'Yes, good job, Ingrid,' Ryan mutters dismissively, and I bristle. I'd rather feel ignored by him than patronised.

'The pictures on my phone are okay,' I add. 'But it might be worth blowing the budget to get one of the freelance guys out to take some decent shots.'

He nods. 'I'll have a look at what you've got then decide,' he says.

I already know that despite the significance of the story, he won't dare eat into his precious budget.

'I'll email them through when we're done here,' I tell him.

'Actually, Ingrid,' he says, nodding in the direction of his office, 'why don't you nip in and show them to me now. We can chat about the interview as well. Try to plan the best way to approach it.'

Suppressing the urge to roll my eyes, I lift my phone and notebook and follow him through to his office. I'm starting to hate spending time in here, especially when there is no one else with me to act as a buffer.

As he sits down, I open the screen on my phone and scroll through my gallery of pictures to find the snapshots I took earlier.

'You've your car back,' he says.

'I do. Thank God. I picked it up this morning.'

'I hope it wasn't too expensive. Clutches can be pricy.'

'It was grand. Stuck it on my credit card.'

'Shame you couldn't claim it on your insurance. Would've saved you a few quid.'

'Yes, but sure, that's life, isn't it?'

'I suppose. If only it had been, you know, vandalised at work instead. You know, maybe with a slur spray painted on the bonnet. I imagine that the insurance would have covered it then.'

I'm at a loss for words. My brain can't think fast enough to come up with an acceptable retort.

'So, the police called me yesterday afternoon, said they wanted to come and take pictures of the car park, check our lighting – stuff like that. I hadn't a clue what they were talking about. Can you imagine my surprise when they tell me it's part of the ongoing investigation into the targeted harassment of one of my own reporters? The one whose car was vandalised in our car park.'

I colour. 'I didn't want you worrying,' I lie. 'It's not a big deal.'

'Not a big deal? Someone breaks into your flat and daubs a threat on the wall. And someone attacks your car at work and it's not a big deal?'

'I'm dealing with it. It's not affecting my work, so I didn't see any need to fill you in.'

'You took Tuesday off and now you're telling me it's not affecting your work? C'mon, Ingrid. Why can't you just admit this is bigger than you? Do you actually not care that you are putting yourself in danger's way?'

'We both know that threats come with the territory,' I tell him, looking him directly in the eye.

'Of course. Badly written letters. Poisonous emails, perhaps, or the odd drunk shouting abuse in the street. But this, Ingrid? You're an intelligent woman – or at least I thought you were. This is a dangerous escalation.'

'It honestly doesn't bother me,' I lie, trying to still the jittery feeling growing in my stomach, threatening to spread out around my body, making my legs jiggle or my eye twitch. 'We can't be intimidated into not running a story.'

'But we're not running the story, Ingrid. We're not going to talk to Jamesy Harte. I've made that clear. I want the piece for tomorrow written as straight as you can make it. Not a single mention of Harte's campaign to have his name cleared. I will be editing it myself, so God help you if I see anything that shouldn't be there . . .'

I want to tell him to go to hell. If we were anywhere else but in this office, I would do.

'Maybe if you listened to what Jamesy had to say, you'd change your mind about him. People don't always get it right, you know. The law doesn't always get it right. If you heard what he told me, how he was set up. If you could see how broken he looks . . .'

'See how broken he looks?' he asks, his face darkening. 'So you've seen him, then? You've spoken to him face to face. Surely he's not in Derry, is he?' He stops, looks at me directly. 'Is that where you were on Saturday? Before you came to my place?'

Damn it. In my fury I forgot that he doesn't know that I met Harte. I could kick myself. I stare without speaking.

'Who do you think you are?' he says, his face reddening with anger. 'The lead character in a John Grisham book? Leave clearing his name to his bleeding-heart campaigners and his legal team. Do your job without risking your safety and that of your colleagues. Write the stories we pay you to write!'

He is in my face, so close I can feel his warm breath on mine. Rage is coming off him in waves, and I swear it must be contagious, because I'm angry, too. I'm so bloody angry.

'I'm doing just that, writing what you tell me to,' I shout at him, refusing to back away from his stale breath and his toxic, proprietorial masculinity. 'But I'll be damned if you control what I do outside working hours. You mightn't have had the ambition to reach beyond this paper, but we don't all have to rot here. If I can further my career, and help a potentially innocent man, then of course I'm going to do it. So yes, I have seen him. You're right, that is where I was on Saturday. Meeting him.'

'Tell me he's not stupid enough to have come back to Derry?' Ryan asks.

I shake my head. 'He has no intention of coming back here. This city let him down. He's living in a shitty bedsit in Portstewart, if you must know.'

'He has some brains, after all,' Ryan says.

We sit in a silence for a moment or two. The wind has gone from our sails as quickly as it arrived.

'Can I go now?' I ask.

'I need to talk to you about something else first,' he says. 'I've been on to HR.'

I baulk, can feel the colour drain from my face.

'Don't give me that look, Ingrid. You know I had to. Any incident on the premises has to be reported straight away. There are implications. Insurance, et cetera.'

Of course – it had to come down to money and not to the actual welfare of the employees. This time I fail to suppress the eye-roll.

I make to leave. 'I really do have a lot of work to do,' I tell him, 'so maybe we could continue this talk later?'

He ignores me.

'Ingrid, there's to be no more lone working here after hours. They've been quite clear on that. You'll have to leave with the rest of us. HR have also asked that all staff leave a note of where they are going when they leave the office and what time they expect to return. You're to keep your work-issued mobile phone charged and switched on at all times during office hours so that you, and the rest of the staff, are immediately contactable.'

I feel my temper flare again. 'This is absolutely ridiculous,' I say. 'It's not how this job works, and you and I know it.'

'It's how it's going to work,' he says sternly. 'I had to talk them down from insisting all interviews be carried out over the phone from the office, so count yourself lucky.'

I snort. 'Yes. I can see how tying my hands from doing my job properly makes me very lucky.'

'Christ but you're insufferable at times,' he says. 'As you can imagine, the new edicts haven't gone down the best with your colleagues, so if you want my advice, you'd keep your head down out there. I've no need to remind you that for every journalism job out there, there are numerous prospective reporters just chomping at the bit to get the chance at a staff position.'

'Are you threatening my job here?' I ask him.

He pauses, steeples his fingers and looks directly up at me. 'No, Ingrid. I'm not. But you need to be careful you don't destroy your career yourself.'

'You need to be careful, too,' I tell him. 'Because if things get nasty for me, they can get nasty for you. I've not been on my own all of these nights here. We've had some adventures.'

I'm ashamed of myself for dragging our affair into it. For being that woman who issues such threats. But I'm angry.

Not waiting for his reply, I get up to leave. If I didn't think it would set tongues wagging further, I'd slam the door to his office as hard as I could on the way out. Instead, I plaster on a look of nonchalance, even though inside I'm seething, and close the door gently before walking back to my desk as if I don't have a care in the world.

Chapter Twenty

Declan

Declan is having a good day. It has taken him a while to recognise the unfamiliar feeling of something close to contentment for what it is, but today he doesn't feel mired in the drudgery of his own life. It could be because his dole money has landed in and while he doesn't exactly feel flush, it's nice to have the knowledge that there's a few quid in his pocket.

He has treated himself to a haircut and a hot-towel shave, and has taken his washing to his ma's to run through her machine. He throws her a few quid for the cost of the electricity, which he knows she will slip back in his pocket later with a wink that says 'Don't be so silly, son.'

He spent some time this morning cleaning his flat. He hadn't realised just how messy it had become, or how stale the air was until he had pushed open his windows and let the cold autumn air flood his living room. He's going to get himself under control, he promises himself. Stop smoking the grass. Stop drinking – or at least cut down on the drinking.

He picked up a parcel from the food bank yesterday, which has taken the bare look off his cupboards, and he vows he'll spend some of his dole on some fresh fruit and veg. He's been feeling so sluggish lately that he can feel himself spiralling and is afraid of how low he will go this time if he doesn't get a grip.

It's amazing, he tells himself, how looking after himself, and his home, has the power to lift his mood so quickly. His flat will never make it into the interior pages of the *Ulster Tatler* or the like, but at least it looks clean now. More homely. Dust motes no longer dance in mass formation in the air as the autumn sun shines through the windows.

He's not sure what has brought about this change in him, but he thinks it might, just might, have something to do with his meeting with Ingrid last week. He thinks that he might message her again. Offer to take her to the exact spot where he and Niall found Kelly's body. Tell her as much as he can about that day, what he remembers.

He has an urge, no, a need to see her again. He can't get the thought of her out of his head. Her blonde hair, her blue eyes. The way she had spoken to him so kindly as they'd sat opposite each other in the café. At one stage she had reached out and touched his hand, and he had revelled in the warmth of it. Ingrid Devlin was a walking reminder of a better time in his life. Of innocent, happy days before Kelly died. Seeing her again has sparked something in him and he can't stop thinking about her.

His ma hands him a cup of tea and he sits opposite her at the kitchen table as the last load of washing runs through the tumble dryer.

'Your brother's coming down again this weekend,' she says, and he feels something uneasy start to bud in the pit of his stomach.

'That's not like him,' he says. 'What brings him down again?'

'I thought he'd have told you,' she says, reaching for a Rich Tea biscuit and taking a bite.

He watches as crumbs fall to the table and she brushes them into a neat pile immediately.

'We're not as close we used to be, Ma. You know that.'

'I don't know where I went wrong with you boys,' she says, shaking her head. 'You were thick as thieves as children and now it's like you can't stand to be near each other.'

'You didn't go wrong, Ma. Our lives are very different is all,' he says, and she offers him a pitying look in response.

'I suppose,' she says. 'But, Declan, you're still young, you know. You've a lot of living left to do. If you just . . . you know . . .'

Her sentence trails off as if she has already exhausted all the 'if you justs' over the years.

'I know,' he says, because he does know.

If he could stop letting that niggle of doubt and self-hatred in. If he could simply stop fucking up his own life.

He pauses. 'So, Niall didn't say why he was coming down?' he asks.

'Oh, he did. He told me. He's been talking to that Ingrid Devlin one, too. I think he's meeting her. I've not told your father. You know he won't like it. I can't say I like it, either,' she says.

Declan feels the fragile casing of his good day start to crack. It could shatter at any second.

'Seems neither of you boys listen to me when I warn you to stay away from her. There's no need to go digging up the past. Let it alone.'

Chapter Twenty-One

Ingrid

There's a crick in my neck, which I'm trying my very hardest to ease by rolling my shoulders and kneading my tightened muscles. Day has turned to night without me even noticing; although to be fair, in the dimly lit newsroom it's quite a common occurrence for time to pass, seasons to change even, without us paying attention.

I've been in my glorious bubble all afternoon. That place where nothing exists except for me and the tip-tap of my fingers on the keyboard – words coming to life on the screen in front of me, creating a story. Giving people a voice. I know that may sound self-aggrandising, but it's what I love most about my job.

I know this is a good piece. Dammit, I know it's a brilliant piece. It is respectful, heart-rending, and contains just enough salacious detail to keep the public reading. It's a balancing act, but one I think I've managed well.

I grimace as I lift the coffee cup from my desk and put it to my lips. It's stone cold. I'm not sure how long it has been sitting, but I know by the growing pressure behind my eyes that I need a caffeine injection, and quickly. I file my story, sending it through the system to Ryan to read and edit, and get up, taking my cup with me and heading for the staff kitchen.

Of course, I'm only a couple of steps from my desk, when my phone rings with that single beep of an internal call. Surely Ryan can't have read the piece and found fault with it already . . . Briefly, I contemplate ignoring the call and going to get my coffee anyway, but I know curiosity will nag at me until I find out who it is and what they want. So I answer, and am surprised to hear Lisa from reception on the other end of the line.

'Ingrid,' she says in a tone which I'm familiar with.

It's the 'appease the public at any cost' tone, which she uses when someone has been giving her a hard time over the phone or, worse still, at her reception desk.

'There's a Liam Doherty here to see you. I've told him that the paper is just about to go to print and you're very busy, but he is really quite insistent.'

I hear a deep male voice in the background, in full rant.

'I don't care how busy she is. I don't care if she's the bloody Queen of Sheba. I want to see her and see her now. And I'll tell you this much, you can either get her to come out here and talk to me, or I'll force my own way through – and there's not a one of you will stop me.'

'Mr Doherty, if you just give me a moment, I'm speaking to her right now to see if she's available,' I hear Lisa say.

'If she's speaking to you on the other end of that phone then she's available. No ifs and buts about it.'

He is becoming irate. His voice is louder and can now be heard through the heavy fire doors that separate us from the reception office.

Tommy and Jim lift their heads, look towards the door and then at me.

'Can you tell Mr Doherty I'll be out in a minute,' I say to Lisa, but there's a shake in my voice.

I've no idea why he's here, but more than that, I've no idea why he is so angry. Sure, he didn't seem to be falling over himself with joy at my presence in his house, but he didn't seem to be against the idea, either. He'd been content enough to let Bernie do the talking. I feel the headache kick in just a little more and fumble in my desk drawer for two paracetamol tablets, which I down with a slug of the cold coffee, grimacing as I do so.

'Everything okay?' Trina asks, glancing between me and the door. 'Maybe you should get one of the lads to go out with you.'

She might have a point. It can be intimidating facing an angry man, but at the same time I don't want to show any sign of weakness. I can handle this.

'I'll be fine. I'm sure it's something and nothing,' I bluff, but I'm uncharacteristically nervous.

I straighten my skirt, put my hand to my hair to smooth it and take a deep breath.

Liam Doherty looks even more wretched than he did at the house. His eyes are bloodshot and his cheeks flushed. He has the look of someone who has had a lot to drink, and as he comes closer, I realise he has the smell of someone who has had a lot to drink on him, too. I notice the car keys in his hand. Has he driven here?

As soon as he notices me he becomes more animated, pointing a bony finger in my direction.

'I want that story pulled,' he says. 'You're not to run it. Do you hear? People have had their pound of flesh from us already and my girl's life isn't for sale. Bernie should never have spoken to you.'

My stomach tightens as I think of the story I have just filed. Think of the hours I've put into it.

'I'm afraid that the paper has already gone to print,' I lie, my voice wavering.

He steps around the reception desk towards me, everything about his stance oozing pain and aggression.

'Well, then you can just get it back from print. Because it's not to run. You can't run it without my say-so.'

I try to keep my ground and maintain an appearance of calm, when calm is the last thing I feel.

'I'm really sorry you feel this way,' I tell him. 'Councillor Duffy told me he spoke to both you and Bernie at length about the story before I did the interview. I'm sure Bernie has told you that I have assured her that I will not sensationalise things one bit. Yes, it covers what happened, but it also allows your family to let the world know about Kelly as the little girl she was, not just the victim of a brutal murder.'

He takes a step closer, leans against the high desk at reception. He is unsteady on his feet. I see a look of panic in Lisa's eyes. Liam is dangerously close to me now. A swing of his hand and he could hit me square across the face. By the anger in his gaze, I'm not entirely sure that isn't what he is going to do.

'Councillor Duffy has no right to speak for my family. He can issue his "advice" all he wants about talking to the press. But I did not agree to this. No matter what anyone told you. And damn it, I still have some say over what happens when it comes to my family.'

'Look, Bernie did tell me this was very difficult for you . . .' I say, trying to soothe him.

He laughs a brittle laugh, which quickly turns into a sound akin to a sob.

'You've no idea. You'll never have any idea. Is that bastard Ryan Murray here? Get him here and I'll tell him exactly where he can shove his story.'

'I'll just ring through to him now . . .' Lisa starts, but I raise a hand.

The last thing I need is for Liam Doherty to start telling my boss just how unprofessional he thinks I am. As much of a pain in the arse as it will be, Ryan will pull the story. These are different times now. No one takes a publish-and-be-damned risk any more. Especially not Ryan, who has been trying to bury this story from the start.

'Let's see if Mr Doherty and I can have a little chat first,' I say. 'Perhaps we can go through to a quiet room and talk,' I say in my most appeasing tone.

'There's nothing to talk about,' he slurs. 'She is not for sale and she is definitely not for sale to the bloody *Chronicle*!' His anger falters, glassy eyes filling with tears. 'She was my baby, Ingrid. You know that. You knew us. You were there!'

His anger is replaced by pain and I feel my heart constrict.

'We just want to help her be remembered,' I say.

He looks down at his shoes. One lace is loose – undone, just like the rest of him. I see his shoulders shudder as his body is wracked with sobs and guilt washes over me. So much guilt. But still, I know I have to do whatever I can to stop this story from being pulled.

When Liam Doherty lifts his head again, he looks at me, his eyes pleading.

'You'll never understand. You'll never feel the pain we do. And this – seeing it again. Reading it again . . .' His voice trails off. 'It doesn't help anyone. I tried, believe me, I've tried to be okay with it, but I can't be. She was murdered. Let me tell you about that,' Liam says, to the room as much as to me. His voice is thick with pain. 'My wee girl. My wee princess. She was the most beautiful wee baby I ever saw. The light of my life. Every single time I saw her, my heart felt full. She made my soul smile.

'And then some monster caved her head in. Left her covered in bruises. Her perfect, beautiful, innocent wee body. And she would've cried out for me, or her mammy. I know she would have. And that monster, he would have let her. He didn't care. Not about her, or us. He broke her and he broke us, too. Then he left her, in the rain and the cold and the dark. In the water. Did Bernie tell you Kelly was afraid of the dark? She was always asking me to leave the big light on. And she lay there in the dark for three days . . .'

He dissolves into heavy sobs, which wrench free from his body with an almighty burst of noise. I see that Lisa is crying. A few staff members have come out of various back offices to see what the commotion is about and they stare at the spectacle with their eyes wide. Some are shaking their heads.

'Please, just come through and sit down. We'll get you a cup of tea. Call a taxi. You can't drive in that state, Mr Doherty. Please. We can talk this through,' I say.

It seems hopelessly inadequate, but it's all I can offer.

He shakes his head but allows me to lead him through to an empty side office anyway, which is dusty, cold and unwelcoming. He sits down and puts his head in his hands while I nod to Lisa to make some sweet sugary tea. I'll give him a chance to cry, I think. To let it all out. And then I'll try to talk him round. As hard as this is, we do need the story. The story does need to be told.

In the meantime, I just sit down across the table from him and listen to his sobs, mixed with the ticking of a clock that is telling the wrong time, and I wonder how long it takes to boil a kettle. It's not that I don't feel for him. Of course I do.

When the door opens, my heart soars with relief. A cup of tea will help. It'll settle him and bring him round. At least I hope it will.

My relief is short-lived, however, when I notice it isn't Lisa pushing her way through the door but Ryan. He looks at Liam Doherty then at me, and he shakes his head. A heavy 'I told you so' hangs in the air.

'Mr Doherty,' he says, prompting Liam to look up. 'I believe you wanted to see me.'

Mr Doherty brushes quickly at his cheeks, straightens himself. 'I never want to see you, Murray,' he snarls. 'But I do want you to drop the story about my daughter. You've had your pound of flesh. Leave her in peace now. Leave us in peace now.'

'I'm afraid I can't do that, Liam,' Ryan says, and there is a steeliness to his voice that makes my blood run cold.

Chapter Twenty-Two

Ingrid

Liam stands up, faces off with Ryan. I don't know whether to keep sitting or stand up between the two of them.

'I do not want this paper or any paper running this story. I do not want this paper to contact my family again under any circumstances,' Liam says. He's slurring his words, his voice shaking with emotion.

'I'm afraid the page has already gone to print,' Ryan says, and I'm surprised that his lie supports my own. 'The presses are running.'

'Well, stop them from running!' Liam says. 'We are withdrawing our consent and we do not permit you to use anything we said to you. You're a powerful man, Murray. You can make that happen at least.'

'Ingrid has put together a very sensitive and respectful piece,' Ryan says. 'It's a piece that shows you and your wife to be very loving parents. There is nothing controversial in it. The story is very much about Kelly, not her killer.'

There's a moment's silence. Liam looks directly at Ryan and then shakes his head slowly.

'Is it not enough that you covered all this at the time? Was that not more than enough for you? We've stayed quiet. We stayed dignified. And believe me, there have been times when I've wanted to scream about our loss to the whole world. Can we not just have that dignity now?'

'The paper is already away to print,' Ryan says again.

I know that's not true. I know we have at least another hour before the presses roll.

I watch as Liam Doherty deflates in front of me. He speaks, his voice quieter now but steady.

'We couldn't protect Kelly then. No matter how we tried. We didn't do right by her then. We want to do right by her now. That's all we want to do.'

'Controlling the coverage of her anniversary is a good way to do this,' Ryan says. 'And that's what we're doing. I know how sensitive this is.' Ryan's voice is softer now. 'I was on the ground at the time, remember?'

'As if I could forget,' Liam spits, but Ryan doesn't so much as blink.

'I was in the position Ingrid here is in now – covering a story because it's right that it's covered. And I can assure you from the bottom of my heart that there will not be one word published in this paper that supports Jamesy Harte's ill-thought-out campaign. He's guilty, and he'll remain guilty.'

'She was my girl,' Liam says, and he deflates even more. Shrivels into the ghost of a man who looks as if he could just blow away on the wind. 'Do you understand that, Ryan? You're a father yourself now. You must understand where I'm coming from?

'My daughter's killer, no matter what he says or does or what life he lives, or what lies he tells, I just want him to know he will get what's coming to him. There's no jail in the world that will compare to what he will feel on the day of reckoning. I have to hope and believe he will know no peace in this life or the next. I have to hope that he rots in hell. He can admit he's guilty, or claim he is innocent until the day he dies, but he can't run from God.'

As soon as I have loaded Liam into the taxi and paid the driver, I rush back into the newsroom and into Ryan's office.

'You haven't sent that page yet, have you?'

'The Doherty piece? I'm just sending it now before we have any more untimely interruptions,' he says, his face set tight.

'Can I just change one thing?' I ask, and I know I'm pushing my luck. In fact, I am at the pointing of hefting my luck over the edge of a cliff.

He pushes his seat back from the desk and gestures at me to work at his computer.

I delete the existing opening paragraph and start to type.

THE FATHER *of slain schoolgirl Kelly Doherty has told* The Chronicle *that he hopes his daughter's killer 'rots in hell' and has 'no peace in this life or the next'.*

Liam Doherty has said he will never forgive the man who murdered eight-year-old Kelly in 1994.

It's a stronger opener. I push my chair back and show it to Ryan. He shakes his head slowly.

'I think I prefer the original, about her being a wee angel.'

'That was watery, Ryan. And you know it. What's up with you these days? Have you lost your nerve altogether?'

'Hardly. If I'd lost my nerve, I'd have told Liam Doherty we'd pull the article. I would hardly have told him it was already away to print. Stop questioning me, Ingrid. You've no idea what we're facing here.'

He reaches over me and hits send on the final article, with my new intro. We watch as the icon on the page turns to green, signalling that it has been sent to the press. My body sags with relief.

'Tell me,' I say. 'Tell me what we're facing.'

Ryan just shakes his head. 'Just go back to work. There's a paper to get out.'

Despite saving the story from being pulled, he sounds defeated.

Chapter Twenty-Three

Ingrid

I deserve the glass of wine I've just poured myself. I've my laptop open in front of me on my small kitchen table, a notebook to my side. There's also a folder of newspaper cuttings and archive material from the original Doherty coverage, and some coloured Post-its so I can plan in earnest.

My book editor, a very serious woman by the name of Jane Thompson, had wasted no time in replying to my proposal about the case and has asked me to put together an in-depth editorial plan, as well as some sample chapters. She is confident, if it is as good as my previous non-fiction works, that she will be able to get it through the acquisitions process.

It might be a problem if the Dohertys are reticent to talk any further, but hopefully there is enough in what they have already told me to fill a couple of chapters. I had mentioned to Bernie that I may work on a book, I'm sure of it, so our interview material is fair game.

I try not to think about Liam Doherty's face. His pleas just to let his daughter rest in peace. That he doesn't want her to be part of any media feeding frenzy. I admit it makes me feel uneasy, especially if I take the line in the book that I believe

Jamesy Harte to be innocent, but I can't allow my feelings to get in the way of my work. That's not how journalism operates.

At the moment I'm trying to piece together the information I have alongside the sources I'm likely to gain access to. It would be great to see the original police reports from the time. I wonder if the investigating officer is still on the force, or if he has retired. I'd love to interview him and get his take on it.

I should go through official channels for this information, but it has served me well in the past to have a friend or two inside the force who occasionally acts as an unofficial source. He can go digging without raising any red flags. He's great for tip-offs, getting background info, finding out what the general feeling in the force is. Yes, Detective Constable Mark Black has proven to be quite useful in the past. That's why I was so flustered when he showed up at my flat after the break-in.

It doesn't hurt that he looks like butter wouldn't melt in his mouth. No one would ever suspect him of passing on information to a journalist. He's a nice guy. A bit naive, but I suppose that serves me well. Occasionally, I do feel a little guilty playing on that naivety, and on his fairly obvious crush on me. I'm not cold-hearted. It's not his fault he's not my type. Too clean-cut. Too good.

I call his number but much to my annoyance, it goes straight to voicemail. He may well be on duty, in which case his personal mobile might be switched off and in his locker. He doesn't always carry it on him while on shift. I wouldn't dare call him on his work-issued phone. I leave a message, not giving too much away, asking him to call me as soon as he can.

Then I set about listening to my interview with Jamesy Harte again. I don't know if it's because of the day's events, or that I spent the morning with the Doherty family and visiting Kelly's grave, but sadness about the whole situation washes over me.

There is no doubt the Doherty family have been left broken

and no amount of time in the world will heal their grief. It's so raw that it's actually physically painful to watch.

But then I think of Jamesy. Small, grey Jamesy with what seems like not an ounce of wit about him. Like he could be manipulated – but I didn't buy that he himself could be a manipulator.

'I was an easy target. I'm not as smart as some of those people. You think I don't know that I'm not clever?' I listen and remember how he had tapped the side of his head as he spoke as if trying to get it to work properly. 'I didn't know big words, or what to say. I didn't have a fancy suit to wear to go and see the judge.

'No one wanted to help me, you know. Because they said I was wrong. They said I was bad and I'd done it. But it wasn't me. I don't know who it was, but I didn't do it. My mammy used to tell me that Derry was the best wee city in the whole world. That we all took care of each other. But Mammy was wrong.'

There is an audible sniff. I remember that he became agitated. His long, skinny finger poking at the melamine table in front of us. His fingernails were bitten down to the quick.

'People only like you if you fit in,' he said. 'You look different, or sound different, or act different and you're out. I was out.'

His voice was laden with rage and grief. It's understandable, if this was a great miscarriage of justice and he has lost seventeen years of his life to jail, and the life he has now bears no resemblance to the life he had before.

But back then, could that desire to be seen, by a community he felt excluded him, could that have really driven him to do something so horrific? No matter how I weighed it up in my head – I couldn't see it. I just couldn't picture him as guilty.

Which of course begs the question – if it wasn't him, then who was it? And why?

I sit back, swill the dregs of my wine in the glass before

downing it. Even though I've only had one glass, I feel a bit woozy. Remembering I haven't eaten since lunchtime, I get up to forage in the cupboards for something quick and easy to make. I'm just heating water to boil some pasta, when the shrill buzz of my doorbell makes me jump.

I lift the handset and say hello. The grainy CCTV image shows a figure I can't quite recognise. I squint, trying to see who it is, but the security light outside seems to be on the blink again. I glance at the door to my flat, locked, with a security chain just in case. I hate that I'm jumpy.

'Hello?' I repeat again, my voice no doubt echoing into the cold night air.

I'm about to hang up, when I hear a male voice answer.

'Hello? Erm, hello, is that Ingrid? I hate these things . . .'

'Who is it?' I ask.

Sure as anything, I'm not confirming or denying my identity to anyone before knowing who they are. Especially not now.

'Declan Heaney,' he replies. 'You know, from school.'

He sounds awkward, hesitant. There's something, I don't know, a little sad about the fact he is identifying himself as the person he was twenty-five years ago.

'We met last week, up in Creggan,' he continues. 'I wanted to talk to you. About you know, the story?'

I have no idea how Declan Heaney got hold of my address. Yes, I'd given him my phone number, but I hadn't told him anything about where I lived. Or at least I don't think I had. I'm not sure how I feel about him being in my space.

Biting my lip, I reply, 'I'm a little busy just now, Declan. Is it important? Maybe we could meet for a coffee tomorrow.'

I hate having a conversation with him, or anyone, over this bloody intercom system. You never know who is walking past and listening.

I hear him sigh. 'I was kinda hopin' . . .' he says before his voice trails off, carried by the wind.

I hear the rain lashing against my windows and even though I'm often accused of not having a conscience, I feel a prick of something akin to guilt or pity.

It's only Declan, I tell myself. I can trust him.

'Come on up, sure,' I tell him. 'Top floor and go to the far end of the corridor.'

'You're a star bar,' he says, and I wonder if I detect a slight slurring in his words.

I try not to think about it too much as I hit the button to unlock the door and let him in. As I wait for him to arrive, I look at my kitchen table and all the paperwork that is sprawled over it, as well as at my corkboard, where I have pinned coloured Post-its with key chapters I want to cover. I take down the green Post-it, which bears both Declan's and his brother's names, slipping it under my laptop. I'm not sure why I feel the need to do it. Declan already knows I want to hear his side of the events of that cold November night, but still, I just feel uneasy.

After shuffling the rest of my papers together into some sort of vague piles, I carry my empty wine glass to the sink and rinse it. Jumping as I hear a knock on my door, I take a deep breath and will myself to stay calm as I go to answer it.

Declan is soaked to the skin. His dark hair plastered to his forehead, a rivulet of water runs from the end of one thick strand and right down his nose. He doesn't seem to notice, or care. His face is red with cold and his hands stuffed deep into his pockets, for what little use that will do him. It's clear that his jeans are waterlogged and sticking to him.

'It's not too late, is it?' he asks, and I definitely detect a whiff of stale beer from him. 'I was out for a walk, you see, and then it started bucketing down and well, it was freezin'.'

He makes for a pitiful sight. 'C'mon in,' I tell him. 'Let me get you a towel and a hot drink.'

I know he needs more than a towel to dry off. He needs to get out of those soaking clothes, but I have a dearth of alternatives to offer him and I'm nervous enough without encouraging him to strip off. I grab a couple of my biggest, warmest towels from the airing cupboard and hand them to him. He has peeled his jacket off and it has landed with an unceremonious thump onto my kitchen floor. I can already see the water leaching from it onto the tiles.

As he reaches out to take the towels, I notice two things. The first is that he is shivering with cold, and the second is that his hands – specifically his knuckles – are grazed and bruised. He's had a run-in with someone or something.

His eyes follow my gaze and he pulls his hands away as soon as he's realised I've seen the state of them.

'You should see the other guy,' he says with a small smile that most definitely doesn't reach his eyes.

I absolutely don't want to see the other guy.

'I'm sorry,' he says. 'I shouldn't have come here. It was just, well, I didn't know where else to go . . .' His voice cracks a little.

'How did you know where to find me?' I ask him, the heavy sinking feeling still leaden in my stomach.

'I . . . erm . . . it's Derry, ye know. I asked around. Heard you lived down here and then looked at the names on the buzzer. Took a chance it was you.'

There's something about how he says this that makes me shiver. Am I really that easy to find? The people who painted my wall found me easily, and now Declan, too. Unless . . . No, that's stupid. I'm letting the events of the last few days get to me too much. Declan wouldn't have any reason to warn me off talking to Jamesy Harte. Sure, he's told me he's not convinced Jamesy is guilty.

'You could've texted or called,' I say as Declan roughly towel-dries his hair.

I can see water pooling slightly at his feet. His trainers are as soaked as the rest of him.

Looking at me with a curious expression on his face, he says, 'I never thought of that,' as if it actually is the first time such a possibility has even crossed his mind. 'You don't mind, do you?'

I could give him the real answer, of course, and say it's a bit strange, but I'm still trying to get a feel for why he is here and what state he is actually in.

'Of course not,' I lie. 'I'll put the kettle on and make some tea.'

'Would you have anything stronger?' he asks, bold as anything, and I lie again.

'Sorry. All out. Just tea here. Coffee if you prefer.'

'Tea will be grand,' he says, looking around, taking in my flat in all its glory.

It's not huge by any means. In fact, it's quite small, but I've spent a lot of money getting it just how I like it. Scandi-inspired, with just a smattering of cosy comforts, it's always proven to be a haven of relaxation for me, from my pale pink velvet sofa, which cost more than a month's salary, to the Eames-style dining chairs.

'Nice digs you've got here,' he says before shuddering with the cold.

I realise there's no way I can let him sit down on that sofa with wet jeans on.

'There's a dressing gown on the back of the bathroom door,' I tell him. 'If you want to take your jeans off, I can throw those and your coat in the dryer or at least hang them on the radiator.'

Again there's a delay, as if he's just realising how wet he is, before he nods and gives a little laugh. 'Aye. I suppose that might be an idea.'

Declan disappears into the bathroom, while I wonder if it's more than just drink he's taken. He seems a bit too out of it for it to be down to a couple of pints of beer. I make the tea, load the cups onto a tray along with some biscuits and carry the lot through to the living area. He comes back, looking ridiculous in my white fluffy robe, and hands me his clothes. It's clear from his expression he's now feeling a little embarrassed.

'I appreciate this,' he says. 'I shouldn't have come.'

'You're grand,' I say. 'Sit down and get warmed up. I'll get these drying.'

When I sit down opposite him a few minutes later, he seems to be lost in thought. He is cradling the teacup in his hands as if drawing the warmth from it.

'Declan,' I say, and he startles at my voice.

'God, I was in my own wee world there,' he says. 'Sorry.'

'Look, it's nice to see you, but I'm a bit confused,' I begin. 'I mean, I know we said we would meet up again some time, but I wasn't really expecting you to turn up at my door.'

'I don't think I was expecting to turn up at your door either,' he says. 'Sorry, this must look all kinds of wrong. I just . . . well, Ingrid, have you spoken with Niall?'

'Your brother?' I ask.

'One and the same. My mother mentioned he might be coming down to Derry to see you.'

There's a hesitancy to his words, something that I can't quite put my finger on.

'As it happens, he contacted me through Facebook and I told him about the book I'm working on. You know, about Kelly.'

'Is that what all that stuff relates to?' he asks, nodding towards my dining table and my notebook.

'It is,' I said.

'I always thought you'd do well in life,' he says.

'Well, I try my best, you know,' I say.

'Aye. I know. Look, I wanted to talk to you about Niall. I know he's my brother – my twin, for God's sake – and I do love him, but he's not the person he appears to be. You know?'

'I'm not sure what you mean,' I say thinking of the perfectly polite and funny exchanges of messages I've been having with Niall since Monday.

He seems very nice. Genuine. Obviously quite different from the snot-nosed little boy I remember chasing me around the streets in Creggan while we played kiss chase or tig, but then I'm not quite the plaited-hair, scraped-knee precocious little girl I was then, either.

Declan takes a deep breath and puts his teacup down on the table. He doesn't look at me when he starts to talk. Instead, he stares at the wall.

'I know people look at me and they see a scumbag.'

'No!' I protest.

He laughs. 'Come on, Ingrid.'

His hands are shaking. I'm not sure if it's from the cold or because of what he's about to tell me.

'Do you smoke?' he asks, looking at me.

I shake my head.

He sighs. 'Do you mind if I smoke? It calms me down.'

I really don't want him to smoke in my flat. I hate the smell of tobacco. It nauseates me and the last thing I want is for it to linger after he is gone.

'I'd prefer you didn't,' I say.

'Fair enough,' he says, defeated. 'Look, as I was saying. People see me and they make their minds up in the first few minutes. There's me, a bit of a scruff. Not always looking my best. Maybe a fag in my hand. Wandering the streets when most people are at work. They see me as a dole artist. A scrounger.'

I shake my head when he looks at me, but I know that I'm fooling no one.

'It's fair enough, ye know. I struggle to keep a job. Bad with my nerves. Sometimes, when people find out what I saw, what we did, they kind of understand. And they soften a bit. 'Til they hear about Niall and his job, and his nice house and nice car. They think, well, that fellah saw it all too, and he's not dossing about. They lose sympathy for me right and quick, you know. But here's the thing, it never affected Niall the way it did me. He . . . well . . .'

'He well what?' I ask.

Declan blinks slowly as if the memory is being played out on the inside of his eyelids there and then.

'There was a stick. He had a stick. And he prodded her, ye know, to see if she was alive or something. I don't know. I mean it was clear she was dead. She was face down. But he prodded her anyway and . . .' He swallows. 'That stick went right through, right into her brain. I can still remember the sound it made . . .'

My stomach tightens. It must have been horrific.

'Niall called for help. I threw up whatever was left of my lunch then I ran to find the grown-ups. I have never been so scared in all my life. But Niall, he seemed to take it in his stride, you know. Like it was no big deal. I mean, she was dead, and rotting and . . .

'He waded into the water and pulled her to shore. I saw his shoulders shaking and I thought he was crying like I was.

'I called to him to come back because I thought he might throw up, too. I knew, even then I knew, it would be bad if he was sick on her. You know, forensics and all that.' Declan raised an eyebrow at me, and I nodded.

'The thing is, Ingrid. When he turned back, he wasn't crying at all. He was laughing. This mad, like hysterical or something laugh. But I swear he changed in that moment. Sometimes, I wonder had he changed long before that and I just hadn't noticed.'

Chapter Twenty-Four

Ingrid

I ask Declan what he means. Tell him it was probably just shock making his brother laugh. We've all done it in horrible situations. Emotion bubbles up one way or the other – and not always the right emotion.

'It's hard to explain,' he says. 'But I'm his twin and I just felt as though everything was different after.'

'Well, it was a massive trauma,' I reply. 'You were only children. It was bound to change you.'

'Hmm, maybe. But I don't know. It's hard to remember, but I've a feeling we were on different paths from before then. He became very serious. Angry even. Always clashing with me da. Before that, it had been fun. Us up there all the time, pretending we were explorers and the like. You must remember that, Ingrid. How we all played in the summer up there. We never showed you our den, though. No girls allowed,' he says with a wink. 'It was like our own wee world.'

I do remember, although after Kelly had died, I don't think I ever went near the place again. I was a timid child – scared of my own shadow, my mother said. But it had never been my shadow I'd been scared of. Before Kelly died, the bogeyman was just a myth; afterwards, he became real. And bad things really could happen.

But before then? Yes, like most of the children from the estate, we had decamped to the country park around the reservoir on the seemingly endless hot summer days. We built dens. We played until the light started to fade and we never really worried about our safety. We lived in an innocent bubble – strange, really, when you think of the political landscape of Derry at the time. The Troubles sputtering to a violent, dark and scary end.

'Well, Niall didn't want to play those games any more. Said they were for babies. He didn't want to hang about with me so much, either. Wasn't cool to have your brother as your best friend, ye know?' Declan raises his eyebrows and looks at me. 'Maybe he knew I was going to end up with nothing to offer the world anyway and wanted to cut his losses,' he sniffs before looking around the room. 'Look, if I open the balcony door here and hang my head out of it, could I have a wee smoke? Just a couple of puffs? Feeling a bit jittery, ye know.'

I can't say that I'm scared of what he might do if I say no, but I don't want any trouble.

'Okay,' I agreed. 'But out the door. Let me get you a saucer to stub the butt out on.'

'You're a star, Ingrid Devlin. You always were a class act,' he says, pulling a small tin from the pocket at the front of his shirt – the one item of clothing that hadn't been soaked right through – and rolling himself a cigarette.

I watch as his long, thin fingers fold the paper, sprinkle in tobacco and maybe something else before he licks the edges of it with the very tip of his tongue and seals it. My skin prickles. The hairs on the back of my neck stand on edge. My body is on high alert.

Maybe I'm more scared of Declan than I'm willing to admit to myself. I seem to be scared of a lot of things just now. People smashing car windows and breaking into my flat. The feeling that something is off-kilter with the world.

He lights the cigarette, inhales deeply before blowing a long stream of smoke out of the balcony door, not that that gets rid of the smell. Smoke blows back into the room on the wind.

'I don't want to think bad of him,' Declan says after a pause. 'He's my brother and I love him, but I also think something's not quite right with him. It's almost . . . well, it's hard to explain, but it's almost as if he doesn't feel things the way other people do. Can't feel sorry for people. Or happy for people. Shit, what's the word I'm thinking of?'

He stares out into the night sky. The rain is still coming down in sheets. I want him to close the balcony door, keep the place warm and dry. And safe.

'Empathy?' I offer as he turns his head to look directly at me. He looks so ridiculous in my white robe, his skinny legs peeping out from under it.

'Yes! That's it. Empathy,' he says. 'I always knew you were good with big words! He lacks empathy. Sometimes I think he has done so well in life because he doesn't ever think about how other people think or feel, or worry about the consequences of his actions.'

I watch as the ash builds at the end of the cigarette, threatening to drop onto my cream carpet. I blink myself back into the present. Into this talk about empathy.

'But he's a primary school teacher,' I say. 'Seems an odd career choice for someone who doesn't seem to care about other people.'

I think of the pictures I've seen on Niall's Facebook page. A very proud, devoted teacher staring back at me.

'I used to joke with him that he liked a captive audience. Well, he likes an audience who have to do exactly what he says even more.'

I don't know what to think. I try to cast my mind back to all those years ago. To the aftermath of what happened. But it just comes to me in pieces, fragments of colourless memories. He sounded perfectly nice in the messages we've exchanged this week, but I know people can easily hide behind words on a screen.

'You're meeting him this weekend, then?' Declan asks.

I nod. 'Friday evening for a coffee.'

He nods, too. 'I don't suppose me telling you to stay away from him would make any difference?'

I don't like where this is going. It must show in my body language, because Declan takes one last long drag of his cigarette and tosses the butt into the rainy night, ignoring the saucer I'd given him to act as a de facto ashtray. He waves his hands as if shooing the smoke out of the room then closes the door.

'I feel like a total prick for asking,' he says. 'But I'm only watching out for you. I like you, Ingrid,' he says, his face colouring. 'I don't want you to get hurt.'

'I'm pretty sure I can deal with him,' I say, knowing that there's no question of my professionalism slipping. He's too vital a source for the book for me to change my mind about meeting him. Declan looks crestfallen. 'But thank you for giving me the heads-up,' I tell him. 'That's very kind of you.'

He opens his mouth and I'm sure he's about to say something just as the alarm beeps on the tumble dryer to indicate it's finished drying his trousers.

'I'll just get those,' I say.

'And I suppose I should be heading on home,' he says, sighing. 'Look, I'm sorry. I shouldn't have come. It's just, you're a good person, Ingrid, and I didn't – I mean I don't – want you getting yourself mixed up in something.'

I cross the room with his warm, dry clothes. His hand brushes mine as he takes his clothes from me. He looks directly at me.

There is something in his expression I can't put my finger on. A darkness, perhaps. He blinks, long, dark lashes — wasted on a man, my mother would've said — brushing the top of his cheeks. The intensity of his gaze is back on me and I see he is moving closer.

I step back, but his hand is on my cheek. His skin is rough, calloused. I can feel adrenaline start to surge in my veins. The fight or flight impulse is getting ready to kick in. But this is Declan. Declan doesn't hurt people. I return his gaze, willing him not to make the move it feels like he is getting ready to make.

Unexpectedly, I feel tears well in my eyes. As I blink, one falls, rolling down my cheek, and I exhale a long, shuddering breath.

He blinks. Pulls his hand away as if he has been burned. Shaking his head, he mutters that he'll just get dressed and heads for the bathroom.

He doesn't come back into the living room when he is done. I just hear the door close as he leaves the building.

I don't go after him.

Chapter Twenty-Five

Ingrid

I'd be lying if I said I wasn't nervous. I haven't felt settled since Declan left and I've barely slept. It takes extra time in front of the mirror and a more liberal application than usual of concealer and Touche Éclat under my eyes to make me look half human.

I opt for an extra shot in my morning coffee, which might add to my jittery feelings, but I need it – otherwise I fear I might fall asleep at my desk.

Thankfully, work has been busy and that has given me little time to focus on the growing bubble of unease in the pit of my stomach. My story with the Doherty family has gained traction and is being widely shared around local social media accounts. I've been asked to speak on local BBC Radio about it, and my editor, Jane, has emailed me to congratulate me and say she is now 'super excited' to work on the book with me.

Ryan is keeping his distance, which is unusual for him. I imagine he's brooding about that awful incident with Liam yesterday in reception. But as much as he will be annoyed at how close he came to losing his lead story and annoying the close-knit Creggan community, he knows that I did the right thing. He knows sales of the paper will be up.

In fact, the wholesalers have put out extra copies to news-agents in Creggan and the city centre. Our website hits are soaring and our Facebook page is hopping with people offering their condolences to the Dohertys. They are sharing their memories of that time, calling Jamesy Harte all the names under the sun. Some are threatening to chase him down and 'do what should have been done years ago'.

I've been kept busy moderating the whole thing. Hiding those threatening comments. Replying to incoming messages to say no, we do not know Jamesy Harte's whereabouts and even if we did, we would not release it to the public. That it is a matter of public safety.

I know I'm lying about not knowing his whereabouts but it's the right thing to do.

By the time 5 p.m. approaches, I'm tired and my nerves about meeting Niall have started to kick in.

He has sent me a message – told me he'll be in Derry for about six and asked can we meet at seven. We've agreed to meet at Starbucks in the Foyleside Shopping Centre, where it's big enough for me to slip off anonymously into the crowds afterwards.

I'm packing up my things, planning to go home first and touch up my make-up (simply because I still look like an extra from *Night of the Living Dead*). I'll change into my jeans, a jumper. My comfy boots. I'll wrap up so that I look the opposite of alluring. I'll be wary.

I'm just about to leave, when my mobile rings. I consider rejecting the call, but my nosiness gets the better of me and I dig it out of my bag to see Jamesy Harte's name flash up on the screen. My stomach lurches. I answer, not saying his name. I don't want to draw any attention to the fact I'm talking to him – certainly not at work, anyway.

'Ingrid?' he says, a panicked tone to his voice. 'I've just seen the Doherty piece online. Saw the Facebook comments. Ingrid. People want to track me down, Ingrid. They want to kill me! Why did you write it? I thought you believed me!' His panic has quickly given way to disappointment.

I walk quickly from the office to where no one can hear me. 'I can't control what people say online. You must know that,' I say. 'And this was always going to get people wound up. You couldn't have expected different?'

'I expected you to tell people you believed I was set up,' he says, his voice cracking.

'I'm not here to tell people what to think,' I say, but I know that will sound like nothing more than a cop-out to him. 'I present the evidence and people can draw their own conclusions from that.'

'So, you'll publish my side of this as well, then?' he says, his voice hopeful.

'In my book, yes,' I tell him.

There is a deep sigh. 'No. No, Ingrid. That won't help. I might not be the sharpest tool in the box, but I know books don't write themselves overnight. Those words . . . what he said . . . He wishes I'd rot in hell, Ingrid. But I didn't do it . . . and I'm so tired of people thinking I did. I'm not a monster.'

'Jamesy, I know this must be really tough. But at the moment we have to go with how things stand. And the court did find you guilty.' I feel cruel uttering those words, but it is the truth. I can't change that.

'The court got it wrong. Everyone got it wrong. Don't you understand?' he pleads. 'I was inside for seventeen years. I have lost what should've been the best years of my life to these lies. All the years I could've been someone.

'Maybe I'd have met someone. Got married. Given my mammy grandchildren. Who knows? Don't you think I wanted that, too? A normal life. Didn't I deserve that? But now . . . now there's another angry mob baying for my blood. What if they find me, Ingrid? What if they track me down?'

The panic has returned to his voice.

'I know it's scary,' I tell him. 'But there's no reason why they would find you now if they haven't found you before. You're far enough from Derry, but could you speak to someone if you feel unsafe? Do you have a probation officer, or social worker? Someone like that. They would be able to give you better guidance than I can.

'There was always going to be some backlash and when your appeal is formally launched, it might get worse. Try to remember, this world is a strange one now. There are a lot of keyboard warriors on Facebook. All bluff and no substance.'

'You don't know that!'

His voice is borderline hysterical now. I can hear him moving about as if he's pacing up and down the room. 'And I know what they'll do. They'll have me lynched. I know it. I know it.'

'Try to stay calm,' I tell him, aware my words are completely inadequate.

'That's easy for you to say!' he yells, and I'm sure he's crying.

I feel wretched. And worried for him. But I remind myself this is not my fault. I only reported on a family's grief. I did my job. And I will give him his voice, even though I've been warned off doing so.

He ends the call before I have the chance to speak again, leaving me staring at the phone, unsure if I've been cut off or have lost signal. I feel a headache start.

Sighing, I glance at my watch and realise I'd better get a move on to be in town in time to meet with Niall. Wryly, I wonder how long it will take before I have him baying for my blood, too.

*　　*　　*

Niall, unsurprisingly, looks like his profile picture. Groomed. Tanned. Wearing a suit that accentuates a physique no doubt earned from hours in the gym. He is the polar opposite to his twin brother. There are no heavy lines scoring across his face. His eyes are bright. His skin has a healthy glow.

He is dictionary definition handsome, but immediately I wonder just how high maintenance he would be. It could get annoying if I was in a relationship with him. I immediately push that notion to the back of my mind. I don't want a relationship with Niall Heaney. I want to talk to him about Kelly and I also want to keep a safe distance. Declan's warnings have been playing through my mind all day.

He spots me and his face breaks into a wide smile. His perfectly straight white teeth are almost too dazzling. Standing up, he reaches to me for a hug.

'Ingrid! Well, this is lovely. It's so nice to see you. You're looking well.'

I think of how I'm wrapped up like an immersion tank in my Puffa jacket and smile. 'Winter chic,' I say. 'It's a brutal night out there.'

He nods, still standing. 'The drive down from Belfast was a bit hairy in places but sure, I'm here now. Let me get you a coffee. Latte? Cappuccino?'

'A cappuccino, please,' I answer and sit down, unwrapping myself from my scarf and coat while waiting for him.

I decide to take my notebook and my phone out of my bag. Make it clear from the outset that this is purely a professional meeting.

He glances at them as he returns carrying two mammoth cups of coffee. 'You don't waste any time,' he says with a smile.

'Well, sure, it's a Friday night and I'm sure you have plans that extend beyond meeting me for a chat,' I smile. 'So, I don't want to keep you too long.'

'I've no plans other than sitting watching *The Late Late* with Mum and Dad and to be honest, you'd be doing me a great favour to distract me from that.'

Niall Heaney has an easy manner. I can tell he would be comfortable in anyone's company. I admire that confidence in a person, perhaps because I like to think I have it, too.

'It would be a sin to keep you away from that treat,' I say with a smile, and he laughs, the corners of his eyes crinkling. 'So, we really should get down to business. You know I've spoken to Declan?'

He nods and if I'm not mistaken, a cloud passes over his face as he does so.

'That must have been interesting,' he says. 'Declan has quite a take on things.'

'About Kelly? And what happened?' I raise my eyebrow.

'About a lot of things. Poor Declan, it's hard to know what went wrong with him.'

'You both experienced an enormous trauma,' I say. 'I'd think that was enough to have an impact on anyone.' I realise I'm mirroring the conversation I had with Declan less than twenty-four hours before.

Niall sits back, adjusting himself in his seat. 'A lot of people witnessed a lot of trauma in those days,' he says. 'I don't want to speak ill of my brother, but Declan has never really helped himself, if you know what I mean. Our parents did what they could to help us. We saw a counsellor for a while. Did he tell you that?'

I shake my head, genuinely surprised. Declan had made me believe they were just left to flounder – which both brothers did in their own ways.

'I decided it wouldn't define me. I mean, I don't think I made that decision consciously, because I was only a child, but I made it all the same. I think I realised that life could be brutal and you had to make the most of it. Declan, he just never got past the realising life was brutal bit.' His voice is thick with emotion as he speaks.

'Can you tell me your memories from that day? The day you found her.'

'Sure, you must remember it a fair bit yourself?' he says.

I nod. 'I remember how it all seemed so quiet. That it was like everyone forgot how to talk except to talk about Kelly. I remember seeing the grown-ups shaking their heads and crying.'

'Do you remember how strange it was in school? We were all there, but none of us were learning. I don't even think the teachers were even trying – they knew we were all distracted. I suppose they were, too.

'I know that when the bell went, I just felt so fed up of being cooped up. Of all the quietness and the sadness. I just wanted to play with Declan and have an adventure, like we usually did.' Niall's eye contact is fleeting as if he is lost in his own thoughts. 'I don't think we thought it through. Well, I know we didn't think it through.

'No one was allowed out to play then, remember? I can only imagine how worried our ma must've been when we didn't land home at the proper time. I do remember it was a total let-down,' he says with a sad smile. 'It was cold and rainy and once we were at the reservoir, we seemed to lose the excitement for it. We decided to give it up as a bad job, you know.'

I nod, scribbling as fast as I can in my notepad, even though my phone is recording everything he says.

'Declan spotted her first. He didn't know it was her, but we knew it was something . . . different. I went closer and I could see her shape, in the water. She didn't look . . . well, she didn't look real. It took a while for my brain to register what I was looking at. I'd never seen a dead body before hers,' he says and sips from his coffee, pausing for a moment to think about what he's going to say.

'To this day, I don't know why I did it. Morbid curiosity, or bravado, or just without thinking, I decided to poke it – poke her – with a stick.' He colours and wrings his hands before continuing. 'I've never forgotten that feeling. Of the stick, when it . . . There was a wound, you know, to the back of her head. That's where I poked her. The stick went right in.'

I grimace and Niall must catch the expression on my face. He looks down as if ashamed.

'It messed me up for a while,' he says. 'How could it not? Everything changed that day. I don't think I was ever the same after, but – and this might sound a little callous, Ingrid. Don't judge me. But I don't think I'd have got where I am in life if I hadn't had that experience.

'I'm only sorry that Declan didn't see it the same way I did. He spiralled, you know. Nightmares. Anxiety. Was very clingy. I remember that. Didn't want to go back and play in the woods again, even though it was so unlikely anything like that would happen again.' Niall shakes his head as if this response from Declan was completely over the top.

'To be fair to him, I didn't want to go back there and play either,' I say and Niall bristles.

'You see, I don't understand that. There was nothing to fear. There were no bad guys hanging around. Jamesy Harte was arrested and in prison. There was no threat any more. People were just feeding off the drama, like they couldn't get enough of it, instead of letting it lie.'

'It was a huge deal!' I remind him. 'It's not something people just *got over*. It had an impact. And it should have had an impact.'

He shrugs as if that is no excuse. 'Perhaps. But it didn't need to change everything. That was letting the bogeyman win, wasn't it? We didn't need to let him win.'

Chapter Twenty-Six

Ingrid

By the time I leave Niall, I'm exhausted. And confused. His version of the aftermath differs from Declan's. According to him, it was his brother who changed — and no matter how much family and friends have tried to help him over the years, Declan still seems intent on a path to self-destruction.

And Niall is far from convinced that Jamesy Harte was framed. In fact, he is adamant that the right man went to jail and he should never have been released.

'Life should have meant life,' he'd said, his eyes darkening. 'He should never have been allowed to see the light of day again. If you'd seen what I saw, then you'd think the same.

'What he did to her, that wasn't accidental. It wasn't anything anyone with even an ounce of humanity could have inflicted on another human being. No one capable of doing that to a child should ever be allowed the chance to do it again.' He'd stared at the table as he spoke as if this was something he'd thought long and hard about.

'And you don't think, as Declan does, that Jamesy Harte was an easy target? Jamesy himself says he was set up. That the evidence against him was circumstantial at best.'

Niall had sipped from his coffee, then shook his head. 'I don't buy that. There was always something off about him, don't you think? He always made me feel uneasy. I remember how he would look at you girls, too. I didn't understand it at the time – probably didn't understand it fully until I was a lot older.

'Then I knew. If it hadn't been Kelly, it would have been someone else. It was only ever a matter of time with him. There's a wrongness in him, and it's a disgrace that he doesn't even have the good grace to put his hands up and admit it instead of dragging all this back up again.'

I found it strange that two brothers with identical experiences of what had happened that day held views that were so divergent. That it had affected them both so differently. I had been so convinced by Declan's version of events that I knew I had gone to the meeting with preconceptions that Niall would be thoroughly unlikeable. But he'd been charming, and warm. But just like Declan, there was something about him that I just couldn't put my finger on.

I'm finding it hard to get my head around a lot of things, I think as I walk across the multistorey car park to find my car. It's down to me to make sense of it, for the book at least, I suppose. But given the day I've had, and the fact that I have been running on zero per cent for the last few hours, I decide to stop trying to unravel it all until tomorrow at least. All I want now is to go home, switch off my phone, slip into my pyjamas and crash over a trashy movie.

So, the last thing I need is to reach my car and see that all four tyres have been slashed. Immediately, the air is pulled from my lungs with fear. It has been a few days since the break-in – I was hoping that whoever was messing around last week has backed off.

Glancing around, aware that I am exposed on all I sides, I try to see if anyone is watching. I look for shadowy figures peering out from behind pillars, hooded people in cars. There are a few people milling about, but none of them look suspect. None of them have that air of evil lurker about them.

There's a harried-looking woman, weighed down with shopping bags. A family with a child clinging on for dear life to a balloon from a fast-food restaurant. Two teenagers in hoodies who seem more interested in how far they can slide their hands into each other's back pockets than wanting to vandalise anyone's car.

I search for the nearest CCTV camera, hoping that there is one close enough that might have caught some footage of whoever has done this. I spot one, just about, which may or may not be pointed in the right direction. My tired eyes strain to focus on it.

I shiver. I'm scared. Tired. And angry. I'm just doing my job. Why can't people realise that? I want to run, but I also want to sit down on the ground and cry. I just want it all to stop.

That's when I notice a folded piece of paper under one of my windscreen wipers, which I cautiously reach for, knowing instinctively it's not going to say anything pleasant. My hands shaking, I unfold it.

Three words are scrawled across it in jagged handwriting. Stark bold capitals, scored into the paper so that the nib of the pen leaves an indentation.

YOU WERE WARNED

I feel the tears spring to my eyes before a flush of anger takes over. I'm not a crier. I am not a person who gives in to emotion. I hastily brush the tears away and take a deep breath, then unlock my phone to call for help. Just as I'm dialling my garage to arrange for someone to fix my car, a security guard approaches me.

'Miss, are you okay? Someone reported that your car has been damaged.'

'Yes, it has,' I say and nod towards it.

I hear his intake of breath. Clearly, he wasn't expecting this. A prang maybe. A bump from someone who hasn't learned how to park properly. A scrape from someone walking too close. Not four slashed tyres and a threatening note.

'Um . . . I think . . . we should call the police,' he says, lifting his walkie-talkie to inform his colleagues before I have the chance to tell him that it's fine. That I'll just get my car picked up by the garage and sort it.

There's no chance of a quiet getaway and of drawing no attention to this mess. I know he's right, of course. The police do need to be informed. And they need to work harder at finding out who is behind this. So far, they've come back with nothing more insightful than, 'We think it would be fair enough to assume this is related to your interest in the Kelly Doherty case, and your interest in Jamesy Harte in particular.'

As luck would have it, DC Mark Black is the officer who arrives, along with that busybody colleague of his, DS Eve King.

'Detective Sergeant,' I say. 'I'd like to say it was nice to see you, but . . .'

She smiles, seemingly not bothered by my words or my tone.

'We heard it was you and after that carry-on at your flat, we thought it better that I came along and had a look. Someone clearly has it in for you, Ms Devlin,' DS King says.

Is there a hint of a smile on her face? Maybe I'm being paranoid. I've every right to be, in the circumstances.

She pulls a pair of disposable white gloves from her pocket. After putting them on, she hunkers down and runs her finger along the cut into the thick rubber of the front nearside tyre. She repeats the process for them all, taking her time. A small crowd has gathered. Someone has their phone out and is either videoing or taking pictures. I ask DC Black if he can move people on and while he makes an effort to do so, it's half-hearted at best.

'We do say that people park here at their own risk,' the security man says, 'but we've never had anything like this happen before. Normally, it's a couple of scrapes or a ding, but not this.' He shakes his head. 'I can check the CCTV, but it doesn't cover every angle.'

DS King stands up. 'I'd be grateful if you could do that. Perhaps DC Black could go with you.'

My heart sinks a little. I don't want DC Black to go with him. I want him here, with his attempts to stop shoppers gawping at me. I feel heat rise on my face.

'Look, I'm sure it's nothing and I don't want to waste police time, so if I can just call my garage to arrange pickup of the car, I'll be on my way and you can be on yours, too.'

'Do you have the note?' DS King asks, ignoring my protestations that it's most likely nothing, reaching into the pocket of her suit jacket and taking out a plastic ziplock bag.

Momentarily, I wonder what else her pockets hold. Is there an unending supply of police equipment, like some weird version of Mary Poppins' carpet bag?

I stare at her.

'The note?' she says again, with less patience. 'We're told there was a note attached to your windscreen. I assume you have it?'

Reluctantly, I take the piece of paper from my pocket and hand it to her.

She opens it and examines it, her white gloves still on, before putting into the bag. 'You were warned,' she reads.

I notice DC Black look at her, then towards me. I do my best not to meet his gaze.

'And you're the only other person who touched this?' she asks.

'As far as I know.'

She tuts, shakes her head. I feel tears prick at my eyes again and yes, I'm still scared, but in this moment my primary feeling is embarrassment.

'This is quite worrying,' she says, her voice a little softer now. 'We're probably at the stage where we should discuss your personal security.'

Personal security? I see it through her eyes. This is another threat. Another attack. Another warning. That it happened on the day the article was printed in *The Chronicle* can hardly be coincidence.

'Surely if whoever is behind this wanted to hurt me, they would just do it. They wouldn't target my flat, or my car. They'd just go for me,' I say, my voice shaking. I'm trying to reassure myself and failing miserably.

She shrugs. 'It's impossible to predict the behaviour of someone who behaves in this fashion,' she says. 'But what we can assume is that whoever it is, they intended to do real damage to your car. From the look of it they used a large knife to slash your tyres. They came prepared. They want you to know they are serious.'

The words imprint themselves in my mind. A large knife and they came prepared. 'Impossible to predict.' I feel a little dizzy.

'Who knew you were going to be here tonight?' she asks, although her words feel distant.

I feel a cool sweat break on the back of my neck; my skin tingles. I shake my head. 'I don't know. I mean . . . I met Niall Heaney, so he knew. And his brother, Declan, and . . . I don't know,' I say.

My words feel thick, wrong, in my mouth. I'm not usually one to lose my cool, but I am at serious risk of losing it now. Adrenaline propels itself through my veins and I find myself gasping for a deep breath of air.

'Look, really,' I say, 'I'd just like to go home now. If I'm not making a complaint, then surely that's an end to it.' I scan the carpark for the quickest escape route.

If I keep an outward appearance of calm I'll be okay, I tell myself. Don't let them know they've rattled me. Don't involve the police. Don't give it the oxygen of attention. My breath comes in short, shallow gasps.

'Ingrid,' DS King says, and I note she is now using my first name.

I feel her hands take mine.

'Take a deep breath,' she says, and I try, but there doesn't seem to be enough air in this car park to fill my lungs.

I attempt to pull away from her. 'Just let me go home,' I plead, and to my shame, tears start rolling down my cheeks – and there still isn't enough air to breathe properly. I hear her order someone to get a chair. There's a commotion of voices and engine sounds, and a tannoy announcement – and it's all just too loud and too much.

'Ingrid, I'm not sure you're hearing me. We need to consider the possibility that it's not safe for you to go home right now. Whether you make a complaint or not isn't really the issue any more. There was someone in this car park, who had in their possession an offensive weapon. Someone who intentionally caused a significant amount of damage to your car and who has left you a threatening note. Emotions are running high, Ingrid.'

Someone guides me to sit down on an office chair, which has been wheeled out from the security hut. I will my breathing to settle. I know I'm inadvertently putting on a show for anyone who can see what is happening. I feel sick. I'm worried I'll humiliate myself completely and throw up. Panic claws at me. I put my hands over my ears to try to block out the noise and stop the buzzing in my head.

I'm aware of a phone ringing, of DS King stepping back from me. I notice her run her hands through her pixie crop, her expression immediately changing. It's more serious. I notice she's looking at me before she catches herself and turns away so I can no longer see her face. But I know, just know, that something bad has happened.

Something really bad.

Chapter Twenty-Seven

Ingrid

I can't take my eyes off DS King and when she ends the call, her hand drops to her side. She stands for a moment, then I see her shoulders rise as she inhales and then turns to look back at me.

Within seconds she is hunkering down in front of me, so that her eyes are level with mine.

'Okay, Ingrid. We're going to get you out of here and go somewhere we can talk. Somewhere more private.'

'What's happened?' I ask, wondering if she thinks I'm too stupid to realise there is more going on than she has revealed.

She raises an eyebrow. 'We just think it would be better to go somewhere away from all the noise and all the nosy parkers. Is there a family member or friend we can take you to?'

'I'd really rather go home,' I tell her, and really, it's all I want, despite what she is saying to me. Despite the fact it may or may not be safe to do so.

'Ingrid,' she says, her voice calm as she leads me by the arm to a waiting police car, 'we really don't advise that at the moment.'

I look at her, blinking, as I take my seat and she shuffles in beside me, away from prying eyes.

'Tell me what's happened,' I say, even though there is a part of me that doesn't want to know.

'Okay. I'm not sure I should be telling you this, but in light of what has just happened here, I don't suppose I've a choice. There's been an incident at the Doherty house.'

My eyebrows raise. The Doherty house? 'What kind of incident?'

She takes a deep breath. 'Mr Doherty has been injured – quite seriously, I believe.'

'How?'

She pauses for a moment as if she's not quite sure what to say next, or if she should be saying anything at all to me.

'He's been attacked, Ingrid. I don't have all the details, but it would appear he is in a bad way.'

'Mr Doherty?' I ask, incredulous. 'Liam Doherty has been attacked? Why would anyone attack him?'

This makes no sense. Surely it can't have anything to do with the story in the paper or Kelly's anniversary? The only person who could possibly be aggrieved by that is Jamesy Harte. He'd been angry and emotional on the phone earlier, but surely not?

'We're trying to find out more,' DS King says. 'But, Ingrid, there is reason to believe it is connected to the recent interest in Kelly's murder. In light of what has happened, and what has been done to your car, we really don't think it would be wise for you . . .'

Something clicks in my mind. I need to get to Creggan. I'm not sure who else will have heard what has happened, but if I can be at the scene first, maybe . . . This is a big story. I reach for the car door to get out.

'I appreciate your concern, DS King, but really, I'll be fine. I should probably be letting you get on with things. Sounds like you've bigger fish to fry than the tyres on my car,' I add.

I think of Bernie Doherty's face, gaunt and lost. She knows

166

me. She might talk to me about what happened. Unless she has gone to the hospital. Maybe I should go there instead . . .

'Ingrid, we really think . . . *I* really think that you should consider your actions very carefully. We don't know who did this to your car. We don't, at this time, know who attacked Mr Doherty. We do know there is a link between the pair of you and, given what else has happened over the last week to you and your property . . .'

DS King has adopted a very stern voice. There's a hint of concern there, but more than that, there's a very clear message that she doesn't want me out of her sight just now. Maybe she knows more than she is letting on.

I need to get to the heart of this story, I decide, even as the panic is still ebbing from my body, and preferably before anyone else. DS King is not going to be easy to get past, though.

A thought strikes me and I take a deep breath.

'Actually, I don't feel well,' I tell DS King, clenching my muscles tightly and jiggling my legs, doing my very best to adopt a 'stricken with panic' look. 'I don't feel . . .' I let my words taper off, breathe in and out in short, sharp bursts, trying to control the flow of oxygen to my lungs.

'Is it another panic attack?' DS King asks, her voice thick with concern.

I shake my head. 'I don't know,' I say, putting my hand to my chest as if I'm in pain.

'I'm taking you to the hospital,' she says, issuing the order for DC Black to drive on.

He looks into the rear-view mirror just as I raise my head to look up. I catch his gaze, his raised eyebrow. I suspect he knows exactly what I'm doing, but I know he won't have the guts to call me out on it.

If DS King won't let me go home, and won't let me go to Creggan, I'll hedge my bets on Bernie Doherty being at the hospital waiting for news on her husband. If I happen to be there at the same time, and I happen to bump into her there, that's just a coincidence, isn't it? I can't be accused of anything. Not when I'm clearly unwell.

I turn my gaze from his quickly, sit back in the seat and allow a tear to roll down my cheek. It isn't hard for me to make myself cry when I need to. I'm well versed in doing exactly what I need to do to get a scoop. As a second tear follows, I realise that I've been holding my emotions in over this past week. It's not hard, at all, to let some out. If I'm not careful, I'll lose control of them altogether and start sobbing.

'We'll be there soon,' DS King says, taking my hand in hers and instructing DC Black to switch on the blues and twos.

I almost feel bad for lying to her, but I push those feelings back.

I spot Bernie Doherty as soon as we arrive at the emergency department in Altnagelvin. Her face ashen, a bloodstained coat in her arms. She is being led down the corridor away from the main doors of the department by a uniformed police officer, and a man with a stethoscope around his neck who appears to be a doctor. I know the relatives' room is at the end of this corridor and sure enough, I see her led to the door of it.

I feel a hand on my arm and I jump, pulled from my reverie by DS King, who is leading me to a seat in the main waiting room on the left. As much as I want to follow Bernie Doherty and talk to her, I can't just feign a miraculous recovery. The room is full to bursting and is uncomfortably warm.

'You'll get help soon,' DS King says as we sit down.

There's a degree of agitation in her voice. She's tense. She probably wants to see what is happening with Liam Doherty as much as I do. My name is called by a nurse. Before I can speak, DS King jumps in, giving my history so that I don't have to speak. The nurse visibly relaxes, having assessed that I'm not a dangerous criminal. But DS King doesn't, and the tension coming off her in waves is making me feel uneasy.

I follow the nurse through to the treatment bays and she asks me to hop up on the bed.

'We'll do some checks,' the nurse says. 'Give you a little oxygen to regulate your breathing.'

She slips some rubber tubing around my head, poking two little valves into my nose. I feel the gentle flow of oxygen. I lie back and close my eyes as she slips a blood pressure cuff on my arm. I feel it tighten. DS King speaks and I open my eyes.

'Right, Ingrid, I'll leave you here for a bit. DC Black will be just outside. I'm going to check in with my team about the Doherty incident.'

The nurse raises an eyebrow. DS King leaves the room and I take a deep breath of oxygen while the nurse takes my temperature.

'It's all go tonight,' the nurse quips. 'And we can't even blame the pubs. Sure, it's not even eight yet. Must be a full moon or something.'

'Is that true?' I ask between breaths. 'Do full moons really bring out the crazy people?'

She nods. 'As far as I'm concerned, yes. But you know, we're only ever a few beats away from crazy all of the time. You never know, morning, noon or night, who is going to come through the door next.' The nurse scribbles some notes on my file. 'Your temperature is fine, but your blood pressure is a little high. We'll repeat this in fifteen minutes to see how you are.

'For some people, it's just being in a hospital that causes the jump. Your oxygen levels are coming up, so we'll just get you to rest here for a bit. I'll see if I can find that police officer you were with and let her know.'

'My car was vandalised,' I say, keen to let the nurse know I'm not one of the 'crazies' she speaks of.

She looks at me quizzically.

'That's why I'm here,' I gabble. 'My car, and then I had a panic attack and I'm probably okay and really it looks like you are all busy enough and I don't need to be wasting your time.'

'It's not wasting our time. Don't be worrying yourself,' she says, her voice gentle. 'Now, try and rest a bit.'

She pulls back the curtain on the cubicle just enough to slip out before she pulls it closed again and I'm left listening to a cacophony of noise all around me. Someone is screaming somewhere – in pain. They don't want to be touched. A male voice, slightly slurred, shouts, 'Don't fucking touch me,' while a doctor or a nurse is trying to soothe them. How that medical professional can keep their voice so calm is beyond me. My patience wouldn't last long.

A baby is crying. A nurse or doctor is talking about how she is desperate for a cup of tea. There is lots of chat about test results and meds and X-rays. A whole world exists outside this cubicle and I want to get out and see it.

This area of A&E is too far from the resus ward or the family room for me to be in with any chance at all of seeing Bernie, or finding out more about what has happened to Liam. I don't care if my blood pressure is raised – if I don't get on top of this story quickly, it will only rise further.

DS King has not returned, so I pull off the blood pressure cuff and the nasal canula that has been feeding me oxygen and sit up. Rifling through my bag, I find my phone and slip it into my pocket. I'm going to go and investigate.

No one so much as gives me a sideways glance as I walk through the bay of curtain-lined cubicles towards the relatives' room. I'm just one more person in the department and as long as I'm not making a nuisance of myself or demanding attention, I'm the least of their worries.

There's a corridor that separates the main department from

170

the resuscitation ward. I keep my head down as much as possible, while trying to look around. There are a number of uniformed police officers standing around and no obvious sign of Bernie Doherty. Thankfully, there is also no sign of DS King, so I brave it to walk towards the family waiting room. Chances are, she will be ensconced there – perhaps with other family members or the police. Can I risk knocking on the door? What will her reaction be?

I hear whispers of conversation around me.

'It was pretty brutal,' one police officer says. 'I've not seen the likes of it before. Someone has it in for him.'

'It's the wife I feel sorry for. She's in an awful state. Imagine seeing that and not being able to do anything.'

As I walk past them, they stop speaking, perhaps aware they have been speaking inappropriately and they have no idea who will walk past them or what they might know. Derry is a small city and it's still the case that everyone knows everyone else's business. News like this, if it got out, would spread like wildfire.

There's only one thing for it really. I should be brazen. The worst that can happen is that I'll be told to get lost. If it happens, it will hardly be the first time and it certainly won't be the last.

I walk to the door of the family room – that private space, with the comfy seats and boxes of tissues on the table to help mop up the tears when the bad news is broken. The place no one wants to be shown to. The place where pain and grief are contained.

Although I half expect to feel a hand on my shoulder to stop me, or to be asked by one of the police officers who I am and where I'm going, it doesn't happen. Before I know it, I'm knocking on the door, turning the handle and letting myself in.

Chapter Twenty-Eight

Ingrid

Bernie Doherty is still holding the bloodstained coat, only now I can see clearly that it is not her own. It must be Liam's. Her grip is so tight, her hands stark white – a direct contrast to the darkness of the coat. Small specks of blood are luminous against her pallor. There is a streak of blood on her forehead. As if she wiped the back of her hand on her brow, mopping away her own sweat with a trail of her husband's blood.

Her trousers are wet, I notice, and her face is as white as her hands, framed by tendrils of her hair, which is now a mass of frizz. Her blue eyes are ringed with red. She has been crying, but now she is rocking – expending her nervous energy in what little way her body will allow her. Her eyes flash directly to mine as if she both hopes and fears that I have news for her on her husband's condition.

'Bernie,' I say, 'I heard what happened. My car was attacked, too.'

She blinks at me as if trying to place me.

'How is he? How is Liam? What did they do to him?' I ask.

'Ingrid Devlin, from Leenan Gardens,' she says, to herself as much as anyone.

Several sets of eyes from around the room focus on me and I look at the other people gathered. There is a man – one of her sons, I think. It's been a long time since I saw him. And a woman, pregnant, rubbing her stomach as if she is polishing a bowling ball. Her eyes are red-rimmed, too, and she is holding a well-worn Kleenex in her hand. Little pieces of disintegrated tissue fall to the floor like sad confetti.

'Ingrid that wrote the story?' the man says. 'The one in the paper today? The girl that started this up again?' He stands up and before I can even register the moment, he is powering towards me. 'Scumbag bitch!' he shouts, and I flinch, awaiting the physical blow that I'm sure will follow this verbal assault.

'Christopher!' Bernie hisses, and it's enough to stop him in his tracks, his hand frozen somewhere between his towering frame and my face. 'It's not her fault. You can't blame her for what happened to your da. She's only doing her job. What happened . . . It was all my fault.'

Christopher Doherty is over six foot tall. He's of stocky build. It's clear he works out and by the look of his biceps, he might take a little something to help him along. I can tell he's normally a guy who wouldn't be seen outside the house without being groomed to perfection, so to see this giant of a man so dishevelled as he starts to cry in front of me, shaking with anger and pain, feels like a physical blow.

I step back.

'I'm sure the only people who are at fault are those who did this,' I say as the pregnant woman places her hand on Christopher's arm and gently guides him into a hug. 'It's okay. He'll be okay. He's a strong man.'

Bernie looks down, releasing the coat from her grasp at last. 'He's not. He's not a strong man. He wasn't strong enough for this and I did it. I only wanted to tell her story. To keep a part of her alive.'

Christopher pulls himself from his wife's embrace, punches the wall – the sound his bones make as they smash into the solid brick is sickening.

The pregnant woman looks crestfallen. She shrinks back into herself, rubbing the roundness of her stomach in a protective manner. I feel for her. She was clearly only trying to help and here she is in the middle of this nightmare.

'And people are talking about her. Remembering her. That's a good thing.' I say.

I want to reach for my phone to show Bernie and Christopher the Facebook likes and the retweets, but sense kicks in before I do. What do they care about stupid numbers on the Internet when Liam is in God knows what state.

Bernie just shakes her head. Tears are rolling down her face. 'No . . . No.'

'We're in shock,' the pregnant woman says. 'It was just so unexpected. So brutal.'

Christopher sits down beside her, like a child in need of comfort, and she takes his non-bruised hand and squeezes it gently.

'Did they tell you what they did?'

It's Bernie's turn to talk. My eyes flick to hers. She is ashen, her fingers still blanched white, wrung together.

'No. No, I just heard he'd been attacked. The police were with me at Foyleside. My car was vandalised. A threat left for me. I took a panic attack and they brought me here.'

Bernie isn't listening to what I'm saying. I can see that. She drops her gaze from mine, looks down at the floor.

'There were three of them. Three big men in their balaclavas. They beat him, right in front of me. I tried to stop them, but one of them pushed me into the chair. Liam kept trying to reassure me he was okay, but all I could do was beg them to stop. One of them, a man with a Belfast accent, said if I spoke again it would be worse for Liam. If I so much as made a noise they would finish him off. So I had to watch . . . and listen . . . And then . . .' she pauses as if trying to find the words, 'one of them went out into the kitchen. I could hear it, you know.'

Her voice cracks. 'Oh, Jesus, I could hear it and he could, too. The kettle boiling.'

She brings her hand to her mouth as if she is going to throw up. It's all I can do to keep standing myself. Dear God, what have they done to him? I watch as Bernie steadies herself, takes a deep breath.

'The other two of them held him down and the third man came back in with the kettle in his hand. I wanted to beg them to stop, but the Belfast one, he just looked at me and told me again to keep my mouth shut or he'd pour it right down Liam's throat and into his eyes. So I had to sit tight and I was afraid to move – and God forgive me, I closed my eyes because I didn't want to see it. I couldn't see it and I heard the screams of him.

'They scalded him with that boiling water all over his chest, right up to his neck, and they held him down while they did it. And I . . . I let them . . . I didn't stop them.'

Her body convulses into sobs and Christopher, this big lump of a man, simply drops his head and cries, too.

I can't deny that the scene, and the news of the barbaric nature of the attack, has my stomach twisting, too. There's a darkness to this that I can't comprehend. Why Liam Doherty? What had he done to deserve this?

'Do you have any idea who did it?' I ask, but Bernie won't or can't answer.

She looks at me and her eyes widen as if she is realising something else. I see it. The fear, stark, as if I'm posing a direct risk to her.

'Oh, God. Oh, God. Don't . . . you can't say any of what I

told you in the paper. Tell me you won't say any of that in the paper? They said if you did . . .'

Her sentence is cut short by the door to the relatives' room opening and the arrival of a distinctly unimpressed DS King.

'You shouldn't be here, Ingrid,' she says. 'You know that. Come on, now. The nurse is looking for you.' Her tone is very much like that of a schoolteacher.

I can't refuse to leave the room, no matter how much I want to. I have to go back to have my blood pressure checked. Even though I'm sure it will be fine. As we walk back down the corridor, I hear DS King give two young officers a roasting, informing them that no one but next of kin should be allowed near the Doherty family. As she directs me through the double doors into the main cubicle area again, I catch a glimpse of DI David Bradley, DS King's superior officer, walking down the corridor, his coat flapping around him, his face grim.

At least, I think, as I disappear behind the curtains and clamber back up on the trolley where I am supposed to be, I've not come face to face with him. This day has been stressful enough without getting a dressing down from the sanctimonious Bradley.

'Whatever Bernie Doherty may or may not have said to you in that room, I'd remind you this is a sensitive ongoing police investigation and we would ask that details of the incident are not reported in the media,' DS King says.

'Have any arrests been made?' I ask.

'Not at this time. I'd suggest you direct any further questions through official channels. I'm not a spokesperson for the police.'

I nod. She's told me all she needed to. There is nothing, legally, to stop me from printing details of what the Doherty family told me. Restrictions only come into play once an arrest has been made so as not to jeopardise legal proceedings. But for perhaps the first time in my career, I feel my nerve leave me. This is more serious than I ever thought it could be.

It was supposed to be a news story. An investigation into something from the past. It was never supposed to bring violence to anyone's door. Were the same people behind Liam's attack as were behind the attacks on my car, on my home? I imagine Liam Doherty, the frail man he has become, being held down while boiling water was poured over his skin. I imagine his skin blistering, melting off in sheets, and I feel sick.

'You've gone very pale,' DS King says just as I reach for one of the cardboard kidney bowls in the cubicle and empty my stomach contents into it.

Chapter Twenty-Nine

Ingrid

By the time I get home, I'm exhausted. My stomach and my throat hurt from the force of being sick. I feel sweaty and unkempt from the heat in the hospital. The plaster that has been put across my arm after a blood sample was taken has started to itch at my skin. I pull it off, revealing a dark bruise underneath.

I walk straight to the bathroom and strip off before standing under the shower and letting the almost too hot water pummel at my tired muscles. A police car had brought me home. DS King had tried, again, to persuade me to go elsewhere, but all I felt in that moment was the need to be in my own space.

But now, as the steaming hot water stings at my skin, I realise there's no comfort here any more. No sense of being safe. Not on my own. I think of the warnings I've received, what has happened to Liam, how scared Jamesy sounded on the phone, and I'm scared. So scared.

I turn off the water and shiver as I walk, wrapped in a towel, to my bedroom, where I dry off and pull on fresh pyjamas and a pair of fluffy bedsocks. My anxiety only grows, so I double-lock my front door and push a chair from the dining area against it, I close the doors to my bedroom, to the bathroom, and pad through to the living room-cum-kitchen. I make a cup of tea but can't bring myself to drink it.

Sitting cross-legged on the sofa, I lift my MacBook and power it up, going immediately to Facebook and Twitter to see what, if anything, is being said about the attack on Liam Doherty.

Twitter doesn't carry much more than the official police line that a man has sustained a life-changing injury in a 'brutal' assault – but Facebook? Facebook is another story. An unofficial 'Derry Scandal' page features a litany of posts, each wilder than the last, from people who claim to be in the know, or people who are theorising about what happened.

I heard it was Liam Doherty. Dragged him out of the house. Whole street was watching and not a being stopped them. Animals. That's what they are.

I heard it was a fellah tarred and feathered for messing around with some wee young one. And the person who told me wouldn't be one for making up stories. Dirty beast whoever he is. They should've cut his balls off, too.

Jesus! The rumours on this page. Derry people love a good gossip. Would you remember there's a human being at the centre of this, and his family, too. For the love of God, don't be spreading your nonsense.

Couldn't have been Liam Doherty. Wee Kelly's da? Why would anyone target him? You'd never find a nicer man. That family have suffered enough. Please, God, it's not him and it's someone who deserves it.

I heard it was just some tout that the dissidents wanted to teach a lesson to.

Naw, I'm telling you now. My ma lives across the street and it was definitely the Doherty house. But no one was dragged out into the street. First anyone knew of it was Bernie running screaming for help into the street. My ma says she was hysterical.

Maybe Bernie had enough of him. I think she's losing the plot. Never been right in the head since that wain died.

So, it wasn't all out there. That was something. And there was no mention of my car being targeted, even though I know a number of people saw the commotion at Foyleside. Then again, I'm not of any significance compared with the Dohertys. Nor am I arrogant enough to think I would garner an ounce of the sympathy or interest they would.

I close my laptop and jump as my phone rings. Ryan's name flashes up. I'm torn between wanting to answer the call and wanting to reject it. I know he will have heard what has happened. Ryan always hears about things. He has his ear close to the ground in Creggan at the moment anyway. I know he'll lecture me. Tell me I should've left well enough alone.

And yet, feeling scared and vulnerable in my own home, I also want to hear his voice. Our relationship, if you can call it that, might be very dysfunctional, but I still find some comfort in him.

I take a deep breath and answer the call, surprising myself to find that even on saying hello, my voice has a wobble to it.

'I take it you've heard about Liam Doherty,' he says. He's brusque and to the point.

'I have,' I say.

'I knew this was a bad idea. Dragging all this up, asking questions. We've put them in the line of fire.'

I bristle. 'We haven't reported anything that wasn't already out there and we've certainly not printed anything that would have warranted this attack on Liam. The piece was well-received.'

Already I'm tired of this conversation. I wanted some comfort from him, not irrational blame.

He sighs. 'Do we know who's behind this? Is it Harte? Have you spoken to him?'

'I spoke to him earlier. This afternoon. Look, I would be 99 per cent sure this has nothing to do with him,' I say. 'He's too terrified to come anywhere near Derry. And I don't think he'd have the wherewithal to arrange anything or be a part of anything. I believe there was a gang involved,' I say, keeping quiet for now about my chat with Bernie.

I can almost hear the cogs whirring in his head.

'Have you been up to Creggan? Are you going there?'

'I'd thought you'd want me to stay out of it,' I say, unable to hide the bitterness in my voice. 'You don't want us "dragging it all up", remember? So no, I've no plans to go to Creggan.'

'Things have already been dragged up and put on display,' he says, his tone sharp. 'This is the here and now. It has just happened. We should have a reporter on the scene.'

'Then call one of the boys, or Trina. I'm home and I'm in my pyjamas and I'm not going out again.'

I know I'm not coming across as particularly professional, but then again, I've done an awful lot of things that cannot possibly fall into the domain of 'professional' when it comes to Ryan.

'It's not like you to walk away from a story,' he says.

'I'm not walking away from it. I know exactly what happened. I've spoken to Bernie Doherty and her son. And my car has been targeted again, so I'm right in the middle of the story.' I spit the words at him, angry that he is goading me.

'You've spoken to Bernie Doherty! When? What did she tell you?'

He hasn't asked about my car or about me. If he wasn't my boss, I would tell him to fuck off.

'I saw her at the hospital. I was taken there, by the police, after I took a panic attack.'

I recall the look on Bernie's face, the fear. Her telling me I couldn't say anything. There was something so raw and real in her expression that I feel a need to protect her.

'She was in shock. She wasn't making much sense, to be honest, but by all accounts, he's in a bad way. And for all I know the people behind that are the same ones who have been targeting me, so there is not one single chance in hell that I am going anywhere near Creggan tonight.'

To my shame, my voice breaks as I finish talking and the sob I've been holding in rises up and explodes from my mouth. It's as if Bernie's fear has invaded every cell in my body. I can feel it. I can imagine the horror she endured. Her helplessness. What these people are capable of, it's inhuman. If those men could do that to Liam Doherty, and make his poor, broken wife watch, then what other horrific acts could they be responsible for?

I can't seem to pull myself together, even though I'm mortified that Ryan is hearing me so vulnerable. This is the last thing I want.

'Ingrid.'

His voice is softer now and for a second I wonder if he will have some comfort for me, after all.

He doesn't. Of course.

'I don't want to say I told you so, but—' he says.

'Then don't say it, Ryan. You don't have to be an arrogant arsehole all the time.'

'I'm not trying to be an arsehole,' he protests. 'You've had an horrific evening by the sound of it. Anyone would understand if you wanted to walk away from the story now. It's not admitting defeat. I'll speak to one of the freelancers. They can take over for tonight. We'll talk again on Monday.'

'Thanks,' I say weakly.

'Do you want me to come over?' he asks. 'I can feed Jen a line about something. I can try and distract you?'

I know what Ryan's idea of distraction is and it's the very last thing I want.

'No. No, I'm grand. I'm going to try and sleep,' I tell him, and we say our goodbyes.

I mull over his words. He doesn't seem to realise that no matter how terrified I am, there is no way I'm walking away from this story; if he thinks that, he is sorely mistaken. I might want to run, but I know now, after what has happened tonight, that there is something huge going on here. Something bigger than Jamesy Harte trying to challenge his conviction.

That level of brutality is only ever born out of anger and fear. Someone is trying to get the message across, loud and clear, that Kelly Doherty's death should be consigned to history – no matter what questions may be asked these days, no matter a family's desire to grieve. No matter what. Someone is spooked. Someone is angry.

Which leads me to believe that someone is hiding something.

My phone rings again. I want to ignore it, but the tone is no less shrill and loud than it was before, so I pick it up to reject the call. My heart thuds, almost loud enough to drown out the noise of the phone, as I see Jamesy Harte's name flash up on the screen.

Chapter Thirty

Ingrid

My finger hovers over the answer button as I try to prepare myself for the conversation we're about to have.

I know I have to answer, even if every sinew in my body is telling me that I don't want to. I may be feeling overwhelmed and scared, but I need to talk to him. I think I need to hear that he is okay. I press the answer icon, put him on loudspeaker and hold the phone in front of me.

'What's happened to him?' Jamesy says before I even have the chance to say hello; his voice is slightly slurred as if he's been drinking.

'Mr Doherty? He's been assaulted. That's as much as I know,' I lie.

I can hear a sharp intake of breath on the other end of the call. 'Is it serious? The police say "life-changing" injury, what does that mean?'

'I know what you know, Jamesy. I'm not working tonight.'

I almost tell him I'm at home but decide against it. I won't give any more information than I need to. Fear is needling at me.

'Can't you find out? Call one of your contacts?'

'That's not how it works,' I say, the third lie tripping off my tongue much easier than the first two. 'There are official channels . . .'

'Ingrid, maybe I'm not the sharpest tool in the box, but I'm not an eejit. I know people like you hear things. You've your sources. There must be rumours about who did it. It's Derry. There's always rumours.'

'Jamesy,' I say, forcing a steadiness into my voice that I most certainly do not feel, 'I am telling you what I know. I don't know who, or why.'

Jamesy sniffs. 'Well, maybe he was just getting a taste of his own medicine.'

He has sounded sad before. Scared. But here is the bitterness of a man whose own life was taken from him.

'Jamesy, I know you must be upset,' I soothe. His bitterness towards Liam makes me uneasy. 'I know you've been robbed of your freedom for years, but surely you can't think Liam Doherty deserves any of this.'

I can hear heavy footsteps as if Jamesy is pacing up and down his room. He sounds agitated. His breathing is heavy. I hear him take a drag on a cigarette.

'He's not as broken as he looks,' Jamesy says at last.

'What do you mean by that?'

'Liam Doherty knows more than he was letting on about who set me up. I'm not surprised, after all these years, it's come back to haunt him.'

'You think he knows you were set up?' I ask, incredulous. Surely it was in Liam Doherty's interest – more than anyone else's – to have his daughter's real murderer brought to justice.

'Aye,' Jamesy says before coughing and taking another drag from his cigarette.

'But why would he stay quiet all these years? You're not suggesting he was involved in her death himself?'

The very thought seems so alien to me. Liam, for all his roaring and shouting, doesn't seem like a man capable of harming his own child. He's a broken man.

'No. No. He didn't do it. But that doesn't make him innocent, either.'

I remember how angry Liam was when he called into the *Chronicle* offices – how he wanted the story pulled. How he said he hoped Jamesy would rot in hell.

Except that he didn't say that, did he? He said he hoped Kelly's killer would rot in hell. He'd never actually used Jamesy's name.

'Who do you think did it?' I ask him.

There is silence at the other end of the phone. The pacing has stopped. I listen, his breath just audible down the line.

'Jamesy?' I say again and wait for his answer.

But the line just goes dead.

I stand up and stretch before walking to the balcony doors, which look out over the inky black water of the River Foyle. The river is swollen, choppy. It's a bitter night and there are no walkers along the quay. I watch as the patrol boat from Foyle Search and Rescue passes, on the lookout for any poor soul tempted to end it all by jumping into those murky waters. I wonder how the volunteers manage, dealing with people in crisis each and every day.

I pull the curtains closed, to fend off the darkness in more ways than one, and then I pour myself two fingers of Jameson and throw it back, allowing the hot spice of the whiskey to burn then soothe my throat. Maybe if I drink enough, I'll fall into a drunken sleep that won't allow me to jump at every creak and rattle through the night.

I'm about to pour a second glass, when the buzzer for the door goes.

It buzzes a second time and I look at the grainy CCTV

image, to see the familiar figure of Declan Heaney looking into the lens.

'Ingrid?' he asks. 'It's Declan. I'm just checking you're okay. After what happened at the Dohertys'? I was just passing . . .' he mumbles. 'Can I come up?'

No, I think. I just want to drink myself into semi-oblivion and go to sleep.

'I'm not sure that's a good idea,' I say.

'Sure, it's only me,' he says. 'I won't be long. Honest. I just wanted to have a quick chat. See if you're okay. And here, I've heard a whisper about what happened at the Dohertys'. It might be a lead for you to follow. But look, if it makes you feel uncomfortable . . .'

I think of him. Harmless — lonely, too. Just like me, I suppose. I think of the contrast in his life compared to Niall's and hit the button to let him in before quickly running to my room and changing into a pair of jeans and a jumper.

When I open the door, I'm glad to see he's not in the same sorry state he was in when he last called. He seems sober. Or mostly sober. And while it's clear he has been out in the rain, he isn't soaked through.

'Wild, isn't it? That craic up in Creggan.' He shakes his head. 'I'm told it was brutal. Derry rumours have them cutting his tongue out, but I don't think that's true.'

'It isn't,' I say before thinking that I really shouldn't say any more. 'I don't know the ins and outs of it, but I do know that's not the case.'

He nods. He's a little fidgety, his eyes darting around the room. He spots the Jameson bottle on the worktop and I curse myself for not putting it away.

'On the hard stuff?' he asks as he slips off his jacket and hangs it on the back of one of my dining chairs.

'Just a nightcap after a busy week,' I say. 'Can I get you a cup of tea?'

'A swig of the Jameson would suit me better, but tea will do,' he says, and I put the kettle on to boil.

I can't help but shiver as it bubbles and whistles. Bernie's description of what happened to Liam is all too fresh in my head. I turn to see Declan look around the flat again before sitting down at the dining table.

'So, what have you heard about what happened?' I ask him. 'You said you had a lead.'

He stands up again. He's on edge and it makes me nervous. I watch as he wanders to the window, pulls back the curtain and looks out for a while.

'Yeah, well. I heard it was mistaken identity.'

This doesn't marry with what Bernie told me. The attack was personal, exceptionally personal, and prolonged enough to know that any mistaken identity would have been noticed.

'Who told you that?'

He taps the side of his nose. 'Word on the street, you know. You've your sources, Ingrid, and I have mine.'

'And who were they really looking for, then?'

I watch his face for any tells, any change in his demeanour or presentation. He stalls for a moment.

'Someone from the next street over. Drug debt, I'm told. Had been warned to pay up lots of times and it seems people finally ran out of patience.'

'Surely drug dealers would know who their own customers were?'

He blinks, his mouth hangs open just a little. 'They never do the dirty work themselves, Ingrid. You know that. They send the heavies in.'

He pulls the curtain back over and sits down on the sofa. I hand him his cup of tea and sit opposite him.

'I'm surprised that you didn't come up. From what I'm told, you're never far from a breaking story. A real Lois Lane,' he says, blowing on the steaming tea and taking a sip.

'I was working elsewhere,' I say. 'And, you know, even journalists get the night off every now and again.'

'Elsewhere? That's right. You were meeting your very own Superman,' he smiles.

It's a sad smile and then he breaks into song – a bastardised version of 'My Perfect Cousin' by The Undertones, replacing 'cousin' with 'brother'.

'I hope he treated you well,' he says, and I can't help but feel this is the real reason for Declan's visit. To check up on what happened with Niall. Perhaps even to check if Niall is here with me.

'It was a business meeting, for all intents and purposes. But he was very polite, yes.'

'I suppose he had a lot to say about me?' he asks.

'No more than you said about him, but with respect, it's not really about either of you. It's about Kelly and what happened to her.'

'With respect,' Declan said, his face serious, 'what happened to Kelly happened to all of us. We were all touched by it, Ingrid. Even you. Every single one of us changed that day and don't tell me you don't know that to be true as much as I do.'

I don't want to get dragged down this rabbit hole again.

'Look, Declan. It's been a bastard of a day, so if there is anything you want to tell me – anything new – then just get to the point and tell me. I'm tired and I'm not in the mood for riddles or trying to make anyone else feel better about things.'

He blinks. Taken aback by the harshness of my tone. To be honest, I'm a bit surprised by it too, but it's clear that Declan Heaney has made up some stuff and nonsense about what happened in Creggan just to come here and find out how my chat with his brother went.

'Sorry for giving a shite,' Declan says. 'I just wanted to check you were okay after you met with him. You don't know him like I do.'

'I don't know either of you, Declan,' I say. 'Not any more. Just because we played together twenty-five years ago, it doesn't mean we have any knowledge of each other now. Niall didn't tell me anything to alarm me. He didn't behave like a madman. The only person behaving strangely is you, coming to my flat again for a second night in a row. We aren't friends, Declan. We're barely even acquaintances.'

He doesn't speak for a moment. Then he stands up and walks to the kitchen, pours his tea down the sink and says he must be going. I don't do anything to stop him. I just want him out of my flat.

I jump as the door slams shut and he leaves, but I refuse to feel bad for how I spoke to him. I just lock the door, pull the chain across and put the chair back in front of it before going to bed.

I can deal with everything else – the car, the Dohertys, how uncomfortable I feel – tomorrow.

Chapter Thirty-One

Declan

Saturday, 26 October 2019

Declan Heaney wakes under a black cloud. For the first few moments of consciousness, he can't quite figure out why. He often wakes up like this — angry at the world for every reason and no reason at the same time. Being angry at himself for waking up to another day is nothing new. But today, today there is something more.

He senses it as he stretches, smells the stench of his own morning breath on his pillow. He senses it as he scratches himself, wondering when it was he stopped waking up with an erection. Is it because of ageing? Or something else?

He thinks about the last time he had sex. It has been at least two years, probably three or four if he's honest, and it wasn't anything to write home about. A drunken fuck on the sofa at a house party with a woman he didn't know and never saw again. Not that he was sure he would recognise her even if she walked past him on the street.

He is never going to be anyone's romantic lead, he thinks. And his mind flits to Ingrid and her apartment by the river. The pale pinks of the cushions on her sofa. The soft lighting of the lamps she has dotted around her room.

There are no bare bulbs hanging pitifully from the ceiling in her world, he thinks. He thinks of how her home smells. A mix of floral scent, of her apple-scented shampoo. Clean, comfortable, warm. He thinks of how her dressing gown felt on his skin while she dried his clothes for him. The thought that it had also touched her skin – maybe her naked skin – stirs his limp dick into action. He feels it start to harden and he wonders whether or not to have a wank. It might lift his dark mood, to imagine the things he could do with Ingrid. The things he could do to Ingrid.

She'd annoyed him last night. She'd been cold. Angry. He knew he probably shouldn't have called at her home again. It was stupid, but the thought that she had spent some time with Niall had set him on edge. He had to check she was okay. Actually, he had to check that Niall was not in her flat. Or in her bed. That would've been too much for him. If Niall got her, too.

Had he not warned her about him? And she went anyway – met him in spite of what he'd said. And then he'd heard about that incident at the Doherty house and that seemed like the perfect excuse for him just to call in. He was only watching out for her.

She was his. She had been so kind to him when he'd bumped into her last week. Chatting to him. Taking him for a cup of tea. Treating him like he was someone important. Someone of use to her.

And she had been kind to him back then, too. When they were children. He remembered that, even if she didn't any more. He remembered how, as they had all walked to the chapel for

Kelly's funeral, lines of children walking in pairs, Ingrid had slipped her hand into his and given it a little squeeze.

'Just be brave,' she had said to him.

He thought then, looking at her, that he could be. He could be brave. He could stop being scared for just a few minutes.

Ingrid Devlin with her blonde hair and her pale skin. Her slender fingers and her gentle curves. She oozed class now. A professional lady. A successful journalist and writer. He'd even seen her interviewed on *The Late Late Show* about her books.

He couldn't stay away even if he tried. He was drawn to her. If he could just explain to her everything he knew about that night then maybe she wouldn't be cross. She wouldn't look at him with the disdain she had in her eyes last night, as if he was an annoyance to her. She might look at him differently. She might give him a chance. Let him do the things to her that he wanted to do. There were so many things he wanted to do. He'd take his time, enjoy every inch of her body. These are things he thinks about as his hand moves faster and faster until he feels his body spasm with the force of his climax, her name on his lips.

Chapter Thirty-Two

Ingrid

The sheaves of paper on my table are mocking me. My laptop remains closed. Normally I'd get up, make myself a cup of coffee then sit down and get straight to work.

This morning, I've made the coffee, but I'm curled on the sofa cradling the mug in my hand and I don't know where to start. It has all become so complicated and I don't know who I can trust any more.

This is darker than I ever thought it could be. Darker certainly than anything I have tackled before. I had tossed and turned all night. Thinking about the Dohertys and their new nightmare. And about Declan and the dejected look on his face as he left. I'd been unnecessarily cruel to him.

And as for Jamesy? I'd try to call him later. Maybe arrange to meet him again. I'd make sure no one could possibly have any clue about our meeting. I'd have to be careful about it. I doubt whoever was behind the attacks on my flat or my car would give me any more chances before I, too, might feel the kind of retribution Liam Doherty had.

Taking a sip of coffee, I realise it has long since gone cold.

The bitter taste makes me wince and I get up to make a fresh cup, which I realise I will probably just stare at again until it, too, goes cold.

I've just flicked the kettle on to boil, when my phone starts to ring. It's Ryan.

'Ingrid,' he says when I answer. 'How are you this morning?'

'I'm okay,' I lie, because I'm still mortified for crying down the phone last night.

'That's great,' he says. 'There's a press conference at Strand Road Police Station at noon about the incident last night. I've arranged for Tommy to cover it. I just wanted to make sure you knew.'

I take a deep breath. 'There's no need for Tommy to go. I'll go myself.'

He pauses. I hear an intake of breath.

'Ingrid, are you sure? Things are getting heavy.'

'I'm sure,' I say. 'And I've only half an hour to get ready if I'm to be there on time, so if you don't mind . . .'

'Okay. If you're sure. Just get what they say. File the copy. Leave it at that. You don't have to make this bigger than it needs to be. It's not worth it. We need you safe. *I* need you safe,' he says.

There's a hint of affection in his voice. I'm shocked by it. This time it's not about health and safety or insurance. It's about his need to have me safe. It's possible that he genuinely does care about me. While that might feel too uncomfortable a shift in our dynamic, right now I'll take it. I need to feel like I matter to someone in the middle of this madness.

'I'll get the copy up on the website as soon as I can,' I say to him. 'And I'm okay, Ryan. I'm not taking any chances.'

The truth is, of course, that I don't know if I'll be taking any chances.

I'm ready to go in just twenty minutes, which gives me enough time to walk to the police station, given that my car is still in Foyleside car park.

It's only when I'm standing at my front door, opening the locks and getting ready to go out, that I realise my heart is thudding and I'm holding my breath. What has always been so familiar to me now feels scary. I don't know what I will find around the next corner. I don't know who to trust. I don't want to go out, but I have to.

I force myself to exhale, trying to calm the shuddering of my breath. I remind myself it's daylight. I will be walking along a busy walkway. I will be safe. I am heading in the direction of the police station. It will be fine.

Putting one foot in front of the other, I fight back the fear. I'm just doing my job. I'm safe, I tell myself. I'm safe.

Maybe if I say it enough times, I'll start to believe it.

I'm not the only reporter at the police station. I didn't expect to be. There are representatives here from other newspapers, from the radio and from the TV. They are huddled together when I arrive, no doubt talking through what each of them has heard so far. I don't think it's a figment of my imagination that they appear to stop talking as soon as I arrive. They look flustered.

'Ingrid,' Aidan Devine from the BBC says. 'Nice to see you. We didn't know if you would make it or not. This is mad, isn't it?'

'Why didn't you think I would be here?' I ask, bristling at the question.

I can see some of the other reporters look down to their feet, desperate not to catch my eye.

'Well,' Aidan says, 'I heard you were in a bit of trouble your-self last night. Your car? And that incident at your apartment block? Do you think it might be linked to all this?'

I shrug. 'I suppose the police will tell us that,' I say coldly. 'But if you're asking in some sort of roundabout way if I'm responsible for what has happened to Liam Doherty, then no. I'm not. I just told their story. That's all. Any of you would have given your eye teeth for that story, too.'

'You've been talking to Jamesy Harte, from what I hear,' Nuala McLaughlin from one of our rival papers says as she pushes a stick of chewing gum into her mouth.

For as long as I've known Nuala, she has been trying to quit smoking, and hiding the telltale smell of cigarette smoke on her breath with Wrigley's Spearmint.

'That has nothing to do with anything,' I say.

'I think Liam Doherty might say differently,' Nuala says.

She says it in a manner to sound like jokey banter, but I know there's a sting in her tail.

'The Doherty family have no problem with me,' I say, and am extremely grateful to see the doors open to the police station and the police press officer, Sue Clarke, walk out ahead of DI Bradley and DS King.

Their expressions are set, serious and sombre. Sue Clarke thanks us all for coming out, especially on such a cold day. We nod and say it's not a problem, even if it is. She hands out paper copies of the statement and if I'm not mistaken, she gives me a sympathetic look. I imagine she knows exactly how I'm caught up in all this mess. I'm sure I'm the talk of the station by now.

Doing my best to show no reaction whatsoever, I take it from her and cast my eye over it. It doesn't say anything that isn't already out in the public domain, and part of me wishes I'd stayed at home and asked Sue simply to email the statement over.

Sure, I wouldn't have been here for any questions, but it's not like I don't have a degree of an inside track on all of this.

I set my phone up to record then join Aidan and Nuala and all the others in a huddle in front of the police. DI Bradley, of course, will do the talking. He stands there, officious-looking in a black overcoat, his salt-and-pepper hair perfectly coiffed.

'If we could have your attention, please,' Sue says, even though we are all already clearly focused on the people in front of us.

'Thank you all for coming,' DI Bradley says. 'At around 20.00 hours last night, police from Strand Road received a report of a serious assault in the Creggan Estate. A man in his sixties had been set upon by three unknown males at his home in Malin Gardens. There, he was subjected to a brutal and terrifying ordeal in which he was savagely beaten before his attackers poured a kettleful of boiling water over him.

'The attack occurred in front of his wife, who the men restrained. The man was taken immediately to Altnagelvin Hospital, where he is currently receiving treatment for his injuries.'

He pauses, for dramatic effect, I imagine.

'The men are described as being in their thirties, and of average height and build. They were wearing dark knitted balaclavas, dark-coloured jackets and jeans. Two of the men had local accents. The other is said to have had a Belfast accent. They left soon after the attack, walking in the direction of Broadway.

'Police are appealing for anyone with information about this attack or for anyone who may have seen anyone acting suspiciously in the area to get in touch. We would say again that the nature of this attack was particularly depraved, and the police will do everything in their power to find those responsible and bring them to justice.'

DI Bradley nods to Sue, signalling that he is finished. He has barely taken a breath before Aidan asks his first question.

'Are the police willing to confirm that the victim of this

attack was Liam Doherty, the father of murdered schoolgirl, Kelly Doherty?'

'At this stage, the victim of the assault has asked not to be identified,' DI Bradley says.

'But the dogs on the street know who it is,' Aidan says. 'There are videos on social media from outside the Doherty house.'

'As I have said, the victim of the assault has requested that he is not identified at this stage,' DI Bradley repeats.

There is a collective sigh of frustration.

'Has Jamesy Harte been spoken to by the police regarding this matter?' Nuala asks.

'At this stage there is nothing to indicate that Jamesy Harte is in any way connected to the events last night,' DI Bradley says. 'And we'd really appreciate it if the media didn't facilitate the spreading of rumours to that effect. I'm going off the record here, folks. This is a very sensitive case, not only in terms of what actually happened last night, but also because of the issues surrounding the Doherty family. No doubt, you'll be aware of Mr Harte's announcement of his intention to try and clear his name, and the increased media attention on the story as a result of the anniversary of Kelly's death.'

I feel myself colour. He's not blaming me, exactly. But he might as well be all the same.

'Our priority at the moment is to find the men responsible and bring them before the courts,' he said. 'Now, ladies and gentlemen, I appreciate your time here today and your co-operation on this matter,' DI Bradley says, cutting off Nuala before she can ask another question.

'That's all we have for today,' Sue says in a voice that makes it clear that the proceedings are over.

DI Bradley turns and walks back towards the police station. DS King stays where she is, though, and as I slip my phone back into my bag, she approaches me.

'Ingrid, do you mind if we have a word? Why don't you follow me in?'

I glance towards my colleagues – God knows the last thing I want is for them to see me being led into the station, in any capacity.

'Give it five minutes and come back in. I understand this is sensitive,' she says, following my gaze. 'But we really do need to talk to you. There's been a development.'

'About my car? Did the CCTV footage show anything?'

She shakes her head. 'No, well. I don't know. I think the area was too poorly lit to catch anything of note. But that's not what we need to talk to you about. It's about Jamesy Harte.'

Chapter Thirty-Three

Ingrid

DS King's face is serious but when she speaks, she thanks me for waiting behind and leads me down a warren of corridors to an office where DI Bradley is sitting behind a desk.

'Ingrid,' he says. 'Sit down.'

'I wasn't expecting an invite into your inner sanctum,' I say, trying to keep my voice light. I don't want him to know I'm rattled.

'Well, it seems today is your lucky day,' he tells me as I take my seat opposite him. 'Look, Ingrid, I'll cut to the chase here. First thing this morning, the police attended the address of Jamesy Harte to speak to him in light of the attack last night.'

'You think Jamesy Harte has something to do with it?' I ask.

DI Bradley pauses. 'Ingrid, at the moment, we are looking at all possible leads and talking to as many people as possible. Including Jamesy Harte, yes.'

I nod.

'The thing is, Ingrid, when we arrived at his registered address, he wasn't there.'

My mind whirs. He could just be out. At the shop. Out for a coffee. Something like that. It doesn't mean anything, I tell myself, but then again, I'm pretty sure the police wouldn't have me in the station talking to them about it if they thought he was out on a normal errand.

'And?' I say, my voice smaller, less confident, than I have heard it in a long time.

'And, well, the police have been unable to locate him all morning. What we do know is that his neighbours heard a door slam and a car leave the street, at speed, in the early hours of the morning. There were signs that Jamesy Harte's bedsit was left in a hurry. There was a full cup of tea on the counter, the TV was left on. And Jamesy's wallet and phone were on his bedside table.'

Anxiety pulls at me, dragging all of my muscles into tight spasms.

'And do you have any idea where he went? Who with?' I ask, even though I know that if they did, they wouldn't have me here.

DI Bradley shakes his head. 'What we do know is that you were the last person Harte spoke to on his phone and that you have been in contact with him over the last few weeks.'

'That's right. I've interviewed him about Kelly's murder and his claim he is innocent,' I say. 'That's not a secret. I've told DS King this before. After the incident at my house, and the car.'

'And he called you last night. What did he want to speak to you about?'

'He'd heard something had happened to Liam Doherty and wanted to know if I knew any details.'

'How had he heard about Mr Doherty?' DI Bradley asks, to the room as much as to me.

'It was all over social media in a matter of minutes,' I say. 'He probably saw it there. Or he had someone contact him. I can't remember if he told me how he heard, but he didn't seem to know a lot about it.'

'And how did he seem on the phone last night? His manner?'

I shrug. 'He was quite agitated, upset even, when I told him I didn't have any more information than he already had.'

'So, you didn't tell him about what you had learned at the hospital?' DS King asks.

I blush. I knew she would bring that up. Of course she would.

I shake my head. 'No. I didn't. Look, I'll be honest. You might find this hard to believe of me, but I've no desire to make things worse for the Dohertys. Bernie asked me not to tell anyone what she told me and I won't. She seems scared, and I understand that.'

I fidget in my seat, pull the arms of my jumper down to my wrists and then I take a deep breath. 'He did say that he believed, and always believed, that Liam Doherty might be aware of some or all of what really happened that night. That he has kept quiet while Jamesy rotted in prison. He said maybe karma had caught up with him, or words to that effect.'

'Has Jamesy given you any reason to believe he still has any contacts in Derry? Anyone here he would have any sway over?'

I shake my head. 'No. Absolutely not. I'd be certain of that. It's been twenty-five years since he lived here. He's been out of jail eight years and hasn't set foot back in Derry. He's too scared to and I believe that fear is genuine. I don't think he has the wit about him to lie to that level.'

DI Bradley nods. 'You think he's genuine? When you spoke to him, you had a feeling he was telling you the truth?'

'I can't be certain, but yes. I do feel he was being honest, and with everything that has happened in the last week, to me and now to Liam, I'm pretty sure he's right. Something else is going on behind the scenes here.'

I watch as DI Bradley glances momentarily towards DS King. If they have any idea of the truth of the matter, they sure aren't letting me in on it.

'How did the call with him end? he asks.

'He hung up on me. He was upset. Maybe I should've called him back, but I was exhausted.'

My face roars red with shame as I speak. DI Bradley makes a note of it and looks back at me. 'Would you allow us access to any notes you have from your conversations with him?'

I stiffen. That goes against every journalistic principle I hold. But if Harte is a danger to others, or himself, or me, then maybe I should. *No.* No, a journalist must protect their sources and their source material, no matter how unsavoury that source might be.

'Where do you think he is?' I ask.

'We're not sure, but we can't rule out the possibility that he is either in Derry or on his way to Derry. Nor can we rule out the possibility that something has happened to him – that he may have been targeted too, in the same way Mr Doherty has, or that he is a danger to himself.' DI Bradley's expression is grim.

I rub my temples. This is all such a mess.

'I really don't think I can give you access to my interview,' I say. 'But I can tell you that there is nothing in what he said to me during that official interview that would indicate he was a danger to himself or others. As for last night, he was agitated, yes. He was upset about the response to the article on social media. Worried it might draw attention to his location. But I really don't think he would do anything to harm himself.'

Oh, God, but I really hope he didn't do anything to harm himself.

'Ingrid, I understand you must be very unsettled by this,' DS King says, her tone conciliatory.

I can't hold in a brittle laugh. 'That's a bit of an under-statement,' I say. The tissue I have been twisting around in my fingers is starting to dissolve. To my shame, I feel tears prick at my eyes.

'You do know you can contact the police at any time if you feel under threat,' DI Bradley says.

I nod. I can't speak because I'm afraid that if I do, I simply won't be able to stop the tears from falling.

'If I can say something to you, though. No story in the world is worth this.'

Of course he would say that, I think, though his concern does look genuine. Then again, I seem to have lost the ability to read people properly just now.

I steady myself. Switch back into professional mode.

'What will you be doing to find Jamesy?' I ask.

'We have officers looking for him at the moment. Checking bus routes and the train station. Needless to say, if he makes contact with you again, we'd like you to let us know immediately.'

I nod. 'And Mr Doherty? How is he?' I ask.

'Medically, he's ill but stable. Emotionally, he's traumatised, as his whole family are.'

I nod.

'Ingrid, we really would ask that you stay away from the Doherty family at this time. They have asked me to pass that message on to you – and to all the media, just so you don't think it's personal,' DS King says. 'They don't want any more attention brought to last night's events.

'At this stage, they have no plans to make any further statement about what has happened and, look, you were there at the hospital. You saw how distressed they were. You heard how awful this is. I know that might make for big headlines, but it's not serving anyone to splash their trauma all over the papers.'

'It is my job to report on the news and this is news,' I say, because that is the truth.

'I understand that. But there are ways to go about this without making things more difficult for the Dohertys. And, Ingrid, you have to consider if you could be making things more difficult for yourself,' DS King says. 'There will be a family liaison officer with Bernie Doherty at all times. We will know if you do try to make contact. You can be sure if we are watching then others are watching, too.'

'You've been targeted three times in the space of the last week,' DI Bradley interjects as if I'm not only too aware that I have already attracted the wrong kind of attention. 'At the moment, we have nothing to identify who is responsible and can only assume the messages left are intended to warn you off any further reporting on this case. Given the varied locations of the incidents, we have reason enough to believe that someone may already be following your movements.'

The lead weight in the pit of my stomach feels heavier. A wave of nausea washes over me.

'We will of course try to find whoever is responsible for this, Ingrid, but you do have to consider how much you want to bait these people,' he adds.

I'm not used to letting intimidatory tactics get the better of me, but this time they just might.

Chapter Thirty-Four

Ingrid

My mechanic has called and told me my car is ready and waiting for me in Foyleside car park with four new tyres. He doesn't ask about what happened; he just tells me I can settle the bill with him on Monday.

'There'll be an extra charge,' he says, 'for a Saturday call-out.'

I don't argue, I just agree that I'll sort it as soon as possible. All I really want to do now is to collect my car and get home, where I can lock the door and stay safe and warm. But there's also a comfort in being among the crowds of Saturday shoppers. The Foyleside Shopping Centre is thronged with families out beginning their Halloween celebrations and shopping for decorations and costumes.

Halloween is not done in any half measure in Derry. It's a week-long festival of family-friendly workshops, events that bring the city's historic walls to life with fire breathers and acrobats, light shows and storytellers. Thousands of tourists flock to the city for the big day itself, which always culminates in a huge firework display over the River Foyle.

It's as far removed from what it was like twenty-five years ago as it is ever likely to get. Back then it was very much a fledgling festival, a night of music in town. Children still focused on their own streets and their own celebrations.

But now, as I walk through Foyleside, I'm surrounded by tired mothers, children dressed as witches and warlocks, princesses and superheroes. The build-up to the Halloween carnival is at fever pitch. There are a number of people offering face-painting and the queue would try the patience of a saint. Actors in costume move through the crowds, engaging with shoppers. I keep my head down.

The further I walk through the centre, the more uncomfortable I start to feel. The adults in costumes are intimidating, witches with long, pointy fingers, a zombie with white contact lenses in. Someone is wearing a *Scream* mask, dressed as the killer from the Nineties movie. Underneath their costume they could be anyone. No one would know.

'This way, my dear!' a woman dressed as an old crone implores, her voice croaky.

I turn my head, coming face to face with someone dressed as The Child Catcher from *Chitty Chitty Bang Bang*. He waves an oversized lollipop in my direction. Sneers. It's all part of an act, but I don't like it.

'Leave me alone,' I hiss, and he steps back as if I've offended him, but I don't care. I walk on.

The noise is too much, it's too warm. Too busy. I see people, street theatre actors, jump out to try to scare other shoppers. The air rings with screams and nervous laughter. It brings me back to that night, when I fell and I heard the screams on the air. 'Stop!' 'Wait for me!' 'No!' My memory is hazy now.

Those voices, back then, were they male or female? Was Kelly among them? Was she calling for help? Imagine screaming for help and everyone thinking it was part of a game. Imagine the horror of realising no one was coming to help you.

Someone brushes against me and I flinch. I look up and

around at the sea of faces and realise any one of them could be the person responsible for the attacks on my car and my home. Among those happy families and young people wandering around with all the swagger of those in their youth might be the person who held Liam Doherty down, or the person who made the call to pour the boiling water over him. Did it even bother them, what they did, what they saw?

God, Jamesy Harte could be in that crowd. Would anyone really recognise him any more? I hadn't. As implausible as I feel it to be in my gut, could he really be behind what happened to Liam Doherty? What did he mean by what he'd told me last night?

I feel as if the air is being squeezed out of my lungs. Each breath is starting to become harder than the last. I keep to the edges of the shopping centre, walk alongside the shop windows. I reach my hand out to steady myself on the cool glass, my palms sweaty. I can feel a cold sweat break out across my forehead. I pull off my coat and scarf, but I still feel much too warm.

I force one foot in front of the other and walk on until I'm passing Costa Coffee on the first floor, when I feel something, or someone, grip my arm. A firm, masculine grasp – the shock of it almost stops my heart. I pull and shrug, try to break free.

'Let go!' I say, but instead of a shout, a strangled yelp escapes my throat.

'Ingrid! Ingrid, it's me. Niall. I just wanted to say hello. See if you heard anything more about Liam after last night.'

I look up and see that the hand does indeed belong to Niall Heaney, whose expression is one of concern. I blink while I try to make sense of what is going on in my head and feel a surge of adrenaline run through my veins.

I see his lips move, but I can't hear what he says over the din of my own heart thudding in my chest, my blood whooshing through my body. I try to focus on him, on his words. On his touch, softer now. On the smell of him, clean and fresh.

'Jesus! Are you okay?'

I just about make out what he is saying, and I nod then shake my head, and without being able to stop myself, I burst into tears.

Niall leads me, very gently, by the hand to the coffee shop in Marks & Spencer, which provides just a little more privacy than Costa on the mall. He sits me down before going to order two large teas. He brings extra sugar, in case I need it 'to steady my nerves', and two scones with jam and cream.

'Eat something,' he says, 'in case your blood sugars are a little low. This might help make you feel a bit better.'

I realise I've not eaten at all today so far and although my throat feels tight and my stomach unsettled, I am actually hungry.

I sip the tea, cut one of the scones in half, and slather it in cream and jam. I take the smallest of bites, trying to assess whether or not I'm safe to eat the full thing or if my stomach will reject it.

Niall doesn't ask me what's wrong. Not at this stage, anyway. He talks about the weather and how underrated a nice cup of tea is. He allows plenty of prolonged silences, for which I'm grateful, because I need to quiet what is going on in my head.

When I feel myself calm down, when I feel able to breathe again without my whole body shaking, he looks at me with concern on his face.

'Do you want to talk about it?' he asks.

Part of me is mortified to have lost my cool again so completely – it seems to be becoming a habit – but a bigger part of me is just so grateful that someone is asking me how I am with genuine concern.

'I'm not sure,' I tell him. 'I think . . . well, I know, it was a panic attack.'

'What brought it on?' he asks.

I shrug my shoulders. 'A combination of things, I think. The noise. The crowds. What happened to Liam Doherty.'

He nods.

'And my car was targeted last night,' I tell him. 'Here. In the car park. After I saw you. My tyres slashed.'

'Jesus,' he says, his eyes widening. 'But surely it's not related to what happened to Liam, is it? I mean, it couldn't be.'

Do I tell him everything? Do I tell him that yes, it could well be related and, actually, it most likely is related? Do I tell him this is the third time I've had threatening messages left for me in the space of a week?

'We believe, the police and I, that is, well, we believe there could well be some connection. This isn't the first time I've been targeted,' I say, my voice small. I've lost my bravado, I realise. My ability to shrug it off as a peril of the job. 'My car was vandalised outside work last week and at the weekend just gone, someone broke into my flat.'

His hand reaches out and touches mine, and I am so very grateful for the warmth of some human contact that I don't pull away.

'Ingrid, this is serious stuff. Are the police doing anything? Are they keeping you safe?'

'I think they've bigger fish to fry at the moment,' I say, 'but yes. Extra patrols, blah-blah-blah. It's not like me to lose my cool, you know,' I tell him. 'It's just been stressful. I thought this was just an anniversary story. Then I thought I'd speak to Jamesy Harte and find out about his quest to have his name cleared. Maybe, I'd get a book out of it. I never once expected that any of this would kick off. Not what has happened to Mr Doherty. Not the attacks on my car and home. Not press conferences and missing people . . .'

'Missing people?' he butts in, and before I've even thought

211

about it, I blurt out that Jamesy Harte has gone missing. 'All of his belongings are still in his flat, from what the police could see,' I say.

'He wouldn't come here,' Niall says, but he looks worried.

I suppose even though he is now a grown man, he believes he saw with his own eyes just exactly what Jamesy Harte is supposed to have been capable of.

'He'd be lynched as soon as he hit the city limits.' Niall swallows hard and puts his teacup back on the table.

'I don't think he has any desire to come back, but that doesn't explain why Liam Doherty has been targeted. That's the bit I can't get my head around. Maybe I have Jamesy all wrong. I know you don't agree with me, Niall, but from talking to him, I couldn't help but believe there was some truth in what he was saying. I just never took him to be the vengeful type.'

'Or the murderous type,' Niall says, 'but believe me . . .' His voice trails off.

An awkwardness has opened up between us, a divergence of opinions that can't easily be brushed over.

'Anyway, look, I've taken up enough of your time,' I say. I'm embarrassed now. Now that the fear has left. I just want to get to my car and go home. 'I really appreciate you being there for me just now. Let me cover the cost of the tea and scones.'

He pulls a face, his expression laden with 'don't even think about it'.

'Okay, then,' I concede. 'Next time.' But of course, I'm not sure there will be a next time.

I stand up and gather my coat and scarf.

'Let me walk you to your car at least,' Niall says unexpectedly.

I shake my head. 'You're very kind, but I'm grand, honest.'

He shrugs off my reply.

'Ingrid. I'd feel a lot better if you just let me make sure that you get there safely.'

I'm about to object again, when his mobile phone rings.

He glances at the screen and scowls. 'Declan,' he mouths in my direction before answering the call. 'Declan, what I can do for you?'

I, of course, can't hear the other side of the conversation, but it isn't hard to pick up the general gist of it.

'I'm in town just now. Yes. With Ingrid, as it happens. We were just having a cup of tea together.'

Niall rolls his eyes in my direction. He's clearly not enjoying getting the third degree from his brother.

'Yes, she's fine.'

Declan says something and I see the expression on Niall's face change. He looks at me with an intensity that wasn't there before. It passes as quickly as it arrives, replaced by a quizzical look instead.

'Okay, I'll tell her. Yes. And will you tell Mum not to put any dinner on for me. I've plans.'

He ends the call, slips his phone into his pocket.

'Declan says to ask if you're okay. You seemed upset when he was at your place last night.'

Chapter Thirty-Five

Ingrid

I don't know why I feel unnerved by Declan having told Niall he called at my house, or by the expression on Niall's face when he speaks to me about it. But I do.

'He called round when he heard the news, wanted to check I was okay,' I say.

'How did he know where you live? Has he been there before?'

Niall's tone is light, inquisitive. If I didn't know that there is little love lost between the two brothers, I would probably think nothing of it, but knowing what I do it feels wrong.

'He's been over once before,' I say, not revealing it was the night before, or what state his brother was in when he arrived.

I wonder if I should tell him that Declan made me feel uneasy last night. That I didn't like how he spoke, or how he looked at me.

'Seems it's not that hard to track me down if you want to find me,' I say.

I think of how Niall had tracked me down himself, almost effortlessly. A quick search on Facebook and we were in touch.

Niall sighs. 'Ingrid, sit down a wee minute again.'

I look to the couple of elderly shoppers who had been eyeing up our table and mouth my apology as I take my seat again. Niall pinches the bridge of his nose with his fingers and takes a deep breath.

'I know I said things last night about how Declan has spent his life, or how he has let his life be defined by what happened, but beneath that I do love him. That said, I can't keep quiet. Especially not now.'

I search his face for any sign of what is to come. I just see a man, lost in thought, worry lines running across his forehead.

'He's not right,' Niall says. 'Not mentally well. My parents have tried to keep it all quiet as much as possible. God knows they've cleaned up enough of his messes to last them a lifetime.'

I'm conflicted about where this might be going. I feel sorry for Declan. I have the feeling he has always been and always will be the underdog, especially when it comes to his relationship with his brother. But the last two nights have also made me uneasy enough to need to know what Niall is going to say next.

Niall leans across the table, gestures at me to come closer. He keeps his voice low.

'He has a record, you know. ABH, breaking and entering – that kind of thing. I'm sure someone at *The Chronicle* might have covered it at some stage. Someone at the *Derry Journal* definitely will have. He was a frequent flyer at the magistrates' court in his time. The reports might not have all the details, but I can tell you, Ingrid – some of the charges relate to harassment of women. At least one of the breaking and entering charges relates to the house of one of his ex-girlfriends. If I were you, I'd be very careful about what I let him know about your routine, your home. Anything.'

I pull back, sit up in my chair. Think of Declan and his smile, and his helplessness. I think about what he has actually done in my presence. It might not have been suitable for him to call at my flat, but he hasn't tried anything on. I've felt uncomfortable, yes, but not threatened.

'Might just be worth asking the police to look into his whereabouts when your car was attacked – and your flat, for that matter.'

I shake my head. No, that's just ridiculous.

'Ingrid.' Niall's voice is low and soft. 'I'm not trying to scare you,' he says, 'I promise.'

'I want to go home,' I stutter, and I don't wait for any further revelations – I just stand up and push my way out of the café, towards the car park.

I'm vaguely aware that he is following me. He's calling my name. Can I take him at face value, or is everyone involved in this entire sorry mess as deceitful as each other?

'Ingrid, please. I didn't mean to scare you,' he shouts as I hurry to my car.

A passing security guard must have heard, because I hear him approach me.

'Are you okay, miss? Is this gentleman bothering you?'

I don't know whether to nod or shake my head. I just stand there like a stupid rabbit caught in the headlights.

'Ingrid, please. I just wanted you to know. I want you to be careful.'

Realising he's not going to be getting an answer from me, the security guard walks behind me. I turn round just in time to see him raise his hand in a 'Stop!' gesture and ask Niall to step back.

'I don't think the lady wants to talk to you,' the security man says in his broad Derry accent, his voice husky as if he has smoked all his life, including his childhood.

'Look, she's upset. Someone has been bothering her and I

just want to make sure she gets home okay. Gets to her car okay. It was vandalised here last night.'

The security guard cops on to who I must be and which car is mine.

'Ms Devlin,' he says. 'Do you want me to walk you to your car? I can ask this gentleman to leave if you want.'

Niall is looking at me. His facial expression pleading for me to believe him.

'Or I can call the police for you?' the security man adds.

I shake my head. 'No. No, I'm fine. Thank you. I'm fine. Niall, I'm fine, too.'

The security guard nods and leaves, and Niall takes a step closer to me.

'I really didn't mean to scare you,' he says. 'But you had to know. You can double-check if you don't believe me.'

I simply nod. 'I'd better go.'

'Ingrid,' Niall says, 'if it's any consolation at all, I think you're incredibly brave. It takes a lot of guts to put yourself on the line like this. I'm not sure I'd have the balls to keep digging, but I suppose that's why I'm a primary school teacher and you're the journalist with the book deal.'

'Thanks,' I say. 'For the tea, and the info.'

'Take care, Ingrid,' he says. 'If you need anything else, get in touch.'

'I will,' I say as I finally leave him and head to my car.

I lock the doors as soon as I'm safely inside and when my hands have stopped shaking, I turn the key in the ignition to start the engine.

The radio bursts into life, much too loud for my current state, and I immediately turn the volume down. It's 2 p.m. and I hear the presenter announce the news is coming next. No doubt they'll lead with the Doherty attack. It wouldn't hurt for me to hear what their top line is.

But instead of launching into the details of last night's assault, the newsreader leads with news that the body of a man has been discovered on rail tracks between Portstewart and Coleraine.

Chapter Thirty-Six

Declan

Declan's hand is throbbing, his knuckles bloodied and bruised. The fist-shaped dent in his wall doesn't look too great, either.

He is angry at himself for losing his cool and lashing out, even if, this time, it was only the wall in his bedroom that bore the brunt of his physical aggression.

Ingrid Devlin is with Niall. In town. Having a coffee.

Of course she is.

He thinks again of how cold she was with him last night. How she looked as if she couldn't wait for him to leave. Even though she had been shaken by what happened, she hadn't reached out to him for comfort like he had hoped she would.

It was the first time he had seen something cold – disgust maybe – in her eyes when she looked at him. He'd been so stupid to think she could see him as anything more than the wastrel he is.

Especially now that she had met with Niall again. For twins, they couldn't be more different. Niall oozes a calmness. An air of confidence only someone who had it easy in life could have. And, even without the money, style and grace his brother carried, Declan knows that Niall will always be better than him. He looks better, almost perfect. And it isn't just the grooming that does it.

There is something just a few degrees off in the symmetry of Declan's face compared to his brother. Something not quite appealing in the smallest difference in the length of their noses, the exact shade of grey in their eyes. Declan is like a factory second version of Niall, a fact that he has never been able to escape.

And now, despite his warnings, Ingrid Devlin appears to have been taken in by his brother's charm, too. What will he have to do to get her to listen to him? How can he prove that Niall is not a good option? He has nothing to offer that could persuade anyone he is the better catch. Women don't see past Niall's charm and finery, his toned body and his shiny shoes.

They can't see the real him.

What else does Declan have to do to prove he can protect her? He'd wanted to offer her a shoulder to cry on last night. That was why he had gone to her flat. Sure, he had lied. He didn't have any leads. He made up all that rubbish about the drug dealers, and she'd known it. She had seen right through him. He'd wanted to own up to her there and then. To laugh it off, maybe. 'Okay, you've got me. I'm lying. I don't know anything new – I just want to check that you're okay.'

Would she have reacted any differently if he had?

Even though he knows it is empty, he opens the door to the freezer compartment in his fridge anyway, hoping there might be something hiding in the back of it that he can use to bring down the swelling in his hand.

There isn't, of course.

His fridge is a virtual wasteland, too. Some milk, butter, half a packet of back bacon and a block of cheese that is going hard around the edges. He'd like to see what *Ready Steady Cook* could do with those ingredients.

That thought raises a smile, but only the briefest of ones. Because his hand still hurts, and he swears it is swelling more and more by the second – and, for all he knows, Ingrid is still with Niall, listening to his twisted version of events and deciding that Declan is a man she should avoid at all costs.

He hates his brother. In that moment, he hates him with every single cell and fibre of his being.

Chapter Thirty-Seven

Ingrid

I know, without having to hear any more, that the body on the train line will be Jamesy Harte.

Most people, of course, have no reason to think it could be Jamesy. Most people don't know that he has been living in Portstewart, or that the police called at his flat this morning to find him missing. Most people don't know that the police were looking to talk to him about what happened in Derry last night, or that when he had gone missing, he had left behind his phone, his wallet and even his keys.

If I can get through to DC Mark Black, I think, I might just be able to have an off-the-record briefing on what they've found. I'll be able to see if my hunch is right. I'm not sure whether I want it to be or not. Jamesy's sad face, his bowed demeanour, comes into my head. His fear at being found. But also what others have told me. That the police believe there's a possibility he is behind the brutal attack on Liam Doherty last night.

I keep a burner phone for occasions such as checking in with illicit police contacts. It's to protect them as much as it is to protect me. A cheap pay as you go that I picked up for thirty pounds in Argos and that only facilitates calls and text messages. It's not registered. It can't be traced (I paid cash, just in case) and there are only a handful of numbers on it. People I know I can turn to for information when none is forthcoming through official channels. I replace it every couple of months, to be extra safe.

As soon as traffic allows, I pull my car over into a lay-by and delve in my glovebox until my hand touches the phone. It needs a quick charge, just enough to allow me to send the message, and it's good to go.

Need your help with train timetable. I'd appreciate a reply asap.

I send it to DC Black's personal mobile. As codes go, it's pretty pathetic. I don't think anyone would kill themselves trying to decipher it, but it gets the point across. I hope. If it is Jamesy, this is a huge story. Bigger than anything I'd originally thought of.

Ryan will wet himself over it, I'm sure he will. He'll forget all about his vow not to bring attention to Jamesy Harte and he'll go big on the story. With my stomach fizzing with nerves, in a heady mixture of fear, adrenaline and excitement I decide to drive straight to Ryan's house.

It's clear when I get there that Jen, and quite possibly the two boys, too, are home. Despite the cold day, there is a bike lying on its side on the grass to the front of the house. Jen's car – a Volvo 4x4 beast of a thing that there is no need for when all you do is drive around city streets – is parked at the top of the driveway, with Ryan's car behind it.

Their house has been decorated for Halloween. Jen is the perfect homemaker. Even though I'm thirty-five I have been known to say I'd like to be just like her when I grow up. Ryan doesn't find the quip particularly amusing.

Pumpkin-shaped fairy lights twinkle from the windows. Yellow fake crime scene tape criss-crosses along the front door.

Small ghost-shaped decorations dance in the breeze and a skeleton is perched on the front step beside a freshly carved pumpkin.

There are still five days until Halloween – the insides of that pumpkin will have well and truly started to rot by then, I think before pressing the doorbell. The usual ring of the doorbell has been replaced by a spooky cackle for the Halloween season. We've all become so Americanised. A far cry from our home-made costumes and plastic bags filled with nuts and apples.

A voice in my head tells me ours were simpler times, but then, of course, I remember Kelly. I remember that night. My mother shaking me from my sleep, asking if I knew where Kelly was. Had I seen her?

I'd shaken my head. Too tired to realise the significance of what I was being asked.

'Think, Ingrid. Think!' my mother had implored, and that's when I'd registered the worry and the fear in her voice.

I'd been asleep and I hadn't gone to bed 'til gone ten o'clock. That meant it was late, and certainly much too late for Kelly Doherty not to be home or for no one to know where she was. I heard a male voice call her name in the street. I blinked, trying to wake up.

'I saw her earlier when we were out collecting. She was at the top of the street. But then my feet got soaked in that puddle and I came home to change my socks and put on my wellies,' I told her. 'I didn't see her after that.'

'And who was she with when you saw her?'

I shook my head. One child in a duffel coat with a fifty-pence mask from the newsagents looked much the same as another child in a duffel coat wearing a fifty-pence mask. I wanted to remember, but I couldn't. I could see my mother's face illuminated by the pale glow of the street light outside our house. She looked as scared as she sounded. Grown-ups weren't supposed to get scared. They were supposed to make it better.

'I don't know, Mammy,' I told her, and I was shaking now myself.

What if something bad had happened? Something really bad? We'd all heard stories of children going missing only to turn up dead later. Was that what had happened to Kelly? Had someone taken her?

I heard more voices join in the chorus calling her name in the street. My mother sat on my bed and took my hand in hers, but her eyes were at the window. She flinched every time someone called Kelly's name and was met only with silence as their reply.

I watched as she made the sign of the cross. 'Jesus was lost, and Jesus was found,' she muttered over and over.

All I could think was that Kelly Doherty's face was going to be staring out at us all from the front of the newspapers in the way all those missing children's faces had been. What if someone was hurting her right now?

The sound of footsteps making their way down a hallway, on expensive tiling, pulls me from my memories and the door to Ryan's house opens. Jen greets me with a smile that doesn't quite go all the way to her eyes. She is drying her hands on a tea towel and there is a trace of flour in her hair. She's been baking. Of course. She's the type to bake.

I can't help but notice she looks tired. I'm not used to seeing her looking anything other than perfectly presented. She's not a stupid woman. She always treats me with suspicion, which is understandable in the circumstances. I'm not sure she knows that Ryan and I have had sex, more than once, but I imagine that living with a man like Ryan, you soon come to suspect every woman who is vaguely well presented. Ryan has a reputation that precedes him, and it's not that of a brilliant editor.

'Ingrid, what can we do for you?' Her eyebrows knit together in faux concern. 'Ryan told me there'd been some unpleasantness and that awful business last night with Liam Doherty. Dear me, what is the world coming to?'

'It's terrible,' I concede, mirroring her painted-on concern. 'But I need to see Ryan, if he's in. About some breaking news. One he'll want published on the website as soon as possible.'

'Is that what has him on edge? He's been like a bag of cats all day. I've been doing my best to keep out of his way.'

She laughs but it's hollow and there's something about the way she rubs at her wrist that makes me feel uncomfortable. I try not to stare at it.

I shrug. 'There's a lot happening, that's for sure. And he'll be under pressure to get the Web clicks rising.'

Jen nods. 'Never a day off any more. Not that he was ever one to leave the job in the office anyway. He always has to be nosying at something.'

'He does,' I say, eager to get past her and see Ryan.

She looks at me for a moment as if frozen and then just as she goes to speak, a beep from my phone tells me someone has sent me a message. Could it be DC Black already? I glance towards my bag.

'I'm sorry. That's probably about the story,' I say.

'Of course. Sure. Okay. Well, Ryan is in his office if you want to go on through. I assume you know where it is?'

I'm pretty sure it's a trick question. I'm not supposed to know where his office is. I'm not supposed to be familiar with this house at all.

I shake my head.

'Top of the stairs, third on the left,' she says before calling to Ryan in a sing-song voice that is just a little too shrill to let him know he has a visitor. I slip my phone from my pocket and look at the screen.

There's no attempt at any code back.

Body not in a state for ID. But believe it's your man.

I nod, feeling strangely satisfied that my instincts were right. The phone beeps again as the message updates.

Foul play suspected.

Chapter Thirty-Eight

Ingrid

Ryan is shocked to see me. His confusion, much like Jen's, is written all over his face.

'Ingrid?' he says, looking up from his desk.

I wonder what he's doing. Is he working? Is he penning some magnum opus of his own? He has mentioned his desire to write a book some day. A memoir of his time in journalism. Something of 'historical importance'.

'True crime is popular, of course,' he has said to me in the past. 'But I want the book I write to be more a legacy project. Something that will outlive me.'

I never bite when he says something like that. I know it's born out of jealousy that I'm out there and making a name for myself already.

'Sorry to interrupt your work,' I say. 'I should've phoned or texted, but I have a scoop for you that you won't want to miss.'

'If it's the press conference, every news agency in the North is already running with that and I can't help but notice it's not uploaded onto our site.'

He looks up at me. He needs a shave; stubby grey spikes of hair line the wrinkles on his face. Out of his usual shirt and tie, wearing a sweater and jeans, he looks old. Of course I know that I'm a good twenty years younger than he is, but what once looked mature and inviting to me now just looks tired.

I shake my head. 'There was nothing in that press conference that wasn't already out there. I was busy chasing something juicier.'

He sits back in his chair, crosses his arms and raises one eyebrow. 'Go on,' he says.

'There's been a body discovered on the tracks between Portstewart and Coleraine,' I begin.

'Yes. I've seen the release. I've even put it up on the site. Because that is what a conscientious journalist would do,' he says, his tone derisory. 'I did tell you if you weren't feeling up to working, I'd get Tommy to fill in.'

'Ryan,' I say, perching on the side of his desk. 'Stop it. I am up to the job. I've been doing the job. I happen to know Jamesy Harte went missing last night. From his home. Which, as I told you, is in Portstewart.'

Now he's interested. He pauses, regards me from his chair.

'That doesn't mean . . .' he begins.

I imagine he's afraid to believe he has such a story in his reach.

'No, it doesn't. But I have it from a source that they believe it could well be Harte and, furthermore, foul play is suspected.'

'Fuck!' Ryan exhales through his teeth. 'And your source? Who is it? How rock solid are they?'

'You know better than to ask who my source is. But I can tell you they've never led me down the wrong road before,' I say.

He walks to the window of his office, his hands thrust deep in the pockets of his jeans, and back again. He is clearly thinking about what to do next.

'What's the thinking? Someone close to Doherty took

revenge? Someone in Portstewart realised who he was and what he'd done? This is messy, Ingrid.'

'I don't know what the story is,' I say. 'I've only just heard about his body. But given what happened to Liam Doherty last night . . . and witnesses said they heard Harte leaving his bedsit in the small hours and getting into a car. His phone, wallet, keys – that sort of thing – were all left behind.'

'And we have the last ever interview with him,' Ryan says, his eyes wide with excitement. 'This is some scoop for us.'

I bristle. This is not how this is going to work. 'Us?' I say.

'Well. You do work for *The Chronicle* and you do have an interview with Jamesy Harte in the bag, don't you? You offered it to me before, so surely you will offer it to me again.'

'And surely this time will be my chance to say no. I've already committed to using it in a book.'

'Ingrid,' he says, his head to one side. He reaches out to me. 'Don't be like that. This would be great for *The Chronicle*. It would be great for us . . .'

I take a step back. 'Ryan, I came here to you with the exclusive about his death. I came here to work with you on getting that to a place where we can publish it. I didn't come here to hand over the interview I did in my own time.'

I stand up from where I've been perched on his desk, but he grabs my arm and forces me back down.

'For Christ's sake, Ingrid,' he snarls, and there is anger in his eyes. 'You know how tough this business is at the minute. Head office will be looking at the numbers again soon and I've no need to remind you that print sales are still in decline, as well as advertising revenue. This could give us the boost we need to save more jobs from the axe. Are you really that selfish you'd keep that from us? Are you really that much of a bitch?'

I look him in the eye. This isn't about jobs, I know that. We both know that any boost now will just bring about a stay of execution. The executioner is still sharpening his axe and getting ready for the next round of redundancies. This is about Ryan wanting to lay claim to something that isn't his.

He has stalled this story at every opportunity and now – now, when the villain of the piece is most likely dead – he wants to go to town. I already know what angle he'll take. After all, you can't libel the dead. You certainly can't libel a convicted child killer who never had the chance to clear his name. He'll use whatever he can from my interview to bury whatever remnants of Jamesy Harte's alleged innocence are left.

'Back off,' I snap, my voice low but just as menacing as his.

He does what I ask and steps back from me, his hands clenched. Frustration is coming off him in waves.

'You told me to keep out of this story altogether,' I remind him. 'Just a wee colour piece for the anniversary, you said. You told me no good could come of it.'

'And no good has come of it, has it?' His voice is raised, his jaw set tight. 'What has happened since you started digging, Ingrid? Jamesy's dead. Liam Doherty is in hospital. Bernie is traumatised. Did you know that her daughter-in-law, Christopher's wife, has been admitted, too? Blood pressure dangerously high and she's expecting. Christ, Ingrid, your own car, your own home have been targeted. And you wonder why I didn't want you near it?

'But you had to win, you had to know more than anyone else. You have brought this fucking mess to a head and the very least you could do is make some sort of half-hearted attempt at cleaning it all up. Make amends, do right by me and by your colleagues!'

He is shouting by now, flecks of spittle shooting forth from his mouth, making me feel sick. How did I ever kiss those lips and find them anything less than revolting? He thinks this is all my fault? And he wants me to give him access to my research material? He has another thing coming.

'Ryan,' I say, doing my very best to keep my voice measured and in control. 'You covered the story at the time. You were there. An adult. Let me ask you, do you believe Jamesy Harte killed Kelly Doherty?'

Ryan straightens himself, pulls himself to his full height. He looks directly in at me, doesn't shift his gaze. I feel the weight of his authority bear down on me. He is my boss, after all.

Still he stares, refuses to blink. But then I see it, a split second when he looks away to the door and back again. It's so rapid I could so easily have missed it, but I didn't.

'Of course I think he killed Kelly Doherty,' he says, his voice matching my measured tone now. The fight gone. The abuse all hurled.

I might have believed him had it not been for that quick glance to the side. The almost imperceptible way he wet his lips before he spoke. The faintest hint of colour in his cheeks. But now it seems obvious to me that Ryan is lying. He knows more than he is letting on.

'Oh, God,' I say. 'You know something, don't you? From then?'

'I know Jamesy Harte isn't right in the head. I know what was found in his house.'

'He says he was set up.'

Ryan snorts, but I know that fake laugh. That bravado. I've seen it many times. Christ, this is why he didn't want me near the story. He's been trying to control it all this time. Surely it's not possible that he's scared, too?

I look at him, the sound of his fake laugh still hanging in the air. The aura of self-confidence around him cracks. The arrogance of the man is a pathetic act. This has never been about *The Chronicle* or my colleagues at all. Nor has it been about not rocking the boat and upsetting the good people of Derry. This is about him covering something up. I'd bet my life on it.

He is not, I realise, the man I thought him to be.

'Ryan,' I say. 'Fuck you and fuck your job. I quit.'

It's my calmness that rattles him. I can see the confusion on his face.

I grab my bag from his desk and turn to leave. Just as I reach for the door, he reaches out and grabs my wrist, tries to yank me back towards him. I feel my skin twist and bruise. My mind flashes to how Jen had rubbed at her own wrist at the front door. This man is nothing but a liar and a bully. I can't believe it has taken me so long to see it.

'You're making a big mistake,' he hisses, his face twisted.

'What are you going to do, Ryan? Smash the windows of my car in? Break into my flat? Slash my tyres? If you don't let go of me right now, I swear I will scream as loud as I can until Jen wonders what the hell is going on up here.

'When she comes up to see what all the fuss is about, I will describe in detail to her how you fucked me over this very desk when she was away for the weekend with the boys. I will tell her all the times you've had your way with me in her home. How we did it on her precious kitchen island, where she is baking you a fucking cake right now. Do you understand?'

He releases his grip, hisses at me that I'm a fucking bitch and that I'm not to say I wasn't warned. I storm out of his house without so much as calling goodbye and get into my car.

I am flooded with adrenaline. How wide does this mess spread? How many people have been lying all these years? How deep will I have to dig to find the truth? Because I'm determined I will find it.

Chapter Thirty-Nine

Ingrid

There are a number of things I could do. I could drive up to Coleraine now, try to find the spot on the train line where Jamesy Harte's body was discovered. I could drive to Portstewart and see if I can see in his bedsit, although I imagine it will be taped off as a possible crime scene. I have no contacts in the PSNI in Portstewart to bend the rules for me and let me in. So I decide both of those are a non-starter.

I'm tense, wound tight by my argument with Ryan. I'm not sure where to go from here, short of calling DI Bradley and telling him I suspect Ryan might know something about the Doherty murder. But it's a closed case and there are so many open cases right now that I doubt he'll care.

Maybe I could tell him that Ryan has been trying to steer me away from investigating this story. That I believe he is tied up in it in some way. I think of the anger in his voice just now and I feel that maybe, just maybe, he could be.

But I have nothing concrete to take to the police.

I'm pretty sure he won't dare make any moves now, though. Hopefully, he's currently sufficiently panicked that he'll behave himself. I don't think he would stupid enough to try anything that might show him in a further dark light.

I think of poor Jamesy and my heart aches for him. He'll never feel the relief of being exonerated now. I don't imagine people will be queuing up to identify whatever is left of him. Not even those who claim they were campaigning for him. It's a sad end to a sad life, I think. An image of him comes to mind: smiling from the garden of his house, waving at us walking home from school. Kelly skipping over and offering him a Kola Kube from the paper bag she was carrying. He smiled and took it. I remember that. I remember him saying they were his favourite boiled sweet, and any time we bought a bag on the way home from school we would stop and give him one.

It's funny how the memories are coming back. Bit by bit.

When I reach my flat, I sit at the table and sift through all of my paperwork and research materials, hoping to find something that I've overlooked before. Something that will help it all to make sense.

DC Black has assured me that he will be in touch when he has more information, but God only knows how long that will take. I tap my pen on my notepad, nervous energy making it impossible for me to sit still. I have to do something.

The little knot of anxiety in the pit of my stomach grows – but I push it down. I can't and won't let it win. I read over my notes until I reach the transcript of my interview with Declan Heaney at the Rath Mor café. It jumps out at me again that he was never convinced that Jamesy Harte was guilty. But he wouldn't be drawn on it.

'Look,' he'd said. 'It's just a gut feeling or something. Naw, it's more than a gut feeling. I really don't think it was him. It doesn't make sense.'

Maybe, if I speak to him again, he might tell me more. Tell me what exactly he meant by 'more than a gut feeling'.

Declan does seem keen to spend time with me. He genuinely seemed to want to help – well, before last night, anyway. But I'm sure I can talk him round a little.

Niall's warning that his brother is an unknown entity rings in my ear. Switching on my laptop and accessing *The Chronicle*'s online archive, I search his name and come up with a plethora of stories – mainly from the petty sessions of the local court. Niall wasn't lying when he said his brother had a record. When I finally click on the story of how he had plagued an ex-girlfriend over a three-month period, calling at her house at all hours of the day and night and flooding her phone with messages, my blood runs cold.

His solicitor told the court that Declan was dealing with 'significant mental health and addiction issues following a child-hood trauma'. That he had been off his medication at the time of his relationship and break-up with the girlfriend in question.

'I cannot argue with you that Mr Heaney does not have a lengthy record,' the solicitor had told the court, 'but it has not been for this type of offending. My client is accessing support from the community mental health team and is willing to engage with probation services.'

That had been four years ago. There were a couple of occasional drunk and disorderly cases reported on after that. I think of him, needy and lonely, with an air of desperation about him. If I'm honest, I don't really think he could be capable of stalking me and threatening me. He's just someone who has fallen about as far as a person can fall and who just wants a friend. I can use that to my advantage.

I scroll through my contacts on my phone until Declan's number comes up. Glancing at the clock on the wall, I see it is now almost three thirty. I don't want him to come to my flat again. I've not lost my mind completely, but I do want to see him. Preferably somewhere public.

I think of that café in the Rath Mor Centre, where we first shared a cup of tea, and I figure if we move quick enough, it will still be open. It would be ideal.

Tapping the call button, I watch as the call connects, but Declan doesn't answer. The phone rings a handful of times before it switches to an automated voicemail message. Swearing inwardly, I hang up and send a text message instead.

Declan, it's Ingrid. Sorry about last night. I was rattled. Give me a call when you get this.

I wait for an answer that I'm sure will be immediate, but my phone stays ominously, and very annoyingly, silent.

I contemplate getting in my car and going for a drive around Creggan, just to see if there are signs that Bernie Doherty might be home, or that word about Jamesy has got out, or, I don't know, just something to quieten all the voices in my head. But I don't want to be brazen about it. I don't want whoever it was who attacked my car to think I'm goading them. If it's the same people who attacked Liam, or who may have targeted Jamesy, it's quite clear they aren't messing around.

I decide to wait for Declan to come back to me. I'm sure he will.

I grab a packet of coloured index cards and start to label them with key points about the case. If I can see the jigsaw puzzle in front of me, something might jump out at me that helps.

All of these people, even Ryan, are tied together by one little girl and the night she died. I just don't know how.

Chapter Forty

Declan

This time Declan lets his anger get the better of him. Taking his keys from his pocket, he walks alongside his brother's car, digging the point of the keys into the paintwork as hard as he can. The screech of metal on metal hurts his ears. He can feel it reverberate through his body as if someone were digging the sharp end of a key directly into his bones.

This is how Niall makes him feel. This is the anger he has for his brother and while he has learned to keep a lid on it over the years, just as he has learned to keep a lid on so much, this time he has to show it. He doesn't want to keep it buried.

He only wishes he were brave enough to walk up to Niall and tell him exactly what he has done. To tell his brother that it was the very least he deserves. That he hopes the bill will take the smug look off his face.

That smile. His teeth professionally whitened, like he thinks he is somebody. Declan would like to knock that smile to the other side of his face.

But he won't. When he thinks of his ma, of how she frets about them both, he knows he won't do it to her. It would break her to see either of them hurt. It's why she has always been so generous with him. There's nothing she wouldn't do to ease his path. It's a pity Niall, with all his money and charm, doesn't feel the same. He'd deny Declan as quickly as he could look at him.

Niall Heaney wouldn't think twice about walking over his brother to get to whatever he wanted, and he'd proven it again today. Meeting Ingrid in town. Was it not enough they'd met last night?

He feels a warm sense of satisfaction as he reaches the front of the car and glances back at the deep groove he has just carved into his brother's pride and joy. He reminds himself that he must not smile. He must not give the game away.

He lets himself into his parents' house, follows the sound of chatter coming from the living room. Niall is, it seems, holding court. Their parents are enthralled by one of his stories about how he – single-handedly, he'd have them believe – turned a failing school around into something hugely successful.

'What happened to your car?' Declan asks, his face a perfect depiction of shock and surprise.

He delights in the change in Niall's expression. The confusion closely followed by a hint of fear, then anger before he rushes from the room and out of the front door.

A litany of expletives carries into the room on the air from outside and Declan watches as his parents make their own way to the front street. His mother stands, arms crossed, hand to her mouth and head shaking.

'Some wee bastard,' his da says. 'I'll ask around, see if anyone saw anything.'

'Good idea,' Declan chimes in, even though he knows full well that no one will have seen anything.

The street was deserted as he walked up it. The wind and rain were keeping anyone with an ounce of sense indoors and in front of the fire.

'At least it's only a car. A car can be fixed,' his ma says, but there's a tremor to her voice.

'There's dangerous people around at the minute,' Niall says. 'Think of what happened to Mr Doherty, and Ingrid Devlin, too. Her car has been vandalised. Maybe I should call the police.'

Declan feels his face flush. That would be the last thing he needs – to get into trouble with the law again. He'd been doing a good job of keeping his nose clean and he had no desire to fall back into old habits.

'There's no need to be getting the police involved,' his da says, and Declan fights the urge to sag with relief. 'It'll be some hood acting the maggot. I'll look into it. Give whoever did it a piece of my mind.'

Despite his advancing years, the thought of Frankie Heaney giving you a piece of his mind is still enough to put the fear of God into most people. Especially Declan. His da has always made a formidable opponent.

'But I'll need a reference number if I'm to claim it on my insurance,' Niall says.

'For the excess you'd pay, and the increase in your premiums, it'll be cheaper for you to do it yourself, and it's not like you can't afford it,' Declan says.

His brother glares at him. Declan is almost tempted to smile. Almost, just to push his brother into losing his temper. There's been a row brewing between the two parties for a long time now.

The air is thick with tension. Declan notices his ma looking between the two of them, her mouth a thin line. Her eyes dull, dark-ringed. She's looking older, he realises. Stressed. He doesn't want to make it worse.

'It's freezing out here,' he says. 'Ma, how about a cup of tea?' She smiles. 'That's a good idea, son. I'll put the kettle on.'

He walks to her, puts his arm around her shoulder. 'You go

in there and sit down and I'll make the tea. Doesn't that sound like a better idea?'

'You're a good son,' she says. 'You are both good sons.'

Declan would like it more if she could just compliment him without the need to compliment his brother, too. Niall gets enough praise.

He knows that makes him a little childish. He hates himself for it. He has always lived in Niall's shadow and no matter what he has tried to do to direct attention his way, nothing has worked. He sometimes wonders if he is invisible.

If he were to disappear right now, he wonders would anyone even notice, let alone care. But he can't allow himself to fall down that rabbit hole again. Not now. He is already low enough without making things worse for himself.

He switches the kettle on to boil, moves around the kitchen setting out mugs, putting biscuits on a plate. He doesn't even hear Niall come into the room and jumps when he hears him speak.

'You need to watch yourself,' Niall says, his voice quiet but still with enough menace to make Declan freeze.

It can't be possible that his brother knows with any degree of certainty that he is responsible for what happened to his car. He decides to say nothing, just to continue with his task of making the tea.

'Are you listening to me?' Niall says.

Declan takes a breath, turns to face him. 'I am. But I'm not sure I've the first notion of what you're talking about.'

'Back off from Ingrid Devlin,' he says, and Declan colours. 'I've seen her today and you're freaking her out. Creeping around. Calling at her apartment like some sad stalker. Is there actually something wrong with you?' Niall taps the side of his brother's head, his words dripping with venom.

Declan moves out of the way, fights the urge to punch Niall.

He wonders just what Ingrid has said about him. Have the words his brother has used come from her lips? A sad stalker. Something wrong with him. Creeping around.

'I've not done anything wrong,' Declan says.

'That's not how she sees it. Do you know that she's even worried that it might be you who targeted her car?'

Declan's fists clench despite his promise to himself to stay quiet. 'Well, she's wrong. For fuck's sake, why would she think that?'

He notices his brother looks delighted with himself. Niall knows he has him rattled.

'And she thinks you might the person who broke into her place. Painted on the walls.'

Declan just blinks at his brother. He can hardly believe what he is hearing. Ingrid thinks he's capable of that? He has only ever tried to help her. He thought she saw him differently from how others saw him. But maybe she is just like all the others. She saw what was on the outside and has made all of her judgements based on that.

'Do you need some help in there?' His ma's voice cuts through their stand-off.

'No, Ma. We're grand. Sit you down,' he calls and then he turns to his brother. 'The pair of you can go to hell. You'll make great company for each other.'

'We do get along very well,' Niall smirks.

Declan brushes past him, probably a little too roughly, and takes the tea in for his mother. He will not let himself down by showing his anger in front of her.

When his phone beeps later with a message from Ingrid Devlin saying she is sorry for how she treated him last night and asking him to get in touch, he hits the delete button. She's so sorry for last night that she's just told his brother she thinks he's a creep. If he never speaks to her again, it will be too soon.

Chapter Forty-One

Ingrid

Declan hasn't messaged me back by 9 p.m. I'm tempted to send him another text, try to call, but I don't want to appear needy. I'm still not sure if I should trust him or not, and I'm worried that if I speak to him now, he might want to call round again.

I've been checking *The Chronicle* website and there has been no update on the body found on the train tracks. Ryan has posted a fairly bland copy of the statement Sue had given out at the press conference about Liam Doherty, but the site is dead apart from that.

I don't know if Ryan has tried to contact me. It might be childish, but I blocked his number on my phone. I have no desire to listen to anything he has to say. Knowing the arrogance of the man, he won't have taken me seriously. He will think I'm just being a 'typical woman' and I didn't really mean to quit my job.

He is probably thinking that I will come crawling back to him soon, or that he can talk me round with false promises of promotions and pay rises on the basis that I hand over my research on Jamesy Harte.

If only Declan would call me back. I check my phone again just in case I've missed a call, but there are no notifications.

I rub the muscles in my neck and shoulders; they are taut, tense. I can feel the beginnings of a headache. Ideally, I'd stand under a hot shower for half an hour before falling into bed, but I am too wired. I need a second pair of eyes on this. Someone to help me make some sense of it. To give me a different perspective.

I look at the notes again and it strikes me that just as Declan is so sure Jamesy is innocent, Niall is equally convinced of his guilt. Niall, who was so nice today when I had a panic attack. When he'd warned me to be wary of Declan, he genuinely seemed to care. He might just be the person to help me see this more clearly.

I'm only calling him about work, I tell myself as I wait for the call to connect. Nothing more.

He answers. 'Ingrid? Is everything okay?'

'Look, there's been a big development in the story, and I sort of wondered if you were still in Derry and maybe we could talk about it.'

'As it happens, I am still in Derry. At my parents' house. Someone took a key to the side of my car and my da's getting a friend of his to have a look at it before I go back. So, I'm here 'til tomorrow afternoon at least.'

My heart quickens. Someone has attacked his car?

'Shit, I'm sorry. You don't think it's the same person who vandalised my car?'

I hear movement and the sound of a door closing.

'Sorry,' he says, 'I was going somewhere more private. I suspect it might have been Declan, so it might well be the same person who attacked your car if I'm right about that, too.'

'Jesus,' I sigh.

'He's not right in the head,' Niall sniffs. 'Look. It's not that much damage, but it goes to show that you really can never know what he is capable of. He's forever getting himself into trouble like this.'

'I've been trying to get hold of him,' I admit.

'Why would you do that?'

Niall sounds annoyed. The tone of his voice makes my skin prickle.

'As I said, something has happened. Something big. Look, I'd rather not talk about it over the phone. Is there any chance we could meet up?'

'After nine on a Saturday night? Everywhere will be rammed. We'll be shouting over the noise,' he says. 'Why don't you just tell me?'

I shake my head, even though he won't be able to see me anyway. 'No, really. It's not the kind of news you break over the phone.'

I realise I don't want to risk his reaction attracting the attention of his parents, or anyone else. This is not the kind of news he will be able to keep to himself once he hears it. For a moment I wonder if I'm making a mistake in trying to get him on board. I know so little about him, but I have to trust my gut and ideally, I'd love to get to the bottom of this before Ryan splashes the news all over the Internet with his own coverage.

'You could come to my place?' I say.

There's a pause. 'Your place? Are you sure?' he asks.

'Strictly business,' I say, trying to keep my voice light.

'That's a shame,' he says. 'But I get it. Big story. Are you sure you're okay? You're not in any danger or anything?'

The concern in his voice is heart-warming.

'I'm fine. I'm here and I'm locked in,' I say.

'Okay, well, let me know your address and I'll be with you as soon as I can.'

I tell him where I live and he starts to say his goodbyes. I'm about to end the call, when I hear an 'Oh, Ingrid . . .' echo down the line. I put the phone back to my ear.

'Yes?' I say.

'If Declan does call back, if he shows up, don't let him in. He was in bad form leaving here earlier and he'd already had a few drinks by then. God knows what state he'll be in by now. Best give him the chance to sober up first.'

The thought of Declan Heaney arriving drunk and angry at my door makes me feel sick.

Chapter Forty-Two

Ingrid

'Jamesy is dead?'

The look on Niall's face is one of genuine shock. In fact, he has gone quite pale.

He hasn't been here long. A matter of minutes, in fact. He arrived twenty minutes after our call, and I was relieved when the door buzzer went to see that it was him and not his brother on the screen, waving at the CCTV camera.

He'd smiled awkwardly when he arrived. 'I'm not sure I can be any help to you, but I'm guessing the something big isn't a good something big?'

I had nodded, invited him through to the living room. Of course it was impossible for him to miss my fairly low-tech attempts at piecing together all the bits of this investigation and everything that has happened since.

'You're really looking at this from every angle?' he'd asked as he examined the index cards, running his finger down some of them while he read. He had paused for just a moment when he reached the card with his name on it and had glanced back at me.

'Fame at last,' he said with a weak smile. 'Or infamy.'

He paused again at the clipping from *The Chronicle* with the report on Kelly's funeral.

'That was a brutal day,' he said before he'd spotted Jamesy Harte in the picture of mourners.

'That man . . .' he said, and I blurt out what I know.

'That man is dead.'

I watch as Niall puts his hand on the back of one of my dining chairs, trying to steady himself.

'Sit down,' I urge. 'I know it's a shock.'

Niall does as I tell him and drops his head into his hands. For a moment I wonder if he is going to start crying, or maybe be sick.

'I can't believe it,' he says, his voice quiet.

I sit down on the other side of the sofa, angle my body towards his. There is more to tell him and I'm not sure how he will react.

'What happened?' he asks.

'Did you see the news at all today? The body on the train tracks?'

Niall sits back in the chair. It's almost as if the weight of my words has pushed him back into the seat.

'Jesus Christ!' he exclaims. 'Did he . . . Was it . . . Did he kill himself? How do you know all this?'

He blinks at me and there is no mistaking it now — there are tears pooling in his eyes. He tries to stop them from falling, but I notice his hands are shaking.

'I mean, the police haven't named him. And wasn't that in Coleraine or somewhere? It could be anyone. I'd heard he was in Scotland.'

I shook my head. 'He never left the country,' I explain. 'He's been living in a bedsit in Portstewart. He's not known as Jamesy any more. He's Jim. I met him there for an interview just last week.' I can hardly believe that's all it has been.

So much has happened. 'I spoke to him last night,' I tell Niall. 'He was so upset with me for the article in the paper. And he'd heard about Liam. He said Liam was part of the whole plan to set him up.'

Niall's skin pales further in front of my eyes.

'So, do you think he was behind what happened last night at the Dohertys'?' he asks, wide-eyed.

I shake my head. 'No. It doesn't add up. I don't think he'd have been capable of arranging something like that. And he sounded too upset, too angry, when he called me.'

Niall pauses. 'So, how do you know the body on the tracks is his? They haven't named anyone on the news. It might be someone else.'

'I have a source in the PSNI and he's very reliable. He confirmed it to me.'

Niall nods, pinches the bridge of his nose.

'Niall,' I say and take a breath. 'My source told me foul play is suspected.'

Niall just stares at me, blinking occasionally. 'Murder?' he eventually asks.

'That's the approach the police are taking. I imagine there will be a press conference about it soon enough.'

Niall exhales slowly, rubs at his eyes. His leg jiggles up and down as if he is filled with nervous energy. He takes a breath and looks directly at me.

'Well, I hope right now Jamesy Harte is rotting in hell. Where he belongs.'

I let his words hang in the air for a moment or two.

'So, you definitely don't share Declan's conviction that Jamesy was set up?'

Niall laughs, a short, sharp burst. 'No, I absolutely don't share my brother's view on that. Jamesy was always creeping around us kids. There was always something not quite right about him.

I know you felt it, too. None of us would talk to him when we were on our own. Our parents wouldn't let us. You remember that?'

I nod, but it's only the vaguest of memories. Everything from then has become blended together, an amalgamation, I assume, of what actually happened, and what I've read and heard since. Our memories are strange creatures, so easily distorted and manipulated.

I barely register he is still speaking, tuning back in only to hear, 'Her things were found in his house. There's no reasonable excuse for that. I don't know what other proof you need.'

Niall shakes his head. 'Ingrid, if you'd seen what I did, on the banks of the reservoir that day, you wouldn't feel one iota of sorrow for that man. It took me years to be able to close my eyes and not see her lying there. I was just a child myself. No child should have to see that.'

His voice is trembling, so I reach out and take his hand. I expect him to pull it away, for some reason. I'm not even sure why. But he doesn't move and that comforts me. We were all so young. We've all carried this with us for so long now. But Niall and Declan have carried it more than most.

'Would you like me to show you where she was found?' he asks after a few minutes of not quite comfortable silence.

I turn my head swiftly to him. 'It was up at the reservoir. I know that.'

'But you don't know where exactly. I know none of us were ever allowed up there again. Not for a long time, anyway. The Dohertys, they didn't want people knowing the exact spot. They didn't want it being made a shrine. Said that wasn't how she was to be remembered.

'I wanted to leave flowers there, but my ma said no. But it might help you,' he says, nodding towards my research on the wall. 'For your book. It might help you get a sense of it. Properly. It hasn't changed that much over the years. Surprisingly. A lot up there has changed, but not that spot.

'I go there still, the odd time. I used to go more. I get a comfort of sorts from it. I suppose that makes me sound a bit weird.' There's that stiff, brittle laugh again.

'I suppose we all do what we need to do to get through it,' I say. 'Maybe it would do me good to see it. Give me a better sense of things.'

'Do you ever feel guilty about it?' he asks.

'About Kelly's death? Yes. Don't we all?'

That's what makes this all so emotional for me. It could have been me, or any of one of us out playing and collecting apples and nuts that night.

I had been wearing a white dress, too. It wasn't a first communion dress. I was too old for mine to have fitted me even if I had wanted to wear it. I think it was a summer dress. And a tinsel crown. A star on a stick, wrapped in tinfoil, just like the one Kelly had.

'I sometimes wonder if we could have done more to protect her. She was younger. Maybe we should've watched over her more. Kept a closer eye on her. Isn't that what community is all about? So yes, I do feel guilty. I don't think I'll ever stop feeling that way.'

'But, Ingrid, we were only children ourselves. We can't carry the weight of that around forever. It's enough that her life was destroyed.'

He stands up, walks back to the wall and runs his fingers down through the index cards again. He seems unduly agitated by the news.

'This really is fascinating, Ingrid. You have everything here,' he says, his tone falsely bright.

'Not quite everything,' I say.

'No, I suppose not,' he says. 'But I suppose once news spreads about Jamesy, you'll know more. God, I hope they're not thinking of bringing him back here to bury. People will be lining up to dance on his grave.'

I look at him, shocked at his words.

'They will, Ingrid. He doesn't deserve to be allowed to rest in peace.'

Chapter Forty-Three

Ingrid

Sunday, 27 October 2019

I can hear the rain battering off my window when I wake. The wind is howling, a vague hint of the banshee about it. I remember being terrified of that mythical Irish creature when I was small. It was one of the kids on the street, possibly even Niall or Declan, who first regaled us with stories of the wail of the banshee – a creature whose cry, carried on the wind, heralded a death.

The first time I'd watched the Disney movie *Darby O'Gill and the Little People* I had been frozen to the spot with fear by the appearance of the ghostly woman, ordering Darby to his demise.

'You hear her, like a really loud wind in a storm, it means someone you love is going to die,' I'd been told, and I'd lived in fear of every stormy day, every whistle of wind through the trees. How loud was loud enough to be the banshee? For a long time, I ran for cover every time I heard the wind roar.

The night Kelly died, the air was still.

I get up, pull open my bedroom curtains just as a fresh squall of rain and hail batters the window, startling me. It may be daytime, but it is still dull and grey outside. The kind of day that looks as if night could call at any second without any regard of the actual time. Cold radiates through the window-panes, even though they are double-glazed. I shiver and close the curtains again.

I climb back under my duvet, reach for my phone and log in to social media. The word, it seems, is out. The death on the railway line is officially now a murder inquiry and the police have identified the victim as Jamesy Harte.

Ryan, or someone in *The Chronicle*, put the story live on the website at 7 a.m. and has shared it on Facebook. Even though it's still early on a Sunday morning, a steady stream of comments have started to flood in. There is something so incredibly inhuman and cold about the number of people responding simply by clicking a Facebook emoji. The laughing-crying smiley face seems to be getting the most mileage.

The comments are filled with vitriol and triumphalism.

Make whoever did this first minister in Stormont. That's how you deal with paedos.

Won't be missed. Shoulda been strung up years ago.

Ha-ha! Hope he felt every second of it. Dirty bastard.

Thoughts and prayers with the Doherty family today – shame they had to wait twenty-five years for proper justice.

Yeeeooo! Best news I've heard all year.

Life should mean life. He never should've got out of jail.

*May Jesus and the Blessed Virgin Mary have mercy on his soul,
and the souls of those who did this.*
– *Mercy? He never offered wee Kelly any mercy. I hope he's
burning in hell right now.*

Public holiday to celebrate the news? We should start a petition!
– *Wise up, you balloon! You only want the day off work after
Halloween to nurse your hangover!*
– *Nothing wrong wi' that! Best holiday of the year! Cannae
wait!*

The comments are exactly what I'd expect from any social media
response. People seem to feel able to say anything and everything.

I click out of Facebook and force myself to get up. For my
sins, I have agreed to meet Niall Heaney up at the reservoir so
he can show me the exact spot where Kelly was found.

I pull jeans and a soft cream jumper from my wardrobe, and
contemplate whether or not to wear wellies. It will be a muddy
mess up there no doubt, so it would probably be advisable. I
put on my ordinary boots for now, knowing I've a pair of
Hunter wellies in the boot of my car. I'd been caught too many
times trudging through fields or flooded areas in heels while
out covering news stories not to invest in a pair.

As I get ready, I think of Niall. How he had stayed at my
flat for more than an hour. He'd declined a glass of wine, opting
for tea. He'd sat on the opposite end of the sofa to me as we
spoke. Every now and then he'd made a flirty comment, but I
think we both knew it wasn't the time for flirting. There would
probably never be a time for flirting between us. Being tied
together by the murder of a school friend isn't, perhaps, the
best start to any potential relationship.

My phone beeps just as I'm searching for my thermal gloves and part of me hopes Niall has seen the weather, thought better of things and is cancelling our meeting.

While it is indeed from Niall, he has no notion of calling things off.

I'll pick up two coffees on the way and see you at the top entrance to the country park in about half an hour. A cappuccino for you?

I reply that I'll see him there, then I click onto my Facebook account just to check the comments under *The Chronicle* story one last time.

One comment seems to be getting a lot of attention. I look closely, see the name of the poster, and my stomach sinks so fast I fear I might pass out.

I did it. It's Halloween − the best time for haunting people. Jamesy was first and he deserved it. But I'm not done yet. Who will be next? When I come for you, you can't say you weren't warned, Devlin!

The comment is posted by someone using the name of Kelly Doherty, the profile picture the same image we have all seen a hundred times of her in her first communion dress. I sit on the edge of my bed and read the message again, my head spinning.

I click on the profile, to see it doesn't offer much information. There are no friends attached to it. Only two items are shared on the user's timeline and one is a link to *The Chronicle* story about Jamesy. The second is a link to the fairly dry press release about the attack on Liam Doherty. The user has commented on that one with 'Daddy needs to keep his mouth shut' and a laughing face emoji.

I screenshot it, intending to contact DS King later. Then I click back to *The Chronicle* page and read the comment again, and the replies below it.

Some people are telling the poster they are sick. Some are

laughing as if it's all a great joke. Some warning that the cops will be able to find out who they are and will be rapping on their door before long. It isn't long before I reach the inevitable comments stating that I'm a horrible person and a scumbag. I'm too big for my boots. I think I am somebody important. I give all journalists a bad name.

I see a second comment from 'Kelly', posted just twenty minutes ago.

Ingrid Devlin met with Jamesy Harte last week. Don't believe her when she says she cares about the Doherty family. She was on that monster's side. Anything to make a few quid in one of her trashy books. She's a bitch.

There may not be people at my door with pitchforks and lanterns, but the social media equivalent is building strongly. I report the comments. Report the user. Part of me wants to call Ryan and tell him to lock comments on the Facebook page to stop this from going any further, but I know he will be loving it. I can imagine him laughing at the folk posting the GIFs of Michael Jackson eating popcorn, saying they're 'only here for the comments'.

All attention is good attention in Ryan Murray's eyes and if the blame is landing on my doorstep and not directly at that of *The Chronicle* then all the better. I might have thought the same myself in the past. That it is all part of the game – if people are commenting, even if they are angry, then people are reading.

For a bleak minute or two I actually wonder if he has planted the comment himself. He is, after all, one of only a handful of people who know I met Jamesy and somehow, I don't see DI Bradley or DS King as Internet trolls.

I'm supposed to be meeting Niall Heaney and I don't want to keep him waiting. I can pretend, as I wrap my scarf around my neck and throw my phone into my bag, that this is just like any other story I've covered. I'm going to do some research. That is all. I won't be alone. Niall will be with me. I will be fine.

I know I will be fine.

Chapter Forty-Four

Declan

The light on the electric box is flashing again. Declan has been doing his best to leave the heating off as much as possible, but it has been bitterly cold. Much colder than it normally is at this time of year. He hopes it warms up, or at least stays dry, on Thursday for the big Halloween parade.

Declan will do what he always does and watch the fireworks from the top of Creggan. He has to keep busy on Halloween night. Every year he has found the day impossibly hard. He would hide away if he could, but he's not good left alone with just his thoughts at this time of year. He has to be busy. Or drunk. Or preferably both. He might just get high, too. Obliterate his reality with whatever he can.

He gets up – his thirst driving him from his bed to the kitchen of his one-bedroomed flat so he can fill a pint glass with water from the tap.

He was smoking last night. The smell of grass still hangs in the air, the taste still in his mouth. He probably smoked more than he should've, and this stuff was strong. A couple of drags and he could feel himself slipping away to somewhere where he didn't have to care about anything or anyone. It was a good place to be.

He'd put on the radio, some dance music station that promised to play 'all the hits of yesteryear'. Dance music from the Nineties and early Noughties had invaded his head. Songs from his childhood, his youth, his sneaking into nightclubs when he shouldn't even have been out of the house. Watching *Trainspotting* when he was twelve in a mate's house on a VHS and not really understanding it but knowing that everyone thought it was really cool. That was when drugs were bad.

He'd tried to believe that, but despite the horrors of that movie, he still felt a glimmer of jealousy and longing when Ewan McGregor slipped into an unconscious state to the strains of 'Perfect Day' by Lou Reed. It had seemed quite blissful to begin with. Imagine what it would be like to escape the horrors in your head . . . To disappear for just a while from this existence. His twelve-year-old brain took a while to realise that an overdose was being played out in front of his eyes.

Not that Declan has tried hard drugs. Well, nothing more than a couple of Es when he was out as a teenager. Like so many before him and since, alcohol is his drug of choice. Grass is just the chaser. Or possibly it's the other way around. He's not fussy.

He downs the pint of water as if he is taking on the lead role in the old black and white movie, *Ice Cold in Alex* and he feels better for it. He'll get dressed and, despite the rain he can hear lashing outside, go down to his ma's. Sunday dinner, again, will be eaten around the family table. If he is lucky, Niall will be on his way to Belfast soon and won't be there to pass comment when his ma slips him the money for the electricity. Or to make any other snide remarks about what Ingrid Devlin does or doesn't think of him.

Of all the things in his life that disappoint him – and there are many, right now – he is most disappointed in her, he thinks as he brushes his teeth and drags a blunt razor over his face.

He never quite manages the fully clean-shaven look. The kind that Ingrid, it would seem, likes.

Yes, he is disappointed in her. He'd tried to be fair. He'd tried to warn her. He thought she'd listened when he told her about Niall. He thought she'd been kind and interested in him. But she is just like all the others. Once Niall walked in with his patter and his big car and his gym body, Declan might as well have been a ghost. He's just a shadow of what could've been.

He slaps some aftershave on his face, feeling it sting as it catches a small nick, and he wipes the steam from the bathroom mirror.

'Wise up, Declan,' he tells himself. 'That'll teach you for having notions about yourself.'

He pads back into the bedroom then digs through his chest of drawers to find clean socks. A thought enters his head. If he could prove to Ingrid that Niall isn't all he seems, you know, really prove it, it might make a difference.

He gets dressed as quick as he can, and not just because it's cold, but because he has an idea. He grabs his coat, his keys, his wallet (for all the good it does him; there's nothing in it but his electricity top-up card) and reaches for his phone – which he vaguely remembers leaving to charge in the living room. He'd switched it off last night before he started smoking. The last thing he wanted to do was get high and start messaging people to tell them exactly what he thought of them. And by people, he meant Ingrid.

Declan doesn't switch his phone on. He just slides it into his pocket, pulls on his hat and leaves his flat – a gust of wind sending a swirling mass of autumnal leaves dancing around his feet.

It's cold. But there's a fire in his belly now. He knows exactly how he can show Ingrid just how wrong in the head Niall is. She won't want anything to do with him when she sees what he has to show her.

Chapter Forty-Five

Ingrid

There is a pale blue Nissan Almera sitting in the car park at the top of Creggan Country Park. It's the only car there, but I don't want to park too close to it. I'm still on edge, and being here on this dark, grey and freezing morning doesn't help.

The driver's door opens and I breathe a sigh of relief when I see it's Niall, carrying two cups of coffee. He is wrapped up against the elements, just as I am, and he grimaces as he looks up towards the sky.

I gesture at him to get into the passenger seat of my car. The least we can do is drink our coffee in relative comfort before we set off on our walk.

'Great day for it,' he says sarcastically as he hands me my coffee and sips from his own.

'I'm not sure this is one of my better ideas,' I say. 'Maybe we should reschedule?'

'Nonsense!' Niall laughs. 'Sure, it's only a bit of rain. Did your mammy never tell you that you're not made of sugar and you won't melt?'

I smile at the phrase half the mothers in Derry must have used at one stage or another. 'She did, but she'd also tell me not to be getting into cars with strange men or going out in a storm in case I catch my death of cold.'

'Well, it's a good thing I got in the car with you and not the other way around, and that I'm not a stranger. Besides, that's hardly a storm,' he laughs as we watch a tree bend and shake in the squall, 'it's practically a summer's day for Derry.'

Niall is upbeat. Almost alarmingly so for 10 a.m. on a stormy Sunday morning when we are about to revisit the scene of one of his greatest childhood traumas. Perhaps the humour itself is a coping mechanism. Laugh it off. Make jokes. It's how we all coped for decades in this part of the world. It's how we still cope now.

I sip my coffee, let the caffeine wind its way into my veins.

'I see the news about Jamesy is out,' Niall says, cradling his coffee cup in his two hands, looking straight ahead of him.

'Yes. Social media is particularly sewer-like this morning,' I say.

'People were never going to grieve for that man,' Niall says. 'I think it's healthy for people to have a place to express their emotions.'

'You clearly didn't see all the comments calling for my head on a block,' I answer, turning to look at him. 'That didn't feel particularly healthy to me. The knives are out. Not to mention a troll account, in Kelly's name.'

He is still staring straight ahead, his gaze on the tree, which is shedding more and more leaves with every gust.

'I saw that,' he says. 'Nothing but keyboard warriors. I wouldn't take it seriously. I imagine it will all blow over now that Jamesy is dead.'

'Unless I prove he was innocent, after all,' I say.

Niall's jaw tightens just a fraction.

'Although, I'd guess whoever is threatening me doesn't want that to happen.'

'Maybe that's because he was guilty,' Niall says. 'I admire your commitment and your sense of righting a great wrong here, but Jamesy Harte was no saint. Don't let championing his innocence be the hill you die on. If you want my advice, walk away from it all now and it will all be forgotten in a few days. People will move on. Find someone else to spew their hatred about.'

I shift in my seat. 'The thing is, I can't just ignore my gut on this. Something isn't right about the whole situation and I want to get to the heart of it. Even if we take Jamesy out of the equation, the Dohertys deserve to know the truth. On a personal note, since I am gainfully unemployed as of yesterday, getting to the heart of this would put two fingers up to my former boss.'

Turning his gaze to mine, Niall places his coffee in the cup holder on my dashboard. 'Well, I can't say I've ever been a fan of Ryan Murray. He's a slippery fucker if ever I met one. He'd fall into the Foyle and come out with a salmon in his mouth.'

'I didn't realise you knew him,' I say, eyebrow raised.

Niall looks at me incredulously. 'Come on, Ingrid! Everyone knows Ryan Murray. He's been sniffing around, acting the big man for years. You want to hear my da about him. He said he wouldn't spit on him if he was on fire. He was only a wee runt when Kelly died. Made a name for himself with all the coverage back then. My da says he's never done an honest day's work since.'

I'm not sure what to say. Ryan may well be on my shit list right now, but I have admired his journalism throughout my career. I don't want to start an argument about it though, so I ignore the dig and put my half-full coffee cup in the cup holder beside Niall's.

'Shall we go on our walk now?' I ask.

'Sure. Okay,' he says. Just as he opens the passenger door of the car, a gust of wind catches it and threatens to pull it from its hinges. He looks at me to check if I'm really, really sure and I nod, get out of my side of the car and change into my wellies, leaning on the car for balance.

'You don't let anything get in your way, do you, Ingrid?' he shouts over the noise of the storm.

'Nope!' I shout, because it's much too easy to find excuses not to do things. I can't let my doubts and fears stop me. Especially not now.

Another gust of wind catches the tree we have been watching, stripping it of its orange-and-gold leaves. It howls as it carries them, spinning towards us, the high-pitched squeal like that of the banshee.

'I do like that about you, Ingrid Devlin. Your spirit, it's very appealing,' he says as he walks beside me.

I notice he is smiling.

'My spirit? Most people call it a stubborn streak,' I laugh, but there is something in his words that makes me feel warm and fuzzy inside.

'Well, I like a stubborn streak. I like someone with determin-ation. I see them as a challenge,' he says, and there's no denying this time that there's something flirtatious in his tone.

We stop walking and I look at him. There's a frisson of something between us. A connection that I can't deny. An attraction that part of me knows is a bad idea and yet, here we are. Together. Conversation flowing between us. Able to banter and laugh even on a day like today, when we're walking on this path to the place that changed everything.

'Well, I am told I can be very challenging,' I say, my eyes on his. 'Always have been, apparently.'

'Yes, I remember that determined wee girl who liked to boss everyone around,' he says. 'Even back then. Everyone followed your lead, Ingrid. I don't know if you even realised it, but it was almost like everyone else was invisible when you were around.'

His words disarm me. The intensity of his stare. I'm filled with the urge to reach out and touch him. Take his hand. Or put my hand to his cheek.

'Are you trying to tell me the world doesn't still revolve around me now? I thought I'd maintained my diva qualities.' It's an attempt at humour, but I cringe at how cheesy it sounds.

He pauses. From the look on his face, I guess he's not sure how to answer me. The moment is lost.

'So, with that in mind, this diva would like to get going before this weather gets any worse,' I say before he can speak.

He blinks as if he is bringing himself back into the present day and points in the direction of the reservoir. 'There's a new pathway down here now,' he says, 'but follow me up through these trees a bit first.'

Under the cover of the trees, the wind doesn't seem as loud. The rain is still falling, dripping through what is left of the leaves on the branches and landing in fat ice-cold droplets on the ground, on my clothes, on my face. I'm glad I put my wellies on, because the persistent wet weather of the last few days has left the ground slick and muddy. I tread slowly.

'Do you remember playing here after school?' Niall asks.

'I didn't play here all that often. Not after school, anyway,' I said. 'My mum was always terrified I'd get into some sort of trouble. Fall into the reservoir, break a bone climbing a tree, something like that. But I do remember having picnics here, in the summer. With my parents and a friend or two. The grass was so long it almost reached the top of my legs. I remember the smell of it.'

'It doesn't smell the same now,' Niall says. 'My memory of playing here is just like this, fallen leaves and branches. Mulch beneath our feet. Thick drops of rain, and the smell of the sap and the trees mixed with that of smoke from the coal-fired chimneys. Declan and I, we'd play here most days after school – go home in a state, our clothes mucked to the eyeballs. My poor mother had the washing machine constantly on the go and was forever drying uniforms for us around the radiators or in front of the fire.'

'What sort of things did you play?' I ask, watching as he looks around him, touching his hand to some of the trees, staring up through the branches to the sky – as if trying to re-familiarise himself with the place.

'All sorts,' he says. 'Some days we pretended we were soldiers. Others we were stranded on an island somewhere. Some days we just threw stones or sticks into the rezzie. Or we climbed trees. We had a den, you know.'

His face is animated as he talks; I can see the traces of the child he was. Wide-eyed with wonder.

'I say it was a den, but really it was just a small clearing and there was a fallen tree, which made for a great bench to sit on. The area was really overgrown, so it was the perfect place to hide, to get cover from the rain. We had a password to get into it, which was ridiculous really, seeing as it was only me and Declan who ever went into it. We were eejits, really.'

'All children are eejits,' I say. 'It's part of their charm. But you never allowed *anyone* else in? I mean, I understand that girls wouldn't be allowed, because we were the enemy, but none of your friends from school or the street?'

Niall shakes his head. 'No, it was our place. We didn't want to share. It was like a safe place to go.' His face clouds with sadness.

'My da,' Niall says, 'he's doing okay now, you know. But he was fond of the drink back then. Probably would be diagnosed with PTSD these days if he wasn't too stubborn to go and see the doctor about it. You know, some of the things he went through in the Troubles . . .'

I knew that Frankie Heaney had a reputation as a hardman. He was someone people didn't want to get on the wrong side of. Even now. He'd been active during the Troubles, served time for membership of the IRA. He'd done things, seen things that most people could only imagine.

'He was no angel. He's no angel now, but at the time, he was under a lot of pressure. Trying to police the community, getting grief from others. Not everyone was happy about the IRA calling their ceasefire, you know. There was a lot of fear and mistrust.

'When I look back on it, with adult eyes, I can see that my da was probably terrified of what his position would be in a new Northern Ireland. Would he still be relevant? Would he still have any kind of authority? And the things he'd done, the time he'd served, what was that all about? So, he was angry, and sometimes he was violent with it,' Niall says.

An image of two scared little boys flashes into my mind. The things that go on behind closed doors that we never know about. By the sounds of it, what happened to Kelly wasn't the only thing that had left the Heaney twins traumatised.

'He didn't know about our den. So it was a safe spot, you know. We'd escape here sometimes when things got really bad at home.'

There's silence then, save for the wind and the rain. Niall has finished talking and I'll be honest, I don't know what to say in response to that. I reach out and take his gloved hand in mine.

'I'm sorry to hear things were tough,' I say, knowing it's woefully inadequate.

'You let it make you or let it break you,' he says. 'I chose one path and Declan chose the other. Maybe he's more like my da than he wants to let on.'

Niall gives my hand a little squeeze before letting go and turning to walk onwards.

I pick my way through the leaves, behind him. We've not walked far, when his voice rings out.

'Here it is,' he shouts, and I follow him to where there is the smallest of clearings amid heavy overgrowth of bushes and grass. 'This was our den,' he says. 'It hasn't aged well.'

He wanders on a bit, turns and heads a little uphill. He seems lost in thought as he walks around. I wonder what memories are playing through his head.

I stay where I am and look around the small space, try to imagine it as it was. Look up at the sky, still heavy with dark clouds. The water's edge is visible from here and I can't help but stare.

'Careful, Ingrid,' Niall says, his breath warm in my ear.

For a moment I think about leaning back onto him, feeling his body against mine.

'You don't want to slip. Bad things can happen here if you slip,' he whispers as his hands press down heavily, uncomfortably, on my shoulders.

His breathing becomes heavier and my blood runs cold as his grasp tightens further.

Chapter Forty-Six

Declan

'Is that you, son?' Declan hears his mother as he opens the door and walks in, immediately hit by a wave of heat and the smell of baking.

'It is, Ma,' he calls back, taking off his jacket and hanging it on the bottom of the bannister.

His mother will give out to him about leaving his coat there, but he'll deal with that in his own way. He knows he can sweet talk her. He has always been able to do that.

'Did you smell these scones baking or what?' she calls, laughing. 'I'll stick the kettle on.'

'I just need to look for something upstairs,' he replies. 'I shouldn't be long.'

He climbs the stairs, goes straight to the room he used to share with his brother. The large mahogany wardrobe is still here, now storing clothes his mother won't wear again but can't bear to throw away. Her 'fancy clothes', she calls them. Outfits she's worn to weddings, dances, celebrations. Her own wedding dress is folded in tissue paper in a box on a high shelf. Beside it, shoeboxes are filled with photos, memorabilia, old school reports, newspaper cuttings.

Declan starts to pull each box down and open them, quickly discarding those that don't contain what he's looking for. He hears his mother on the stairs and soon she's by his side.

'What on earth are you doing? I hope you're going to clean all that up after yourself!'

'I'm looking for something,' he tells her, tearing open the lid of another shoebox, only to find it filled with old birthday cards.

He's getting frustrated now. He can feel it well up inside him.

'Well, what are you looking for? Maybe I can help you find it before you wreck this house of mine altogether!'

'The time capsules,' he says. 'Remember, you made me and Niall do them before the new millennium.'

'The ones you were disgusted to do because you were fifteen and thought you knew everything there was to know about everything?' she says, raising one eyebrow.

'Aye. Those ones,' he says, probably a little too harshly. He sees the way she winces at his tone, feels immediately guilty. 'Sorry, Ma. But it's important.'

'What on earth could be so important about them that you need to storm in here at just gone ten on a Sunday morning and start pulling my house apart?'

Declan bites back the urge to shout at her. God knows she has been shouted at enough in her life. Memories wash over him of a different time. A different kind of household, where angry voices were a regular feature.

'It's just something I remembered that I need. To prove a point to someone.'

She eyes him suspiciously.

'Declan, you've not got yourself into some sort of mess, have you? Because I don't know how much more of that I can take.

You've been doing well, don't be going down that road again. All that trouble . . .'

The worry lining her face makes him feel guilty for everything he has put her through, but she has to understand it's not all of his own making. Things happened and things changed him. Things he has never been able to talk about, because if he did it would blow the whole family apart. He couldn't be responsible for that.

'I'm not in any bother, Ma,' he tells her. 'Honestly. It's just something I want to get my hands on. You know, Ingrid being around here and all this talk of Kelly Doherty, it's just made me remember some stuff, you know. From back then. Not bad stuff,' he hastens to add. 'But I want to look over a few things anyway.'

'It's a bad business. No good will come of it,' she says. 'And Jamesy Harte dead. Murdered, they say.' She blesses herself. 'So much heartbreak.' She shakes her head. 'Look, your da will be home from Mass after eleven, if he doesn't stop to chat to some of his cronies. I'm sure he'll help you look.'

'I don't need to be bothering him with this,' Declan says, because the very last person he wants involved is his da.

Not, at least, until he is sure what he's going to do. And he needs to see Niall first. Needs to confront him.

'You know, I think I might have put them up in the attic. Beside the Christmas decorations. I don't suppose it will be long before we're taking those down. Your woman at the top of her street will have her tree up come Friday. It's the same every year. As soon as Halloween is done and dusted, she goes full North Pole. I wouldn't want to be paying her electricity bill.'

His ma laughs and he laughs with her, but he's already thinking he needs to get up into the attic and have a look around.

'Where's the pole for pulling down that ladder?' he asks her.

'For the attic? I think it's in the built-in wardrobes in my room. You don't really want to be climbing up there, do you?'

He's already heading to her bedroom and retrieving the pole with the hook on the end that he will use to haul the folding ladder down from the roof space.

'Would you not just sit and have a cup of tea with me?' she asks, and he hesitates.

He loves his ma. He really does. He loves her more than anyone in this world. She's the only woman who has ever treated him with respect and never thought worse of him when he stumbled and wound up in trouble again.

'I will, Ma. As soon as I've had a look up here. Why don't you ask Niall to have a cup of tea with you? He's still about, isn't he? Is he watching one of those Sunday morning politics shows and pretending to be some big brainbox?'

'No, he's not here. He's worse than you. Off out this morning all wrapped up. Said he had to go and take that Ingrid Devlin somewhere. He wanted to show her something. I said why couldn't the wee girl wait 'til that storm had passed, and he laughed at me. The cheek of him. You know what he said to me? "I'm not made of sugar, Ma. I won't melt." He looked all delighted with himself.

'You don't think there's something going between the two of them, because I'm not sure how I feel about that. I mean, what happened to poor Liam Doherty was bad enough – and wasn't it off the back of that story she did for that paper she works for?'

Declan notices his ma's tone has changed again. She is worried. She is twisting her hands.

'Don't be going up into that attic, son. Come and have a wee cup of tea with me. There's treacle scone there. I know that's your favourite.'

But he can't. He has to get up into the attic now more than

before. And then he has to track down Niall and find out where the hell he has taken Ingrid on a morning like this and he has to make sure he can get Ingrid to understand exactly what is going on.

'I'll get a cup of tea in a wee bit,' he tells his ma, doing his best not to show her just how rattled he is. 'Just let me look up here first. Sure, don't I have the ladder down and all?'

She nods. 'Okay, son,' she says.

She is a meek woman, he knows that. She wouldn't argue.

'You would tell me if you were in trouble, wouldn't you?' she asks.

He reassures her he's fine. If only she knew it isn't him she should be worrying about.

Chapter Forty-Seven

Ingrid

'Jesus Christ, Niall. You scared the heart out of me,' I swear, my heart thumping.

Treat it as normal. Don't show him I'm scared.

I try to turn and pull myself loose from his grasp, but I lose my footing on the slick leaves and mud and start to slide down the hill. I feel his hands grab at my arms, squeezing so tightly I know he will leave a bruise.

Looking up, straight into his eyes, I know there is a pleading in my expression. He pulls my arms, drags me closer to him.

'I did warn you,' he says. 'Something tells me you aren't one for walking about in the woods much. There are so many hazards.'

'I don't have much call for it,' I stutter, righting myself and trying to regain my composure.

It dawns on me that despite the caring person he has appeared to be, or how much I have felt a growing attraction to him, I don't know him – and certainly not enough to trust him. I'm scared, I realise, and wish that I was anywhere else but here.

'You have to be careful, you know,' he says as he lets go of me.

I can't speak, so I just watch as he starts to descend the hill sideways, one careful footstep after another. He reaches up to take my hand and help me towards him.

'It's just down here. Where we found her. We were walking towards Glenowen.'

His pace has slowed, his voice is low and I struggle to hear him over the howl of the wind, yet I don't want to get closer to him. Not now.

'I picked up a stick,' he says. 'I can't really remember why. I might have been using it as a pretend rifle, or a lightsabre, or just using it to batter the leaves from the trees.'

Even though I know it has been twenty-five years since Kelly Doherty's body was found on the muddy riverbank, there is a part of me that feels nervous as we approach the spot. As if she might still be there. Maybe some echo of her is. The wind roars through the trees as if warning us away. The sky seems darker, the clouds heavy with the threat of rain.

'Did you usually walk this way? Was it not quicker to go back the way you came?' I ask.

Niall doesn't answer. He has walked a few steps on, closer to the water. It's overgrown now, fenced in, but I can still see the muddy bank.

'She didn't even look like a person. Just a thing. An object. Like, I don't know, a doll, or a plastic bag, or rubbish or something. She was face down. You wouldn't have known her. Her hair was darkened. And her dress was dirty. Even the parts of her legs I could see, they didn't look like legs, not at first. They were a strange colour. Grey and blue and bloated. Still, I couldn't really make out what I was seeing, or who she was. I think . . . well, don't they say your brain can shut down almost when you experience something like that?'

'I think so, yes,' I say, making sure to keep a few steps back from him.

Crouching down, Niall reaches his hand to the wet ground and picks up a leaf, examining it closely. Not quite sure what to do or say next, I stand still, feeling the wind whip my hair around my face. I tuck the loose strands back under my hat.

I think of her body. How small it must've been. How fragile, lying there at the water's edge, her face down, mouth and nose filled with sludge and mud and water. I've seen enough. I want to go.

Niall rubs at his face. If I'm not mistaken, and I really don't think I am mistaken, he is rubbing away tears. My heart aches for him in that moment and trying to push my own fear aside, I reach out and touch his shoulder to guide him back to a safer place.

He lets out a shuddering breath, stands up, and that intense look is back.

'Ingrid,' he begins, and his left hand brushes against my right cheek.

His touch, though gloved, is gentle, but my body tenses.

'Maybe we should head back to the cars,' I say. 'I don't think this weather is getting any better. It might even be worse, if I'm not mistaken.'

I am trying to keep eye contact with him, but it's hard. It's intimidating. I remind myself to be professional. To hang in there.

He blinks. 'I just think . . . well, the mind, it plays tricks on you, doesn't it? I read an article about memory, how you can be convinced things happened one way when they couldn't have. Memory is unreliable.'

I shrug. The rain starts to fall heavier now. I can see it pooling in the wells of the muddy footprints we've left.

'Do you believe in the bogeyman?' he asks.

It's such a strange question, it makes me smile at first. I shake my head, then remember the memory I can't quite place of the man on the street and his beckoning finger, and the way I didn't know if it was a dream or real but how my heartbeat quickens every time I think of him.

'When I was a child, yes,' I tell him. 'We all did. Didn't we? That blasted "Who's At The Window" song – it scared me stupid when I was wee. There was once when I was convinced I saw him, too. Not long after Kelly had died, I think. It's all so muddled in my head. A man dressed in black in the street, in the middle of the night. He looked right up at my window.'

'Did you see his face?' Niall asks, his face stony.

I shake my head. 'He was in the shadows. I told my parents about it afterwards; they told me it was most likely just a bad dream.'

He sighs. It's a sigh that is laced with pain and regret. His body slumps.

'I used to think it was a dream, too. I think it was easier that way,' he says. 'It was so hazy. I was so scared of what would happen if people found out. I'd be in so much trouble. The kind of trouble you can't come back from.'

'Niall.' I say his name again, but he is lost in his thoughts.

'I didn't mean for any of it to happen. It wasn't my fault, you see. I'd had a fight with my da and, well, you know what he was like then. He'd gone mad because I'd cut up one of his old shirts to make a Frankenstein costume. It was an old, battered thing. Ma thought he wouldn't mind, but of course he did. He'd pick a fight in an empty room when he got into that state.

'I came home from collecting all my nuts and apples. Pure delighted with myself. And there was my da and all his cronies with him. All drinking and having a great time to themselves. He noticed the shirt right away and of course he couldn't let it go. Even though his friends were there. All those big men and not a one of them telling him to go easy.

'I remember it, you know. Me standing there shaking with fear while he put me in my place, roaring and shouting about what a wee bastard I was – and I think I was supposed to be grateful, because he didn't lift his hand to me.'

The rain is getting heavier, landing with heavy thuds on the ground, rattling what little leaves are left on the trees. The wind howls and wails, and I shiver as he speaks. I don't know if it's the cold or what he is telling me. I know this isn't leading anywhere good.

'I ran out of the house,' he continues. 'It was late. I didn't think there were any children still about,' he says. 'I was so angry and upset. I don't think I'd have recognised my goal-keeping hero, Packie Bonner, if he had appeared in front of me. I just wanted to get away.

'I heard a man's voice calling after me – could've been my da, but I wasn't for stopping to find out. I ran all the way here, well, up towards the den, you know. I was so angry, Ingrid. So fucking angry with him. I wanted to hurt him and his pals. I wanted to break something. I didn't know . . .'

He pauses and my heart is beating so loudly now. Between that and the wind, I can barely hear him. While I want to know what he is going to say next, knowing it will be of help to solve the mystery, there is still a part of me that wants to put my fingers in my ears. I can't bear to hear what I think is coming next.

'Niall . . .' I'm saying his name, but I don't know why. He isn't listening to me. He is in his own world, in the centre of his own storm.

'I didn't know . . .' he repeats. 'She was on her way home, in the dark. I couldn't understand why she was on her own, but she said she'd just dropped her wee friend off at home, and was heading home herself. When she saw me upset, she was like a wee dog nipping at my ankles.

'I told her to go home, that her mammy and daddy would

be worried about her. I told her loads of times. But she followed me, asking me what was wrong. I remember that, her eyes widening when she heard the angry voice calling my name. She asked if I was in trouble. I told her it was none of her business. But she was persistent.

'She followed me right up into our den and I was angry at her, because I didn't want her to know where it was. She was such a pain in the arse. And there she was, standing in the middle of my safe space, and she was asking questions.' He mimics a child's voice. 'Why are you crying? Did you get in trouble? What's wrong? And I was just so very, very angry.'

Chapter Forty-Eight

Declan

A single light bulb hanging from a wire from one of the rafters casts a soft glow around the attic. It's freezing up here, Declan thinks, and he can hear the house creak and the slates rattle as the storm rages outside. He uses the light from his phone to see into the darker corners of the attic until he spots the old artificial Christmas tree surrounded by boxes of baubles and tinsel and tangled lights. Pushing those out of the way, he finds a large brown cardboard box, on which he sees 'Boys' stuff' written in thick black marker in his mother's handwriting.

He pulls the box forwards and picks at the end of the thick tape holding it closed until he gets enough purchase to pull it back. His mother has stored things methodically. There is a box of sports medals, garnered at every sports day and summer scheme the twins attended over the years. There are badges from the Boy Scouts, lovingly unpicked from uniforms the boys had long outgrown and stored in a Tupperware box. Photo albums stacked neatly on top of each other. A few football sticker books he had no idea she had kept. And nestled at the bottom, two shoeboxes, wrapped in brown paper and too much Sellotape, with his name on one, Niall's on another.

On both, in block capitals, they had written '1999 Time Capsule. Do Not Open!' Declan remembered how he'd hated putting it together. He'd rolled his eyes at his mother. He was fifteen. He was in his too cool for school stage, facing detention after detention, sneaky cigarettes out of his bedroom window. He thought it babyish, stupid to put together a time capsule. He'd done a half-hearted job. He knew that.

He could still remember what he threw in his. A copy of *The Chronicle*. His Oasis CD, which he'd outgrown and no longer listened to. Some badges he'd taken off his school bag, bearing names of bands he liked – or thought he should like. Nirvana, Radiohead, Stereophonics. The battered Casio watch that no longer worked and his old Tamagotchi that he had been religious about taking care of for six months before moving on to the next craze.

He knew Niall had made more of an effort with his, because Niall always made more of an effort with everything. He'd started to come out of his angry young man phase and instead had become an overachiever, much to his chagrin. Niall had written a letter to his future self, which Declan had rolled his eyes at. He'd put in a school report, his prefect badge, one of his old Action Men, a Liverpool FC key ring, and other bits and pieces.

As Declan tears open the brown paper around his brother's box, he hopes he has remembered correctly. He hopes that there, among the items his brother could not give away but wanted to hide, he will find a small bracelet. Beads of brightly coloured plastic bound together on elastic. Worth nothing, but everything.

It was the reason Declan never believed Jamesy Harte was guilty. The reason he hated his brother, and hated himself even more. Because he'd been too scared, always, to confront Niall about it. To ask him what had happened. To tell his brother he hated him for bringing him to play at the den on the day they found Kelly. Because he'd realised that Niall had known where she was all along. He'd left her there. It broke him to think his brother was capable of such horror.

He could never be best friends with someone who had killed a person.

And how else would Niall have got the bracelet if he hadn't been the one to kill her?

It was the day after she was found when everything had clicked into place for him. That was the day he realised what Niall had done. In that moment the bottom fell out of Declan's world. Everything that he thought was true was destroyed.

He'd been watching TV. The police appealing for information. An image of the cheap, tacky plastic bracelet flashed on screen. A solemn voice intoned that it was believed Kelly was wearing the bracelet on the night she had gone missing, but it hadn't been found on her body.

'God love them, but it's probably lying at the bottom of the reservoir,' his mammy had said.

But Declan knew it wasn't. He knew Niall had it. In his coat pocket. Declan had found it when he lifted his brother's coat by accident the day after Halloween, slipping his hand into the pocket. He didn't realise then, not yet, how important it was, or what it meant. Not until now, watching the TV.

He thought of the rage his brother was in on the night he ran off. The silent procession of his da, Niall and two of his friends back down the street an hour later.

His stomach lurched, right then, in front of the TV in his cosy living room, while he sat on the sofa beside his mammy. His brother upstairs.

That was when Declan realised monsters existed and sometimes they existed right beside you. Sometimes they looked just like you. And Declan knew he could never, ever tell anyone, because losing his brother would be like losing a part of himself.

But, it seems, he lost him anyway.

And now, now he has to open up and tell the truth. For him, for Jamesy, for Ingrid. He might be angry with her, disappointed with her, but a large part of him still wants her enough to do what he needs to do to protect her. No matter the consequences in his own family. He has covered for Niall for too long.

Chapter Forty-Nine

Ingrid

I can no longer hear the noise around us. I can only hear what is happening right here and right now in the eye of our own storm. I can feel the adrenaline surge through my body, the fight or flight instinct telling me to run. It is almost painful not to, yet I have to hear what he is going to say next.

'You hate me,' he says suddenly, his voice quieter.

I shake my head, not trusting myself to speak.

'I was only ten,' he says. 'Just like you. You remember that, don't you? We were so young. So stupid. So naive. Not like kids these days. I had no wit about me, my whole life ahead of me, and I was just so scared. I couldn't speak. It wasn't that I didn't want to tell people. I did, but what would happen to me if I did? And my mum? And Declan? They didn't deserve that. To have their lives destroyed. I know our life was far from perfect, but that would have blown it to pieces. I was young, but I knew that much.'

I can't find any words. I try, but nothing comes to me except that I am standing in front of a man who has kept the darkest secret anyone could keep for the past twenty-five years. He has built a successful life, while Kelly and her life stopped. I think of Bernie – broken, bloodied, terrified. I think of Liam Doherty lying in hospital. I think of Jamesy, torn to pieces on a railway line. So many lives destroyed.

And this man in front of me is responsible and could've stopped it.

It dawns on me, as he stands, tears trickling down his face, that maybe he has tried to stop it in his own way. Maybe he's the one who has tried to kill this story, bury any mention of it. Maybe he knows who targeted my car. Who held Liam Doherty down. Who pulled Jamesy Harte from his bedsit in the middle of the night.

'You can still do the right thing,' I say, my voice shaky.

He shakes his head. 'No. No, Ingrid. You don't understand. I can't do the right thing. I can't tell anyone and you can't, either.' He reaches for my arm. I feel his grip again. 'Look at me, Ingrid. Do you understand? You can't tell anyone. This is bigger than you and me. People will get hurt. You'll get hurt.'

Chapter Fifty

Declan

Declan slips the bracelet into his pocket and closes the box back up, pushing it back into the corner. As he makes his way down the ladder, he hears the front door open and then slam close.

'Frankie, is that you?' His ma's voice rings out again.

'Who else would it be?' his da answers, but it isn't in a joky way.

There is an anger to his tone that takes Declan right back to that night. He stops, waiting at the top of the stairs, trying to gauge what has his da angry.

'Did you know, Kathleen?' he asks.

'Know what?'

Declan recognises his mother's tone of voice, the one she used to use when his da needed placating, as he so often did back then in those angry years, before he got support. Knocked the drink on the head. Found a forgiving God who assured him he wasn't going straight to hell.

'That Niall was off meeting that Devlin girl! I was told at Mass my car had been seen up in the country park. And herself's car, too.'

Declan freezes. The country park. Why would they be there? What was Niall at?

'No, I didn't know, but I think he's a bit long in the tooth for me to be checking his every move anyway. So what if he's meeting her? It's probably to do with Jamesy Harte being murdered. I've no time for that man and what he did, but still, it feels sad, doesn't it?'

'I told him to stay away from her,' his da bites back. Angrier. Louder.

If that bastard raises a hand to his ma, Declan won't be long raising his own hand to him and knocking him out cold. He's not a frightened ten-year-old any more. He has spent too long being frightened of his da. And frightened of his brother. Both of them sauntering around as if they don't have a care in the world.

'Is he stupid or something? Does he have a death wish? Because God alone knows that Devlin one must have. How many times does she have to be told?'

'I don't know what you're talking about,' his ma answers.

Declan hears the tremor in her voice.

'Don't lie, Kathleen. You're not as stupid as you look. You know as well as I do what happened back then . . .'

His da's voice drops to a whisper and Declan strains to hear it, but he can't. He closes his eyes as if the act of closing off one of his senses will make the others work harder, but it's just mumbling – and then his ma crying and the slam of the front door again.

A sob from his ma lets him know it's his da who has gone out.

'Jesus Christ,' he hears her sob. 'Jesus Christ, I didn't know. God forgive me, but I didn't know.'

He thunders down the stairs. 'What didn't you know?' he asks her, but she looks as if she is folding in on herself with grief.

Has his da really known all this time about Niall and done nothing? Has his da been covering up for Niall, even now, doing whatever he needs to do to stop the renewed interest in this case?

His da, he knows, is still able to summon up some heavies at a moment's notice. Many people still feel a loyalty to Frankie Heaney. He still holds some sway. If he'd wanted a car window broken, or tyres slashed, he wouldn't have struggled to find someone to do it. If he'd wanted to rough someone up, he could have found someone only too willing to do it for him.

His ma can't speak. She is shaking her head and he wants to comfort her, but if this is what his da is capable of, and his brother, and both are in the country park with an unsuspecting Ingrid . . . His stomach turns.

He reaches for his jacket at the bottom of the stairs and pulls his phone from the pocket. With shaking hands, and thick, useless fingers, he paws at his phone, trying to unlock it and find her number. He needs to warn her. He needs to get her away from Niall.

Chapter Fifty-One

Ingrid

I'd wanted to crack this story. Of course I had – but not like this. It was never meant to be like this. Niall's grip on me is firm and there is a wildness in his eyes.

'I shouldn't have said anything,' he says suddenly. 'Shit! Ingrid, tell me,' he says, shaking me so that I almost lose my footing, my boots sliding in the mud. 'Tell me you won't tell anyone. I need you to tell me that now!'

'People will understand,' I tell him, knowing that they won't.

People never understand when it comes to the murder of a child. It is beyond the realm of comprehension and understanding. But I have to say whatever it takes to get out of this park and away from Niall.

'Why don't we walk back to the cars,' I say. 'It's so cold here and I'm wet through. We can talk somewhere warm and dry at least. I can help you.'

It's only a little lie – one designed to make sure we both get away safely. It's for the right reasons.

To my relief, he nods, defeated, and for the first time since he and his brother came back into my life, I see the resemblance between them again. It's in the slumping of Niall's shoulders, as if he is carrying the weight of the world on them. The same weight Declan has always looked as if he were carrying.

We walk in silence, the air thick with everything that has been said and that still needs to be said. I'm afraid to speak, to do anything that might drag Niall from his silent reverie and back into the moment.

When my phone rings I jump, fumbling in my pocket to try to silence it, but my hands are too useless in my gloves. They won't swipe across the screen. Niall stops, turns and looks at me.

'You can answer it, you know,' he says.

'It's okay. I don't need to,' I say. My teeth are starting to chatter with the cold now. 'It won't be important. I can call whoever it is later.'

The ringing stops and inwardly I sigh with relief, as we continue on our walk to the cars. However, the relief is short-lived when my phone starts to ring again. Again, I fumble to try to turn it off.

'Just bloody answer it,' Niall shouts, stopping and staring at me.

He is agitated, his eyes wild.

I take it from my pocket and see that it is Declan's number on the screen. How much of all this has he known? Has guilt been the source of his self-destruction? My hands shaking, I pull off one glove. Swiping my finger across the screen, I hold it to my ear and I'm aware that Niall's eyes never leave mine. I don't want him to know who I'm talking to, so I do my best to turn the speaker volume down. I can barely hear the voice on the other end.

'Ingrid?'

There's an urgency to Declan's voice, but the last thing I need is to get caught up in a conversation with him. Not now. Not here.

'Yes. Actually, I'm a little busy right now. Can I call you back in a bit?' I'm aware my voice sounds funny, as if I'm speaking the lines from a play.

'Ingrid, are you with Niall? At the reservoir?'

'Yes,' I say faux cheerfully. 'That's right.'

'And he's okay? Everything okay?'

'Well, you know. Things could be better,' I say, my voice light still, even though Niall is starting to look agitated again. He's obviously keen to get moving.

'Okay,' he says. 'Can you get back to the car? I'll meet you there. Try to keep calm.'

'I can certainly try to do that,' I say. 'I'll call you later, if that's okay.'

'Ingrid,' he says, 'stay safe. I thought I was doing the right thing . . . I didn't think he would . . .' His voice trails off.

Glancing up at Niall, who is still staring at me, my heart sinks further.

'Okay. I know what you mean. We'll chat later,' I say and end the call.

'Anyone important?' Niall asks.

'A work thing. Nothing that can't wait,' I say.

'Was it Ryan Murray?' he asks.

'No.' I shake my head. 'No. Nothing to do with him.'

Our strange stand-off is broken by the sound of a voice, deep and loud, calling Niall's name. He looks at me, his eyes wide. Reaching out to grab me again, he steps closer, but I step back. It's getting harder and harder to stay calm.

'No. Ingrid, get over here. You don't understand,' he says, and his voice is angry now. Scared.

The voice rings out again. He closes his eyes, shakes his head, and when he looks up, I can see that he is shaking. The over-confident alpha male I have come to know over the last few days has been reduced to a terrified little boy.

'Please,' he says, and reaches out a third time.

This time he grabs me by the wrist and starts to pull me back in the direction from where we've come.

'You have to come with me.'

But I don't want to. I want to get to my car and I want to get home.

The voice rings out again, closer this time. It's not Declan, I know that. It's deep, angry.

'What's going on?' I blurt. 'Who is that?'

'It's my da,' he says. 'Come on! You don't understand.'

He pulls so hard on my wrist that it hurts and I slip again on the leaves, crashing to my knees.

'Get up!' he shouts. 'You have to get up.'

'Niall, stop! You're hurting me. You're scaring me!' I can't pretend this is normal any more. I can't pretend I'm not petrified.

But he doesn't seem to hear me.

'You don't understand,' he wails. 'You have to come with me. If he sees you . . . Come on! I know where we can hide.'

He is pleading with me now, pulling me back to my feet.

'Let me go!' I shout and pull away from him, breaking the hold.

'You stupid bitch!' he shouts. 'You don't get it! You won't be safe. He has a fierce temper. Kelly, come on!'

It's her name that makes me freeze to the spot.

When I look back at him, I see a man reliving a childhood trauma right in front of my eyes.

The voice, his father's voice, rings out again and I see him flinch. He hauls me along the path, babbling all the time.

'She was only trying to get away, just like you. She was trying to run. But he didn't care. He grabbed her, threw her to the ground as if she were a piece of dirt, and it was my fault. It was all my fault. But I knew if I opened my mouth and told

293

anyone what he did, he would kill me. Him and his cronies, they would kill me. Those big brave men. They'd do whatever they had to do to protect him. He told me that. He told me "Son or no son, you're dead if you speak." I had no doubt that he meant it.'

Shock hits me with such force that I struggle to breathe, but as I turn to run, I find myself face to face with Frankie Heaney, his expression a snarl.

'You were warned, wee girl. You can't say you weren't warned.'

Chapter Fifty-Two

Ingrid

Frankie Heaney's face radiates anger. His brow furrowed, his muscles tense. He does not shout. He probably knows he doesn't need to. There is enough menace in his low, quiet voice to get his message across.

My eyes dart around him, trying to figure out if there is a way I can push past him and run to my car. So it had been him. He had pushed her and he had let Jamesy Harte take the blame. As had Niall. And Declan, what had he known?

'Mr Heaney,' I say, knowing that I am about to lie. 'I'm not sure what it is that you're talking about. Is this about Kelly? About the vandalism to my car?'

He reaches out his hand and pokes one long, bony finger at my chest. Jabbing and bruising, pushing me backwards.

'You just couldn't keep your nose out of it. There's no story here, Ingrid,' he says. 'There never was. Not beyond what the courts found. Kelly Heaney was murdered by Jamesy Harte and now he's dead, too.'

'Murdered,' I say, my voice barely audible. 'Jamesy was murdered.'

'He'll not be missed,' Frankie Heaney scowls. 'He should've kept himself to himself when he got out.'

'Da.'

I hear Niall behind me.

'This is nothing to do with Ingrid. Just let us get back to our cars.'

His voice is pleading. All of his cockiness and self-assured bravado has seeped into the muddy ground with the rain.

'You're right there, son,' Frankie says, not shifting his gaze from mine. 'This has nothing to do with Ingrid here and yet, she can't seem to leave it alone. We've tried to tell her.'

'She will!' Niall says, his voice thick with fear. 'Won't you, Ingrid? You'll drop all this and you won't mention it again.'

I see the cockiness that had been in Niall's expression now mirrored in his father's. Frankie Heaney feels powerful here. With his threatening tone and his jabbing finger, and his trembling son who is too terrified to stand up to him. Frankie Heaney is a bully. A dangerous man. He's not the reformed character he claims to be. His tendency to violence, I can see, lurks not too far under the surface.

I realise, in that moment, that it doesn't matter what I say. If I stand up for what I believe, tell Frankie Heaney and his threats to go to hell, he will do whatever it takes to silence me. Just like I fear he did what he needed to do to silence Jamesy, and Liam, too.

And if I agree to drop it, let Jamesy and Liam down, let Kelly down, too, I know that he will never believe me. He doesn't want any of this getting out – and he'll make sure it doesn't. I'll forever be looking over my shoulder for when he decides to make certain of my silence.

'Well?' Frankie Heaney asks, still jabbing, stepping closer, his breath rancid on my face, his frame wider, taller than mine.

He looks down at me and I wince.

'Please, Ingrid,' I hear Niall plead. 'Just tell him you'll let all this go.'

I also know one other thing. I'm sick of letting bullies win. From Ryan Murray and his smug manipulation, to this man in front of me who somehow thinks he has a right to get away with killing a child. And not only get away with killing her, but also with letting her body lie in cold water for days while her family endured hell.

A fiery rage rises up inside me. As Frankie Heaney tries to jab at me again, call me 'wee girl' again, warn me off again, I grab that finger and bend it back so far that he cries out.

'Go to hell,' I tell him in as low and menacing a voice as I can manage. Two can play at his game.

'You stupid bitch!' he shouts, his free hand reaching round to grab at my hat, maul at my hair, try to drag me down.

I feel the strands pull from my scalp, like scalding hot needles. My neck is at an unnatural angle. I try to kick out, to disarm him with a knee to his groin, but the ground is too wet and too slippery, and I lose my footing, his fist still grasping my hair.

'All I ever asked anyone to do was to keep their stupid mouths shut,' Frankie is shouting. 'You're not going to ruin this now.'

I'm aware of the rain and the wind, and Niall shouting, and his father not even speaking. He's pushing my head back, turning me so he can bury my face in the mud, the leaves and the dirt; and the wind is still howling, the banshee is still calling and I can't breathe.

Chapter Fifty-Three

Declan

Declan can't just wait in the house for Niall to come back. He can't just assume everything will be okay, because he knows full well what his brother is capable of now, and he knows that his da isn't much better. Is it any wonder he's a mess himself? Yet, they're the ones who swan about as if they don't have a care in the world.

His ma is still crying and he feels awful for leaving her, but he knows that – while his da is out, at least – she is safe. She will be fine.

He pulls on his coat and hat and heads for the door.

'I'll be back in a bit, Ma. Lock the door and put the chain on. Don't let anyone in. Not even Da,' he calls without looking back and walks towards the country park before breaking into a run.

He feels it in his bones that something is very wrong. Just as he did that night.

From the moment he and Niall had got home that night, everything had felt off. There was tension in the air, along with the smell of beer and cigarettes and the sound of big men mouthing off and acting like they ruled the world.

He'd known better than to become involved in any of it and had gone straight to his room, where he'd sat on the floor dividing his spoils into neat piles of nuts and apples and withered grapes – deflated after being torn from their stalks.

He'd heard the argument start between his da and Niall earlier. He'd pulled his knees to his chest and wished that just once, his da didn't have to ruin everything, or that just for once, Niall would learn to keep his mouth shut and not rattle his da's cage.

The slam of the door had followed. Declan had looked out of the window and willed Niall to run faster, because he could hear his father roaring at his ma, saying he was going out to find 'that wee bastard' and 'teach him a lesson'. Declan could hear the loud voices of his da's friends – angry men with sour faces – jumping to the beat of his da's drum. All these big men who had nothing better to be doing with their time than chase a wee boy. He willed his brother to run away and never look back.

The door to their room had been thrown open with such force the handle slammed against the wall, cracking a hole in the plaster. The change of energy in the room had been enough to push Declan flat against the wall, without his da so much as taking a step inside.

'Where would he go?' his da shouted.

Declan had blinked, unable to find his voice, the fear weighing so heavy on his chest.

'That spoiled wee shite of a brother of yours – and don't tell me you don't know, Declan Heaney, or believe me, it won't just be him who feels the leather of my belt.'

His father may well have been slurring his words, but his intention was clear, and Declan was ashamed that he wasn't brave enough to stand up to him.

'The rezzie,' he whispered.

'Speak up!' his da yelled and he had repeated himself, but louder this time.

When his da had stormed out of the room and out of the house afterwards, Declan had cried until he was sick.

He has carried the weight of that all of his life, he thinks as he sprints up Westway. He doesn't want to carry any more guilt. Whatever happens at the country park, with Ingrid and his da and Niall, the one thing Declan knows is that he has to make sure of it that no one else is hurt.

As the wind pushes against him, doing its best to slow him down, he thinks of how he saw his da and one of his cronies – that fucking bastard Murray – walking back down the street later that night. The night Kelly died. They walked each side of a solemn and broken-looking Niall. He'd heard them come in the front door. He'd asked Niall if he was okay when he had come to bed, but Niall hadn't replied. His brother had just climbed into bed.

The next day, when the news broke that Kelly was missing, Niall didn't even flinch. He remembers that, how his brother just took another bite of toast under the gaze of their da, who sat at the breakfast table with a mug of coffee in hand.

When he'd found out about the bracelet, he'd been too scared to ask Niall about it. He had never dreamed, even after everything that happened, that Niall could've been involved. He couldn't bear to think of his brother that way.

But everything in Niall changed then.

Declan pushes on, through the car park, where he sees both Ingrid's and his da's car – but both are empty. Ingrid and Niall, and presumably his da, are somewhere in the country park.

He runs down the path, occasionally sliding, the rain running down his face in thick rivulets. He'll head for their den first, maybe. Or the riverbank. He doesn't know which. He feels sick to the very pit of his stomach, there's a stitch in his side and his lungs are burning. He can't remember the last time he ran anywhere and his legs are begging him to slow down.

But he messed this up so much once before and he doesn't want to, he can't, mess it up again.

Over the din of the wind, and his own laboured breathing as he pushes his body on, he hears shouting. It's a man's voice. He runs towards it, rounding a clearing just in time to see Niall pull his father away from a figure. It's Ingrid, prone on the ground, face down. She isn't moving.

'Help me!' Niall shouts, and Declan runs towards his brother and his da. He helps Niall restrain their father until he stops fighting.

Subdued, Frankie Heaney falls to his knees, his two sons either side of him, restraining his arms.

Declan is aware, vaguely, of Niall calling for help, asking for police and an ambulance. Aware of his father snarling and making threats – but for now, at least, Frankie Heaney is powerless to do anything more than shout and foam at the mouth.

But Declan isn't really taking any of that in. He is just fixated on Ingrid, who hasn't moved. Who is lying so still. He wonders if the colour will leach from her body in the same way it did with Kelly. He closes his eyes to try to block out the sight of Ingrid in front of him, but he knows it won't help. She will be burned into his brain in the same way Kelly is.

Chapter Fifty-Four

Ingrid

My chest feels like it is in a vice. My neck aches, the muscles across my shoulders burn. I am wet and cold, and my hands are shredded from the stones and grit on the ground as I tried to fight my way free. One of my fingernails is missing – torn from my nail bed during the course of my fight.

The skin on my face feels as if it has been grated and I have already realised I'm bleeding from several deep cuts.

I have wet myself. I can feel the coldness of my own urine soaking through my jeans. My voice is little more than a whisper, my throat swollen and sore.

But I am alive.

A paramedic has wrapped me in a warm blanket, which hasn't managed to stop my shivering yet, and has attached an oxygen mask to my face. I have so many questions I need to ask, but I'm too broken for now.

All I know is that when I came to, it was with the paramedic calling my name. I had blinked, looking all around me, trying to make sense of where I was and with whom and what the hell had just happened.

I can see Declan now, his face as white as a ghost. He is

talking to a uniformed police officer. There is no sign of Niall or Frankie, although my head is ringing as a mixture of voices clash around me. It's possible they are here somewhere. It is possible Frankie Heaney is still a free man.

A murderer, and a free man.

My head thumps and my eyes feel so heavy. I just desperately want to go to sleep. The doors to the ambulance are closed and we start to move. I can no longer fight my need to close my eyes.

Chapter Fifty-Five

Declan

For the last twenty-five years of his life, Declan has believed the most horrific untruth about his brother. It has coloured every single interaction with him. Everything about the boy that he once saw as a part of himself.

It has made him angry and unsure of the world. It has made him unable to trust anyone. It has destroyed him. He has been eaten up by a secret he thought he was keeping. Broken by the guilt of knowing an innocent man was in jail. Terrified that at any moment the truth would come out and his mother would break under the horror of it. Angry that his brother seemed to be able to carry on with his life as normal.

He contemplates all of this as he sits in an interview room in Strand Road Police Station. He knows his brother is in another room. His father elsewhere. DI Bradley is sitting opposite him, having brought him a cup of coffee and a sandwich, which is stale.

'I'm sorry about the food,' DI Bradley says. 'There's not much on offer today.'

Declan just shrugs. He sips at the coffee, but he can't bring himself even to try to eat the sandwich. He's afraid it will get stuck in his throat.

'Are the clothes okay?' DI Bradley asks.

Declan nods. The grey prison-issue tracksuit they've given him is a bit big but clean, warm and dry. His own clothes were soaked through.

They talk through what happened at the reservoir and Declan tries to remember every little detail. But it all happened so fast. He didn't even think, he just did what he needed to do.

'And you went to the reservoir because you thought Ingrid was in danger?'

He nods again.

'I'm afraid you need to say the words,' DI Bradley says, nodding towards the tape recorder.

Declan apologises. Answers again. 'I thought . . . I thought that Niall had killed Kelly. And he'd been covering it up all these years. When my ma told me they's gone to the country park together, I panicked. I knew I had to get to them. All the threats she'd had. I thought he must be behind them or something.'

'And why did you think he killed Kelly?'

Declan reaches into the pocket of the baggy tracksuit bottoms, retrieves the bracelet he'd fished out of his wet clothes while changing. 'This was Kelly's,' he says. 'Niall had it. All those years ago. He'd run away that night because Da was roaring and shouting and threatening to beat the living daylights out of him.'

'Why was that?' DI Bradley asks.

'Because Niall used one of his shirts for his Halloween costume. He'd cut a ragged edge on it to make it look like Frankenstein's shirt. We didn't think Da would mind. He never wore that shirt any more anyway.'

'But he did mind,' DI Bradley says.

'He humiliated Niall. And all Da's pals were there, drinking and carrying on. And Da was roaring and shouting at Niall. I don't blame him for running away. I didn't see him again until an hour or more later, when I saw Da and a couple of his mates walking down the street.

'Niall looked as if he'd seen a ghost. He came in and went up to bed and I asked him, because we shared a room, you know, I asked him what had happened. He told me to "Mind my own fucking business," and then he wouldn't speak about it.

'But I found the bracelet the next day. I didn't know whose it was. I didn't know it was Kelly's until later and then all of it made sense then, you see. That he'd done it. He'd killed her and Da was covering it up for him.'

'And why did you never come to the police with this information?' DI Bradley asks. 'I understand at the time that you were just a child yourself, but over the years? You could've come to us at any time.'

Declan shakes his head. 'It would've killed my mother. And Jamesy Harte was in prison. I was scared I'd get into bigger trouble for not telling. Then, well, then I just learned to live with it.'

DI Bradley shifts in his seat, sips from his own coffee cup. 'And the version of events Niall told us today. Do you think they're plausible at all?'

Niall, it seems, has told police that yes, Kelly Doherty had been on her way home when she saw he was upset. She followed him to the country park, even though he kept telling her to go home. She was there when Frankie had turned up, shouting the odds and threatening to take his belt off to Niall. Kelly was crying and shouted that she was going to go and get a grown-up, but Frankie was so enraged that he screamed at Kelly to go home then pushed her.

He hadn't meant to kill her. He was drunk, didn't realise his own strength. Didn't know she would fall and strike her head so violently on a rock that she would smash her skull.

Niall expected Frankie to get help. He'd left his ten-year-old son sitting in the dark as the life drained from Kelly Doherty body to get help. So Niall couldn't understand why, when he came back with a friend, the two men just stood looking at Kelly. He begged them to call an ambulance, but Frankie had grabbed him by the shoulders, shaking him violently. He shouted that she was dead and he was fucked if he was going to take the blame for it.

Niall had sat, snivelling on the ground, while Frankie Heaney and his friend had rolled Kelly's body into the reservoir and pushed it out into the deeper water. He'd watched her float at first, her dress billowing around her, and then she had sunk out of his sight and he was told never to mention it again. In fact, Frankie had told him if he so much as breathed a word of what had happened, he could be made to disappear just as easily.

'You say you saw your da walking back down the street with Niall later that night?'

'Aye, I did,' Declan says.

'And there was another man with him?'

Declan nods. There was. A smug shite just like his brother, who had made a successful life for himself despite everything.

He stops for a moment, realises he has to reframe how he thinks of Niall from now on.

'Declan? For the recording?' DI Bradley says, pulling him away from his thoughts. 'Do you know the name of this man?'

Declan thinks of the scene again, Niall being marched down the street, his da on one side, Ryan Murray on the other. He doesn't hesitate in naming him.

'He was just a reporter then, no big shakes. But he liked to think he was somebody. Connected, you know. There were a lot of them. Hangers-on. Trying to stay on the right side of the big Frankie Heaney.'

His voice is laced with bitterness and he doesn't care. His da has destroyed more lives than he dares to imagine.

'There were others that night, too,' he continues, listing the names of those he can remember. 'They mightn't have been at the reservoir, but they were there. Out with my da.'

'Was Jamesy Harte there that night?' DI Bradley asks.

Declan shakes his head. No, Jamesy wasn't there. Jamesy didn't mix with those people. Jamesy kept himself to himself. A heavy sense of sadness floods through Declan's body and he feels himself sag under the weight of it. Tears spring to his eyes. He's just so tired of all of it.

'Jamesy had nothing to do with any of it,' he says. 'He wouldn't have hurt a fly.'

'You do know you're not under arrest here,' DI Bradley says. 'We're just trying to piece together what happened. Today, and back then. When Kelly Doherty died. What you're telling us, it's very helpful. Are you okay to continue? Can we get you another coffee?'

Declan nods. Asks for five minutes to have a smoke and to settle himself. It's still raining when he stands outside sucking the probably poisonous smoke from his counterfeit cigarette into his lungs.

He stubs his cigarette out, goes back inside and takes his seat.

'All I can tell you about today,' he begins, 'is that it was Niall who was trying to pull my da away from Ingrid when I reached them. Niall was shouting at him that he wouldn't let him do it again. He wouldn't be scared of him any more. He said too many people had been hurt. It had to stop.'

DI Bradley takes notes, nods reassuringly at him.

'That's really helpful, Declan. Thank you,' he says before

nodding to a female detective in the room and standing up to leave, saying he will be back shortly.

'How's Ingrid?' Declan asks his retreating form, unable to get the image of her prone on the ground from his mind.

'She'll be fine, I'm told,' DI Bradley says with a small smile. 'She'll feel like she's been hit by a truck for a while, but she'll be back to herself soon enough. That one has nine lives.'

Chapter Fifty-Six

Ingrid

Thursday, 31 October 2019

My curtains are open and from my sofa I watch the bright lights and sparkle of the fireworks illuminate the sky. It's loud but there's a comfort to it. To the noise and the life and the fun below. To all of the families walking along the quay in costume, enjoying the festivities. All those people who don't feel scared. Who don't have a need to be worried.

I wasn't brave enough to go out in it, but I'm okay where I am, on my sofa with a blanket over my knee and a cup of hot chocolate in my hands. I'm still bruised and sore after Sunday's ordeal. My throat still aches every time I swallow. My cuts still sting in the shower.

I'm still shell-shocked, if truth be told.

But I know that I'll be okay.

I still can't quite believe that what started as a piece on the anniversary of a murder turned into something that has sent shock waves through the city, through the country even. Layer after layer of corruption and lies and the worst that people can be have been uncovered. And poor Liam Doherty, his life destroyed all over again.

It's hard to make sense of something that is so very senseless. An argument between a father and son. A father with a brutal temper who hurt a little girl but who never meant to kill her. But what he did, this big man who is really just a pathetic coward at heart, was unthinkable. Sinking her body into the water. Threatening his son to keep quiet. Framing an innocent man – a man who had done nothing wrong except be a little different. Spending twenty-five years covering his tracks and making sure no one ever found out. Even if that meant making sure Jamesy Harte was dead. Even if it meant setting his heavies on me.

And Ryan? The man I had once respected, the man I had let into my bed? He'd helped. He'd told them I'd be alone in the office the night of the first attack. He'd told them where I lived. It scares me that when they came to my flat that day, they wouldn't have had any idea if I was there or not. What would they have done if I'd been home? I feel sick at the thought.

When I think of Liam Doherty – what they'd done to him. Would they have done that to me?

Out of all of this, the attack on Liam is probably what will stay with me. It's what had made no sense. Why him? Why a grieving father?

No matter how I tried, I couldn't get my head around it. That is until DS King had arrived to talk to me and had filled me in. She told me that Liam Doherty had admitted he had known, almost from the start, that Jamesy Harte's conviction was based on a series of lies. That Frankie Heaney and his cohorts – and yes, that included a young reporter called Ryan Murray – had conspired to make sure there was no way Harte would escape conviction.

They'd arrived at the Doherty house when it was still reverberating with grief and shock and had removed some of Kelly's belongings to plant in Jamesy's house. They'd told Liam to tell the police that Jamesy had been inappropriate with his daughter. 'Obsessed with her.'

They'd told Liam, who was broken and struggling to find the strength to exist, that they had no doubt Jamesy had done it. That he was a dangerous man. A pervert. They'd planted horrific images in his mind and left them to fester. They'd told this father, living through his worst nightmare, that if he didn't agree to helping them plant evidence, Jamesy would get away with it. He might even kill again.

But over the years Liam's doubts had grown. He'd found himself in a hell of his own making, guilt nagging at him that it was because of him that Jamesy had his freedom snatched from him.

He'd seen Frankie Heaney, still thinking he was the big man, walking about laughing and joking without a care in the world.

When Councillor Duffy had arrived at the Doherty house at my behest and told them it was time for them to speak to the press – and for Liam to say what a monster he thought Jamesy was – well, Liam had just broken down. He'd refused to do the interview. Bernie thought he was just grieving, but the truth was he was no longer able to lie. He couldn't look himself in the mirror knowing what he'd done.

He couldn't look himself in the mirror without knowing who had really killed his daughter.

There was something in Frankie Heaney's demeanour, though. For all his bravado, he couldn't look Liam in the eye.

When Frankie had heard Liam had been at *The Chronicle* office, drunk and shouting the odds about wanting to 'do the right thing' now, he'd decided it wouldn't do any harm to send a warning. He insists things were never meant to get violent but refuses to tell the police the names of the attackers.

'They were only supposed to scare him a bit,' Frankie told DS King.

Guilt that I had unknowingly been a part of it, that I had pushed the Dohertys to talk, now lived in me. As did my guilt about telling Ryan where Jamesy was living, thinking I was just a reporter confiding to her editor and not feeding information directly to the enemy.

And my contacts book that had gone missing and turned up in Ryan's office? Well, it seems you can find anything you want in one of those. Even Jamesy Harte's mobile number. I had been so very, very stupid.

'You couldn't have known,' DS King had said, and I'd seen the compassion in her eyes.

But I should have known. It was my job to read people.

I had failed.

I had admired Ryan Murray. I had let him into the most private corners of my life. I had trusted him. Looked to him. Wondered whether or not I loved him. Now, seeing him for what he is really is, I feel ashamed to have been taken in by him.

I had questioned whether or not I was wise to believe in Jamesy's innocence.

I had thought Liam Doherty to be little more than a drunkard.

I'm doing my best to cope with my guilt. I can't bring myself to speak to either Declan or Niall again. Not yet. Not until I feel stronger. I do wonder how they are, though. Wonder how they are rebuilding their relationship. How their mother is. I can't imagine the nightmare they've lived with these last twenty-five years.

But I can't fix that for them – and I have to figure out to how rebuild my life.

I need to figure out how to make a better life. One with real friends. One with real meaning.

Trina is going to call over tomorrow after work. She's bringing some Chinese food and a bottle of wine. We're going to try to have a normal conversation. No work talk. No Ryan talk.

I'm told Christopher Doherty's wife has had her baby. A little girl, who they've called Kelly. I wonder if they are looking out at the fireworks tonight, too. I wonder if they will tell her that the world is a good place and that monsters aren't real. That the banshee is just an old legend. That the bogeyman will not come rapping at her window to steal her away.

I curl my feet up under me and the words of the childhood song that scared me so much come back into my head.

> *Who's at the window, who?*
> *Who's at the window, who?*
> *It's the wee bogeyman with a sack on his back*
> *Come to take Ingrid away.*

I get up, walk to the window and draw the curtains against the dark night and the falling stars of the fireworks.

Epilogue

Niall

I believed an innocent man to be so vile that for twenty-five years I allowed my father, the true villain of the piece, to cover up for his own crimes while celebrating the fact he had got away with seeing Jamesy Harte sent down for murder.

'You know it was an accident, son,' my father had said as I'd watched the blood seep from the back of Kelly's head as she lay on the ground.

It was strange how her expression changed. How her eyes were glassy. Her jaw sagged open. Even though I was only ten and had never seen a dead body before, I knew that she was gone just by looking at her.

I was crying. Sobbing. Tears and mucus from my nose running down my face. I couldn't bring myself to rub them away. I was shaking so violently.

'You don't want me to go to jail because of an accident, do you?' he'd said.

And no, I didn't want him to go to jail because of an accident. I wanted him to go to jail because he was a violent bully.

'It would kill your mother,' he'd said. 'And there'd be no one to earn any money. You would be out on the street. That's not what you want, is it? I can sort this out. Just you wait and see.'

And he had. Him and the friend he had gone to for help. Both of them taking it in their stride as if death and cover-ups were nothing new to them.

I'd cried, sat on the ground beside Kelly and held her hand while I had waited for my father to come back with help, and while he and his friend – Ryan Murray – had planned what to do next. I'd willed her to move. I'd willed this to be a nightmare. When I realised it wasn't, truly realised that, I had slipped the small bracelet from her wrist and dropped it into my pocket. I don't know why. Maybe to remind me that life could be cruel and horrific.

It was relatively easy to convince myself my father was telling the truth when he said Jamesy Harte was a very bad man, who did bad things to children and who the police had never been able to catch before now. I came to hate Jamesy and everything he stood for. I think a part of me even started to believe that Jamesy was guilty, after all, and those things I'd seen that night on the banks of the reservoir were just echoes of a nightmare.

I realise now, of course, that I had needed to hate Jamesy Harte so deeply so that I could live with myself all these years.

We have all lost so much. Suffered so much. It's hard to think of that. To think of how my relationship with Declan has been fractured. How my mother has suffered over the years, when she could have been free of him. To think of Jamesy, taken from his house and led to his death by some connection of the man I called my father.

So many people destroyed by one night of the year.

I kneel at Kelly's graveside – a place I have refused to visit all through my life – and I tell her I'm sorry before I place her coloured plastic bracelet on her headstone.

It's quiet here today. The early winter sun is bright in the sky and warm where it falls across the marble of her headstone. A feeling of immense peace washes over me. I hope with all of my heart Kelly feels it, too.

Acknowledgements

This book was part written, and entirely edited, during the COVID-19 lockdown. All my usual writing routines went out the window as, like so many, I combined home-schooling, stemming the worry of a global pandemic and not being able to escape to the beach for some fresh air.

I therefore appreciate even more the work of the people who worked behind the scenes to bring this book to life. All those who kept up the same level of support, enthusiasm and professionalism as usual while working in home offices and dealing with the strange 'new normal'.

Most of all to my editor Phoebe Morgan, who once again has helped me polish this book and bring the characters to life. And thank you Phoebe for your never ending support. It really means the world.

Thanks to all the Avon team, and to all the fabulous people at HarperCollins Ireland who work tirelessly for their authors, but most of all are just really nice people to work with.

Thanks to all the brilliant booksellers, who faced their own uncertain times, but kept pushing all our books and offering their support. Special thanks to Dave at No Alibis, Jenny at

Little Acorns, Bob at Gutter Bookshop, Heidi at WH Smith Ireland, and the staff of Eason, Foyleside. Thanks also to the staff of NI Libraries, especially the Central Library in Derry.

No one understands the strange writing life like other authors, and I have some of the best author friends in my corner. Even if that corner is at a social distance these days. Thanks and love to John Marrs, Louise Beech, Marian Keyes, Anna McPartlin, CL Taylor, Liz Nugent and Brian McGilloway.

Special mention to my writing work wife, Fionnuala Kearney, who has picked me up and dusted me off more than anyone should have to. Fionnu, I am grateful for your friendship every day.

To my family and friends; Mum, Dad, Lisa, Peter and Emma, assorted partners and the best nieces and nephews in the world, Abby, Ethan, Darcy, Arya, Thomas and Finn, not to mention the hairier family members Henry and Ben. Thank you for being you.

Thanks to Julie-Ann & Marie-Louise for *Derry Girls*-themed Afternoon Teas.

And to my lifelong friends, forged in the newsroom – Erin, Cat & Bernie. This seems as appropriate a place as any to say that Ingrid Devlin is not based on any living person and the experiences in the *Chronicle* newsroom are not based on any lived experience!

To my family – Neil, and my two amazing children (even if they don't think I'm cool anymore). Thank you. I love you. To the two cats, Alfie and Purry – thanks for not vomiting in my shoes. And to Izzy, my beautiful pupper, thank you for sitting at my feet during long writing sessions.

Thanks also to all the media, book bloggers and book lovers who spread the word about my books. And of course, to you, reading this. I would be nothing without your support.

To the lady who attended my book signing in Eason, Foyleside and asked if I could name a character after her – Sue in the police press office is after you.

Finally, this book is dedicated to my agent Ger Nichol, who has been by my side for fourteen years and fifteen books. I cannot thank you enough, Ger.

Credits

Editor: Phoebe Morgan
Copy-editor: Claire Dean
Proofreader: Simon Fox
Editorial Assistant: Bethany Wickington
Production Controller: Catriona Beamish
Cover Designer: Claire Ward
Marketing: Ellie Pilcher
Publicity: Sabah Khan
Sales: Caroline Bovey
Audio: Rebecca Fortuin and Stella Newing
Contracts: Florence Shepherd

Every family has its secrets . . .

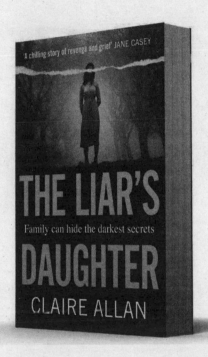

**A gripping suspense novel about
deadly secrets and lies.**

Available in all good bookshops now.

I disappeared on a Tuesday afternoon.

They've never found my body . . .

A unputdownable serial killer thriller
with a breathtaking twist.

Available in all good bookshops now.

Just how far is a mother willing to go?

A gripping psychological thriller
from the *USA Today* bestseller.

Available in all good bookshops now.

You watched her die.

And her death has created a vacancy . . .

A gripping psychological thriller
that will have you hooked.

Available in all good bookshops now.